Brodie

USA TODAY BESTSELLING AUTHOR

HEATHER SLADE

Brodie

Second Edition

ISBN 13: 978-1-942200-45-1

MORE FROM AUTHOR HEATHER SLADE

BUTLER RANCH

Kade's Worth

Brodie

Maddox

Naughton

Mercer

Kade

Christmas at Butler Ranch

WICKED WINEMAKERS' BALL

Coming soon:

Brix

Ridge

Press

K19 SECURITY SOLUTIONS

Razor

Gunner

Mistletoe

Mantis

Dutch

Striker

Monk

Halo

Tackle

Onyx

K19 SHADOW OPERATIONS

Code Name: Ranger

Coming soon:

Code Name: Diesel

Code Name: Wasp

Code Name: Cowboy

THE ROYAL AGENTS OF MI6

The Duke and the Assassin

The Lord and the Spy

The Commoner and the Correspondent

The Rancher and the Lady

THE INVINCIBLES

Decked

Undercover Agent

Edged

Grinded

Riled

Handled

Smoked

Bucked

Irished

Sainted

Coming soon:

Hammered

Ripped

COWBOYS OF CRESTED BUTTE

A Cowboy Falls

A Cowboy's Dance

A Cowboy's Kiss

A Cowboy Stays

A Cowboy Wins

For KAB

Table of Contents

1

She closed the car door and zipped her jacket. The blue sky and bright sun were misleading. This close to the ocean, the wind could be fierce, even on the sunniest days.

From where she stood in the gravel parking lot across the street, she saw a man walking toward her small town's only supermarket. There was something familiar in the way he held himself. His worn barn jacket was taut across his shoulders, but hung loose over his narrow hips. Although his jeans were more metro than ranch, his boots were all cowboy, and so was his black, felt Stetson.

Peyton took a deep breath. It wasn't the first time her mind played this particular trick on her. She looked left and right, once she got inside, but didn't see the man who'd probably been a figment of her imagination anyway.

Growing boys needed milk and orange juice, so before she'd even left the first aisle, her cart was half full. She was reading over her shopping list, on her way to the produce section, when her eyes met a pair of hauntingly familiar deep, blue eyes—eyes of a man she thought she'd never see again. Her disappointment was palpable as she scanned his face. The eyes were familiar, and maybe even the way he held himself had her heart skipping a beat. But the man standing in front of her, whose eyes took in every inch of her in the same way her gaze traveled from his face to his hands, was not who she thought he was.

He raised and lowered his chin, "Hey."

Peyton nearly closed her eyes. She knew the deep timbre of that voice intimately. "Sorry, you look so much like someone—" What could she say? Someone she used to know?

"Yes," he murmured.

"Get that a lot?" She tried to laugh, but the pain she felt whenever she allowed herself to think about Kade Butler brought her closer to tears than laughter.

"No, I don't."

"I'm sorry, you don't what?"

"Get that a lot."

"Oh...uh...well." Her hands gripped the shopping cart handle, but before she could move it forward, he grasped the wire basket.

"I've been looking for you."

"Excuse me?"

"Name's Brodie. Brodie Butler."

Peyton closed her eyes just long enough that the tears she thought she held at bay flooded over her lids and down onto her cheeks.

"I'm sorry, Peyton. I didn't mean for it to happen this way."

"But you meant for it to happen?"

"As I said, I've been looking for you."

—:—

It took a minute before Brodie recognized the woman standing in front of him. He'd only seen photos of her, and not very many.

"Find Peyton," his mother had told him. "We need to give this to her."

"He's been gone over a year, Ma, and you haven't heard a word from her since the funeral."

"I don't care. This belongs to her."

The "this" his mother had referred to was a box of his oldest brother's belongings that he'd asked their mother to make sure was given to Peyton if anything happened to him.

"I have something for you," he explained. "From Kade."

"No," she whispered. "I'm sorry, but I can't." She left him and her grocery cart in the middle of the aisle, and walked out of the store.

Brodie followed her outside and watched as she crossed the street and climbed into a little black BMW. He sat at one of the tables in front of the market and waited to see if she'd drive away. He heard the engine start, but the car didn't move. He leaned forward and rested his forearms on his knees, weighing whether to stay or leave.

—:—

It wasn't as though she'd been hiding. She lived in a small house near Moonstone Beach, in Cambria. Right after Kade died, Peyton spent a lot of her time in the guest house on her parents' ranch. The boys still stayed there most weekends, when Stave, the tasting room she managed since she'd graduated from college, was open later.

There were few secrets in Green Valley, where many families had owned their ranches and vineyards for generations. If Kade's family was looking for her, she was easy to find.

She'd heard stories about Brodie, but hadn't met him until today. She wasn't aware of his strong resemblance to his oldest brother. There were differences though. Brodie's chiseled face, while similar to Kade's, was thinner, more angular, with a dusting of scruffy facial hair. Peyton had never seen Kade without the dark, reddish-brown goatee he kept neatly trimmed.

She looked across the road, where Brodie waited for her. If he thought she would get out of the car and walk back across the street, he was wrong. Whatever he had of Kade's, he could keep.

No matter where she went, she saw him. That's why she'd thought her mind was playing tricks on her again today. So often, Peyton thought she saw Kade walking on the beach, or driving past Stave. She'd blink her eyes, and either he'd be gone, or she'd realize the person she thought was him, wasn't. More memories? More things to remind her of her loss? No, thanks.

She'd come back to the market later, after she picked the boys up from school. Maybe she'd even let them pick out something for dinner they could heat up themselves, since cooking dinner at home was just one more thing that reminded her that the only man who had succeeded in convincing her to give love another try was gone.

—:—

Brodie watched as Peyton backed up the car and drove in the opposite direction, to the back exit of the parking lot. It would've been easier to go out the front, but then she'd be facing where he sat.

He knew where she was going, but he wouldn't follow. It wouldn't be fair, especially since he'd seen firsthand how close to the surface her pain sat. He went back inside and ordered a pastry and a cup of coffee from the bakery. Rather than sit and watch the cars go up and down the main drag of the village, he drove across the highway, parked alongside Moonstone Beach Road, and watched the waves crash along the shore.

There were several surfers out this morning, waiting for waves in the bone-chilling Pacific Ocean. Even in a full wetsuit, Brodie wouldn't have joined them. Maybe he would've ten years ago, but when he surfed now, he preferred the warmer water found a couple of hours south, closer to Santa Barbara.

***

"Don't be such a pussy," his brother Maddox had said the first time Kade brought him along to their favorite surf spot.

Kade smacked Mad, that day, and told him to leave Brodie alone. He glared at Naughton too, daring him to tease their youngest brother.

Kade was nine years older than Brodie, six years older than Naughton, and three years older than Maddox. Brodie was twelve the first time his brothers brought him along on the forty-five-minute drive from their ranch on Adelaida Trail, over the rolling hills of Highway 46, to Moonstone Beach.

"He watches, Kade. You don't take your brother in when it's nigh fifty degrees in that water."

Kade winked at Brodie. "Yes, Ma."

His brother had been home on leave for two weeks and was flying out again the next morning. Brodie begged Kade to let him go with them that day. The words he spoke would haunt him in the years that followed.

***

"I never know if you're coming back. You promised to teach me to surf. What if this is our only chance?" It made him sick to recall his callousness. He was only thankful his mother hadn't heard.

Kade had joined the Marines right out of high school, eventually serving in one of the elite Force Recon companies. He'd gone on to be one of the few priors who also underwent Navy SEAL training as well as attending Special Operations training in Fort Bragg—with the Green Berets. He hadn't stopped there. Kade had also earned a degree as a physician's assistant.

As one of only a handful of men with that level of specialized training, he became part of Delta Force, officially known as 1st Special Forces Operational Detachment-Delta, the most highly trained elite force in the US military. The Special Missions Unit performed various clandestine and highly classified counter-terrorism missions around the world. His brother had saved an infinite number of lives in his years of duty, but lost his own a year ago, on what was to be his final mission.

The first time Brodie heard Kade mention retirement was after he'd been seeing Peyton for several months. For three years, his rotation had been two months on, two months off. It became increasingly difficult for him to go back when his two-month leave came to an end. The mission was no longer his top priority. Peyton was becoming more important to him.

Brodie scrolled through the photos on his phone, looking for the last one taken with all of his siblings. His father had taken it the Christmas before last. Two months later, his parents answered their door and heard the devastating news every parent with a son or daughter serving in the military prays they'll never hear. Kade had been killed in action.

Brodie thought about looking through the contents of the box his mother wanted him to deliver to Peyton, but felt as though he'd be invading their privacy.

The cold wind stung his face with sand, and he buried his hands in his jacket pockets. It was a degree warmer for every mile between here and his family's ranch, thirty miles inland, but today he welcomed the chill of the ocean air washing over him. It reminded him he was alive. His brother wasn't, but he was, and that meant he had a promise to fulfill.

"I gave him my word, Brodie," his mother had said when she asked him to find Peyton.

—:—

Peyton looked up from her computer screen when she heard the back door open. "Hey, Alex."

Her best friend and marketing director for both the tasting room and the Westside Winery Collaborative, sat in the chair next to Peyton's desk.

"How are you not cold?"

Alex wore jeans with tan, four-inch heel boots and a black, sleeveless, silk tank. "Hot Hispanic blood runnin' through these veins, girlfriend."

"It's forty degrees, the wind off the ocean makes it feel closer to twenty, and you never get cold. I'm always cold, even in the summer."

"No meat on your bones; that's your problem."

"You're such a hypocrite. You weigh less than I do. You always have."

Peyton and Alex had been friends since they were teenagers. Her parents became friends with Alex's when they bought a ranch and decided to turn half of it into vineyards. Alfonso Avila, Alex's father, sold Peyton's dad rootstock and helped him produce many fine wines through the years.

She and Alex had been scrawny "beanpoles" when they met—tall and lanky, before both their bodies matured and filled out. Apart from their stature and thin but curvy bodies, they were total opposites. Peyton was a green-eyed blonde, and Alex had long dark brown, almost black hair, and eyes that matched.

"What's with the scowl this morning?"

"Sorry, it's been a crappy day so far."

Alex checked the time on her phone. "Already? Everything okay with the boys?"

"They're fine, Auntie Alex. No, this has nothing to do with the boys."

"What, then? Spill."

"I ran into Brodie Butler at the market this morning."

"Oh. *Shit.* I'm sorry, honey."

"I wasn't very nice to him, and now I feel bad."

"I didn't realize you knew Brodie."

"I don't. Or I didn't. He introduced himself."

"I know it's hard to see Kade's family—"

"He said he had something for me. Something from Kade."

"Oh. *Shit,*" Alex repeated.

"I left."

Alex nodded her head.

"No, Alex, I mean I walked away. Right out of the market. Poor Louie probably wonders why I left a cartful of milk and OJ right there in aisle six."

"Not a big deal, Peyton. Seriously, forget about it."

"I'll apologize to Louie later, but what about Brodie? I owe him an apology too."

"No, you don't. What made him think confronting you in the supermarket was a good idea?"

"He didn't confront me. I don't think he expected to see me there."

"You're right. I'm sure he drives thirty miles out of his way daily to go to a grocery store a tenth of the size of the store located less than ten miles outside the gates of Butler Ranch, because...I don't know...Louie's selection of mortadella is better?"

"You aren't helping. I feel bad enough as it is, Alex."

Alex reached over and rested her hand on Peyton's. "I'm sorry, honey."

"Tell me what I should do. I don't want to call the ranch."

"Why not? Kade's parents ask about you all the time. I'm sure they'd like to hear from you."

"No. I can't."

"Then, I will."

"Would you?"

Los Caballeros, the thousand-acre ranch owned by Alex's family, bordered the Butler Ranch. The Avilas and Butlers hadn't always gotten along, but when Alex's father passed away, a few years ago, the longstanding feud between Laird Butler and Alfonso Avila was set aside.

"Of course I will. Do you want me to offer to take whatever Brodie wanted to give you?"

"No! God, no. Just tell them...I can't. I'm sorry, but I can't."

"Can't what? I'm lost."

"Whatever it is, I don't want it."

"Peyton—"

Peyton walked out of the small office before Alex finished her sentence. She didn't want to hear it. It was more than that; she couldn't hear it.

When Alex followed, Peyton covered her ears.

"Jesus, what are you? A ten-year-old? Stop this."

Peyton walked out the back door of the building and got in her car. For the second time this morning, she ran away.

Instead of going home, she parked her car near the trail that led down to Moonstone Beach. A good long walk on the beach would help clear her head, and then maybe she'd be able to find the grownup living inside her, and stop acting like the child Alex had called her out as.

—:—

Brodie saw the black BMW pull into the parking lot at the opposite end of Moonstone Beach. It was a common car in the little seaside village, but there was no mistaking the woman who climbed out of it. He watched Peyton take the steps that led from the asphalt lot down to the beach.

When she reached the area that was almost directly below where he sat, he waved. Surprisingly, she waved back. More surprisingly, she ran up the path that would lead her directly to him.

"I owe you an apology," she said, approaching him. "I could give some lame excuse, but the bottom line is, I was rude to you, and I'm sorry."

"I'm sorry too, Peyton. I honestly didn't expect to run into you at the market. Although I didn't have much of a plan when I drove into town this morning."

Rather than look at him, Peyton looked out at the sea. "You probably think I should be over him by now, especially since we weren't together that long."

"That isn't what I think at all." Brodie wished he could see Peyton's eyes. Even if she'd look in his direction, her dark sunglasses hid them from view.

"Kade made our ma promise that I'd deliver this box to you if anything happened to him." Brodie pointed to the plain cardboard box sitting on the ground near his feet.

Peyton put her hands in her jacket pockets. He thought for a minute she'd walk away from him again. Instead, she leaned against a rock near his.

"I know it makes me seem like a terrible person, but I don't want it, Brodie."

"You might change your mind someday."

"Your brother knew me well enough, at least I thought he did, that he wouldn't have done this."

Brodie waited to see if Peyton would continue. They sat in silence but for the steady rhythm of the waves crashing on the sand.

She took several deep breaths, but didn't speak, so he did. "Tell me why he wouldn't have done this, Peyton."

Brodie watched as she took three more very intentional deep breaths, and then turned to face him. Again he waited for her to speak, and again she remained silent.

Finally, Peyton shrugged her shoulders and stood. "I'll see ya around, Brodie."

He didn't follow her down the path, and didn't move from where he sat until long after he saw her drive away in the opposite direction, toward the highway that would lead her back into town.

Brodie picked up the box and carried it back to his truck. He opened the door and set it on the passenger seat. "Guess it's you and me for a while, box." He patted the top, and then splayed his fingers, as if by doing so, he could take in whatever of Kade's energy remained in the belongings he'd wanted Peyton to have.

2

Stave had officially opened ten minutes ago, but no one would be in to taste wine this early in the day. Peyton usually arrived somewhere around ten and, typically, didn't see customers until one, or later, especially on Mondays. Most of the tourists left town Sunday night, but she and Alex had decided to stay open on Mondays in case there were stragglers who wanted to order wine before going home. Stave was closed Tuesday and Wednesday instead.

She kept herself busy, taking inventory, placing orders with wineries on behalf of customers who'd joined case clubs or just wanted a few bottles shipped to them, and planning the events Stave sponsored every week.

When her father had asked her to manage what was then a simple tasting room, shortly after Peyton graduated from college, she expected it to be more of a summer job. Almost thirteen summers later, it had become her life, along with her two boys, Jamison, who was ten, and Finn, who celebrated his eighth birthday a week ago.

"You're back." Alex stood near the tasting bar with her arms crossed in front of her.

"I'm sorry, Alex."

"Forget it. And forget Brodie Butler and Kade Butler, and all the rest of the bullshit. We have a wine dinner to plan. Okay?"

There was a dinner club that met at Stave once a month on a Monday night. It was a locals-only group, many of whom owned restaurants or retail shops in Cambria, or one of its neighboring seaside villages. It gave the wineries in the collaborative an opportunity to introduce new wines for the restaurants to consider adding to their lists.

The dinner was prepared by a guest chef in Stave's kitchen. Each one took a great deal of work, but the commission Stave made on wine sales was well worth the effort. Planning started four weeks out and began with a chefs' meeting.

"Who's coming in today, Peyton?"

"Peter Wells from Lark. I'm surprised you forgot."

"Right. Peter." Alex rested the back of her hand on her forehead. "Damn, that man is hot."

"Speaking of temperature, whatever happened with you two?"

"Tepid. The ingredients looked better than the entrée turned out."

"You're mixing metaphors."

"Yeah? Who cares? It just wasn't there, ya know?"

“I know,” Peyton sighed.

“He’s had a thing for you since college. I think he found me lacking as a substitute.”

“Not interested.”

“You’re kidding? Not interested?”

“Stop it, Alex.”

“All right, all right. What’s he makin’?”

Peyton pulled out the folder for the April dinner. “Pasilla chile stuffed with shrimp and provolone as the starter.”

“Oh, gawd, I just remembered how hungry I am.”

“I’m thinking of pairing it with the Charbono.”

“Whose?”

“Harrington’s.”

“Mmm, yummy.”

Although she found herself thinking more about Brodie, getting lost in wine and food pairings was exactly what Peyton needed to get her mind off Kade Butler.

* * *

After graduating from Cal Poly San Luis Obispo with a degree in Agribusiness, Peyton had received several job offers from wineries in Napa Valley, but she preferred the slower pace of the Paso Robles wine region.

Her original plan was to work at her parents' winery, Wolf Family Vintners, but working in their adjunct tasting room appealed to her more.

After a few months on the job, Peyton approached her dad with ideas for expansion. Rather than offering wines solely from their family winery, she encouraged him to open it up to all the members of Paso Robles' Westside Winery Collaborative. The tasting room sales skyrocketed, as did their profits. When a restaurant in the west end of the village closed its doors and the space became available for lease, Peyton approached her father again, only this time, Alex came with her.

Her dad raised his hands in surrender after Alex told him the collaborative's board had also asked her to serve as their marketing manager.

"This is your baby, Peyton, make sure it thrives. You too, Alex."

Peyton and Alex renamed what had first been the Wolf Family Vintners Tasting Room, and then the Westside Collaborative Tasting Room, to Stave, for the thin, narrow, shaped pieces of wood that form the sides of a cask or barrel. An average barrel had thirty-one staves, the same number of wineries in the collaborative.

Between Alex's and Peyton's efforts, the westside wineries' sales far outpaced those of the other sub-regions.

One of the first wine dinners held at the new Stave location featured wines made by Maddox Butler from Butler Ranch Winery. Peyton met Kade the night of the dinner, when he came as Maddox's guest. From that night on, he made a point of visiting Stave whenever he was home on leave, and soon he and Peyton became friends.

Kade asked her more questions than he answered, although Peyton didn't ask very many. She knew he served in the military, in special operations, but no other details. He was often gone for weeks at a time, and then home for several weeks. It wasn't long before she started paying enough attention that she knew when he was leaving and when he expected to be back.

After a particularly long Friday night, when a group of tourists decided to hang out far past closing time, Peyton got an email from Kade. He told her he'd be gone two weeks longer than he'd originally anticipated, but hoped to see her the night he got home. She responded by jokingly asking if he was suggesting they go out on a date. A few minutes later, another email arrived from him, saying that yes, he was. Peyton panicked and didn't respond. With two young boys and a heart that still hadn't mended from her divorce, she hadn't given dating any thought, and didn't plan to.

The next time Peyton saw Kade, she wasn't sure what to expect, but when he came into Stave his first night back in town, their conversation felt the same as those they'd had before the awkward emails.

The night he told her he was flying out again, Peyton told him she'd miss him.

"How much?" he asked.

"A lot," she confessed.

"Then, go out with me when I get back."

* * *

"Yoohoo, Peyton," Alex nudged her.

"Sorry, uh..." She caught the look that passed between Alex and Peter. "I think we should start with something lighter."

"Uh-huh," Alex smirked.

Peter looked lost, but offered to serve his signature oak-grilled artichoke instead.

"Perfect. Then, we'll start with the Falanghina."

Alex came back into the tasting room after walking Peter out to his car.

"I thought you were leaving too." Monday was Alex's day off. She only came in if there was a wine dinner scheduled, or they had pairings to put together.

"I asked him to come back next week, for another planning session."

"Alex! Why? We're fine. He doesn't need to trek all the way back up here. We can finalize the wine pairings without him."

Alex stood with her arms crossed in front of her, as she had earlier.

"Oh, wait. You want him to come back so you can hang out. I get it."

Alex shook her head. "Nope."

"Then, why?"

"Because, Peyton. It's time."

"No."

"Why not?"

There were so many reasons, Peyton didn't know where to begin. Her boys were at the top of her list. It had taken months before she was comfortable enough to invite Kade to spend time with them. They weren't any more ready for her to bring another man into their family mix than she was.

Jamison was three, and Finn had just turned one when Lang Becker told her that having kids really wasn't his "thing," after all, and he was leaving her for another woman who didn't have any. He dropped out of their sons' lives then, and never dropped back in.

And Kade, well, their relationship had been complicated, and now that he was gone, she didn't have it in her to try again only to have another man leave her and her boys behind.

Plus, Peter lived in Santa Barbara, a two-hour drive if there wasn't any traffic, and there usually was. They'd rarely see each other. Why bother starting something that had nowhere to go? She had two other guys in her life whose company she enjoyed immensely, and she didn't have enough time with Jamison and Finn as it was.

"I told you before I wasn't interested."

"Peyton, come on."

"No, Alex. If there ever comes a time when I'm ready to jump back into dating, you'll be the first to know. Until then, the subject is closed."

Alex groaned, but appeared to give up her argument. "At least we'll get another meal out of him."

"Peter Wells is a phenomenal chef, I'll concede that much."

Peyton finished cleaning up the tasting room while Alex focused on the kitchen. All the while, she couldn't get Brodie Butler, not Kade, off her mind.

—:—

Brodie pulled up to the ranch gates and waited while they creaked open. His father had them programmed to close each night at sundown, and not open again until sunrise. Their phones were programmed to open and close the gates as well. Sometimes he thought his father had missed his calling. The guy was as tech-savvy as anyone Brodie had known when he worked just north of Silicon Valley.

He parked his truck in front of the ranch house where he, his three brothers, and two sisters grew up.

* * *

The house had been built by his grandfather, Broderick Butler. Broderick emigrated from Scotland in his early twenties and had settled on the Central Coast of California, where he found work as one of several hundred craftsmen hired to construct Hearst Castle. There, Broderick met his wife, Brodie's grandmother, Analise, a seamstress who also hailed from Scotland.

The two scrimped and saved until they had enough money set aside to purchase the ranch land that was passed down to Broderick and Analise's only son, Laird—Brodie's father.

The main house was built in the style of a historic Scottish Highland farmhouse with a dressed granite facade under a slate roof. The four front dormers were embellished with black shutters, which repeated on the windows of the main level. After inheriting the ranch from his parents, Laird added a porch, which wrapped around all three sides of the u-shaped abode so, regardless of the season, he and Sorcha could sit there in the sunlight. In the center of the u-shape sat a courtyard with a small pond and an archway that led to a path to the original barn, which had been converted into part of the winery.

Laird added two Scottish-style stone cottages, both two-storied replications of the main house. Like the original barn, many of the other outbuildings had been re-purposed for the winery. What had once been a hayloft was now an apartment with a barrel room below.

***

When Brodie moved home after Kade died, instead of living in the apartment where Kade had stayed when he was on leave, he relocated into one of the stone cottages with Naughton. Maddox lived in the other smaller one that sat closer to the winery operation.

His sister Skye, who was two years younger than Brodie, lived in Paso Robles with her husband and Ainsley, the youngest Butler sibling, who was completing her doctorate at Stanford.

There was usually a crowd for dinner at the ranch house, so his mother made enough food that, if he and his brothers wanted to eat with them, there'd be plenty. Maddox sometimes invited winery staff to join them too.

When Brodie climbed out of the truck, he saw his mother and father sitting on the front porch swing.

"Is that my Brodie?" his mother asked in her thick Scottish accent.

She'd met Laird Butler when he was traveling around Scotland right after he graduated from college. They'd met at the beginning of his trip, and were married three months later. Even in her late sixties, his mother was still a beauty, with fiery red hair and deep blue eyes that he and all his siblings shared.

"Yeah, it's me, Ma."

"Did you find Peyton, then?" she asked.

Brodie didn't want to tell her that he'd found Peyton and she'd refused to take the box, but she'd know he was lying if he told her otherwise.

"What's this?" his father asked.

"Nothing to worry about, Laird. Brodie was delivering something we found of hers."

Well, if his mother was going to lie to his father, maybe his lying to her wouldn't be so bad after all.

"Sorcha, you best not be meddling."

"O' coorse nae." His mother stood. "We'll talk after dinner, Brodie."

Before he could follow her inside, his father motioned for him to have a seat. Brodie sat across from him at the small table where his mother and father often shared their afternoon tea.

"Tell me what this is about, Brodie."

"Ma asked me to deliver some things to Peyton Wolf that belonged to her, and some other stuff from Kade."

"Ah. You were unsuccessful, then." His father pulled a tobacco pouch from his pocket and filled his pipe.

"How'd you know?"

Rather than answer, his father nodded and lit the pipe.

"She wouldn't take it."

"I see."

"I don't want to tell Ma."

"Excuse yourself near the end of dinner. She won't be bringing it up in front of me."

"Thanks, Da." Brodie got a chill and shivered.

"Your ma made shepherd's pie. It'll warm ya." His father set his pipe on the porch rail and motioned for Brodie to follow him inside.

"I saw Peyton Wolf today," Brodie told Naughton later when they were back at the house.

Naughton nodded but didn't answer.

"She misses him."

"We all do, Brodie."

"How serious do you think she and Kade were?"

"No idea."

It wasn't unlike Naughton to be reticent. He always said he liked working in the vineyards because he preferred the solitude.

"Didn't you know her first husband?"

"Yeah, Cal Poly grad." Naughton shook his head. "Cheated on her before *and* during their marriage."

"That's right, she went to Cal Poly too."

Naughton had graduated from the university in San Luis Obispo with a degree in viticulture, the science of grape growing. Brodie had followed his older brother Maddox to UC Davis, where they'd both majored in enology, the science of winemaking. Brodie went on to get a Wine Executive master's, which combined enology and viticulture with business management.

"She was an ag-biz major though, more like what you do. Lang was a vit major, but he never took it seriously. Not even sure how the guy graduated."

Brodie thought he heard Naughton say something under his breath, but he didn't quite catch it. Sounded like his brother called Lang a dick.

"He and Kade got into it pretty bad one night."

That surprised Brodie as much as it didn't surprise him. Kade had been a big guy with a nasty scar that ran across his left cheek. It made him look like a bad mother. When he wasn't on a mission, he worked out two or three hours a day, and even when he was, that was how the guys killed their down time. Kade hated going out to bars because, inevitably, some drunk asshole would try to start a fight with him. Lang sounded like just the kind of douche that would've been in Kade's face.

"Older brother walked away from the physical stuff, but he didn't hesitate to let Lang know exactly what he thought of him."

"What happened?"

"He basically called him out as a loser and an asshole for abandoning his kids, and for what he did to Peyton."

That was the thing about Kade—as intimidating as he was physically, his unexpected intellect inflicted more damage than his fists would've. He was one smart son-of-a-bitch, and Brodie missed him so much, he ached. He could only imagine how Peyton must feel.

"It wasn't long after, that Kade told me they got Lang for not paying child support. Courts get after those bastards for shit like that."

"She's better off without him."

"Yeah, but Kade told me she didn't care about the money. What she cared about was her boys not having a dad."

Kade would've filled the role, and now he was gone too. *Shit.* No wonder Peyton didn't want his stuff.

When Naughton buried his head in a horticulture annual, Brodie went outside. It was damn cold, but he needed to walk off talking about his brother. How many nights had he gone on this same walk, wondering if his brother was okay?

All of them looked up to Kade; all of them missed him in their own way. As far as Brodie was concerned, there wasn't a finer man to emulate than Kade Butler. He was forty years old when he died and, as far as Brodie knew, had never been serious enough about anyone to talk about marriage until he met Peyton. Maddox and Naughton hadn't been either. Only Skye was married, and fortunately for the rest of them, she was pregnant with her second child. Her oldest was a little girl, Spencer, and she'd recently found out she was having a boy this time around. With one grandchild and another on the way, their mother stopped nagging the rest of them as much.

After his morning run-in with Peyton at the beach, Brodie didn't feel like going back to the ranch. Instead, he drove down to Morro Bay and had lunch. After that, he hiked around Whale Rock Reservoir, managing to kill enough time that it was almost dark by the time he drove home. Through it all, he couldn't stop thinking about her.

Closing his eyes, he could remember everything about how she'd looked this morning. Brodie was surprised by how tall she was, five feet seven or eight he'd guess. Her blonde hair was pulled back, away from her face, and her pale green eyes reminded him of the sage that grew wild on the hills of Butler Ranch. She had on a heavy, gray sweater that stopped short of the black belt that looped through the worn jeans she had tucked into knee-high, black riding boots.

Right after Kade died, he found photos of her with his brother, on hikes with her boys, and kayaking. There was even a shot of her holding a surfboard, wearing a full-body, neoprene pink and gray wetsuit that covered every inch of her yet left nothing about her body to the imagination.

From those photos, he knew she was pretty, but in person, she was beautiful. *Beautiful and badass.* It was no wonder Kade fell in love with her. Any guy would.

Brodie had no idea what his next move would be, but he knew there would be one. Whether she wanted his brother's stuff or not, there was no way Brodie could stay away from Peyton Wolf.

Naughton was opening a bottle of wine when Brodie came back inside.

"This is their 2013 Cab Franc," he handed a glass to Brodie before breathing in the aroma from his own glass and giving it a hard swirl. "Anise, blueberry, vanilla, tobacco."

Brodie picked up the bottle. Wolf Family Vintners. He took a sip. The palate had that distinct, oily mid-texture you only got with Cab Franc. It was soft on the palate with extracted tannins on the finish. Nice. More than nice. It was a beautiful wine. Made by a beautiful girl's family.

—:—

"Hey, Mom?"

"Yeah, sweetie?"

"You forgot the juice."

It was the third time Peyton walked from one side of the little market to the other because she forgot something. And it wasn't because she didn't have a list.

"You okay?" Jamison asked her.

He was her sensitive child. He picked up on even the most subtle nuances. At first Peyton had tried to hide her feelings from him, but then one day, it occurred to her that her son would benefit more from her emotions than her lack of them. What was wrong with being sad because you lost someone you cared about? It was real, and that's how she wanted her boys to see her. Real.

"I saw someone from Kade's family today, sweetheart. So I'm a little distracted."

"A little?" he smiled.

Peyton ran her hand through his hair. "How'd you get so smart?"

"Genes."

She pulled him close and hugged him hard. "I love you so much, kiddo."

"Same."

It was an expression Peyton got used to. She heard Jamison use it with his friends too. Evidently, "I feel the same" required too many words.

Finn was another aisle over, talking to Louie, who owned the market. It was one among many of the things Peyton loved about their little village. She didn't have to worry if her son was not right next to her. It wasn't as though she'd let him too far out of sight, but there was comfort in knowing that the locals knew her boys, and they knew the locals. They had more people who looked out for them, and loved them, than most people had in a lifetime.

"Whatcha' talkin' about?" she asked her youngest son.

"Louie says R2-D2 is a better droid than BB-8. I say, no way."

It figured that Louie, who had to be in his seventies, would have *Star Wars* droids behind the cash register counter.

Peyton went back for the orange juice Jamison had reminded her to get, while he joined the droid discussion. It was the kind of conversation Kade would've had with them. The three of them would argue, but he'd never get impatient with them. God, she missed him.

"Saw you with Brodie this morning," Louie muttered.

"Sorry about that, Louie."

"About what?"

"Leaving the way I did."

Louie shook his head and patted her hand.

"Thanks, Louie."

"Who's Brodie?" Jamison asked on their drive home.

"He's Kade's brother."

"Oh."

"I miss Kade," Finn said from the backseat.

"I do too, buddy." Peyton looked over at Jamison sitting in the passenger seat next to her. "You okay?"

"Miss him too," Jamison whispered. It was easy to see her son was fighting back tears.

"It's okay to feel sad, Jamie. You too, Finn. I feel sad too. I feel sad a lot."

"Maybe Brodie will wanna hang out with us," Finn suggested.

Peyton cringed but had to admit, she'd been thinking that way too.

What was wrong with her? He sought her out to give her the stuff Kade had wanted her to have. That was all there was to it. He looked so much like his older brother, Peyton transferred her lingering attraction for Kade to his likeness.

"Don't be dumb," Jamison scolded his brother.

"Hey, now, Jamie. There's nothing wrong with wishing someone could replace someone else you lost, although it rarely works out. We loved being with Kade, and we miss him. We wish he was still here, but he isn't, and his brother is. But they're two different people, Finn." Peyton looked in the rearview mirror to make sure he was still paying attention.

He was looking out the window, but nodded.

"I get it, Mom."

Finn didn't want her to read a bedtime story. He wanted her to tell him stories about Kade. Some of the stories she told were real, and some were greatly embellished. To Finn, Kade would always be the superhero who saved them, and the rest of the world, from the bad guys.

She and Kade had shared a love of reading. They could sit in the same room for hours, both reading, no conversation necessary between them. When he left on a mission, Peyton read whatever books he left behind. His taste in literature had been vastly different than hers, but she learned a lot about him, and what he did, from the books he chose to read. Some of the stories she told Finn came from those books.

When she checked on Jamison after Finn fell asleep, he was asleep too.

Her boys needed a man in their lives. They had her dad, but they only saw him on the weekends. She thought about moving back to the guest house full time, but the forty-five-minute commute every morning and night would've worn her out. She could hardly manage the five-minute drive home after the tasting room closed.

Peyton washed her face, brushed her teeth, and climbed into bed. She closed her eyes and thought about Brodie sitting on that rock above Moonstone Beach. He hadn't been waiting for her. He hadn't known she'd decide to take a walk after she stormed out on Alex. What had brought him to the spot where she and Kade often sat and watched the sunset? How could he have known?

She woke, a few hours later, and turned off the television that had lulled her to sleep. It seemed as though she dreamed about Kade every night, but tonight, she dreamed about Brodie instead.

The next morning, when she was making breakfast for the boys, she saw a text alert on her phone. It was a message from Brodie, asking if he could see her today.

Why?

I'd like to talk to you.

Not sure.

Peyton sent a text to Alex, asking if she'd mind if Peyton skipped the morning run they'd talked about.

Morning what? she answered, and then added, *JK, you know I'd rather sleep.*

We can meet, she responded to Brodie.

Moonstone?

What time?

You tell me.

Nine?

Perfect.

Why not take another walk down Heartbreak Road? She was beginning to know its dead end all too well.

3

Brodie moved the plain cardboard box from the front passenger seat of his truck to the floor in the back. It wasn't the only reason he wanted to see Peyton, and he didn't want it to be the first thing they talked about.

After a night of tossing and turning, he got up this morning knowing that, if he wanted to sleep tonight, he had to see Peyton today. He didn't have a plan other than he wanted to see her, spend time with her, get to know her a little, and then force himself to give her the box, and close that chapter of Kade's life.

When he pulled up to the same parking spot as yesterday, Peyton's car was already there, but she wasn't in it. Brodie got out, walked to the edge of the boardwalk, and looked north and south. He spotted her a ways down the beach, near where Santa Rosa Creek spilled into the Pacific Ocean. She was walking away from him, but turned around and waved. He waved back. He'd thought about stopping at Louie's again this morning for coffee and another pastry, but wanted to wait to see if Peyton would like to have breakfast with him. It was a long shot and would probably take far more time than she intended to spend with him, but he took it anyway.

Rather than waiting for Peyton to walk back, Brodie ran down the path and met her partway.

"Wanna keep going?" she asked.

"If you do."

They continued walking down the beach until they reached the rocks of the state preserve.

"It gets a little rough through here," Peyton began. "Maybe we should..."

"What were you going to say?"

"Maybe we should turn back."

"You're not just being nice, are you? Have you heard my stomach loudly reminding me that I haven't eaten breakfast?"

"Neither have I." Peyton smiled, and her cheeks turned the slightest bit pink.

Brodie looked at his watch. "What time do you have to be at work?"

"We're closed today."

"That's great! I mean, that you don't have to hurry in to work, but I don't want to keep you if there's something else you need to do."

"Nope, not a thing. I've got all day and nothing on my calendar. Except picking up the boys."

"What time is that?"

"Not until five. They're both in basketball after school."

Since Peyton did not take advantage of a single out he gave her, he stopped offering. "How about breakfast, then?"

"I'd love it."

They talked about the business of winemaking, a subject they were both passionate about. Brodie told her he was impressed with the work she'd done since taking over Stave. Peyton gave most of the credit to Alex, but he knew better.

"Where should we go?" Brodie asked when they got back to where her car and his truck were parked.

"Do you mind a drive?"

"Not at all." How far away was she thinking? And did he have a protein bar buried in his truck somewhere?

Brodie looked over her black BMW 4 Series. "How fast does this little number go?"

"Zero to sixty in a little over four seconds. Wanna drive?"

"Your car? You're kidding!"

Peyton tossed him the key fob. "I get to drive it every day."

"The Coupe is a little faster than the Gran Coupe, but only by about a tenth of a second, and a four-door is much better for the boys," she said once they were inside.

"I can't believe you have two boys and your car stays this immaculate."

"Yeah, well, they aren't typical boys, I guess."

Brodie backed the car out and got his bearings on Moonstone Beach Road. It would be another story when they hit Highway One. "Which way?"

"Mind going down to Big Sky?"

"Love that place. I never think of it."

Peyton leaned back against the seat and closed her eyes. "I miss it, and I never seem to have time to drive all the way down to San Luis Obispo. When I am down there, I always have somewhere else I have to be."

"What's your favorite thing to have for breakfast?"

"In general, or at Big Sky?"

"Both."

"In general, yogurt and fruit, sometimes with granola."

"Ugh, too healthy!"

"You forget how much food I have to taste all day."

"Is wine considered a food group these days?"

"No, but the chefs who put on our events don't make *wine;* they prepare *food.* The wine dinners are a big part of what we do at Stave."

Brodie glanced over at Peyton. She had been smiling, but it quickly disappeared.

"I met Kade at the first wine dinner Stave hosted. In the years that followed, he came to a lot of them."

There was the elephant in the car with them. Brodie had wondered how long they could go without one of them bringing up his brother. "I remember him talking about them."

"You've never been."

It wasn't a question, and she was right. He hadn't been to one of Stave's wine dinners, but he'd heard a lot about them. As much as he wanted to attend one, he'd stayed away, the last few months, out of respect for Peyton.

"I've heard they're spectacular."

"Maybe you could join us sometime."

Brodie glanced over again. She wasn't looking at him. She was looking out the window, not caring whether he answered.

"Back to breakfast. What's your favorite thing at Big Sky?"

"That's tough. If I could only have breakfast there one more time, I'd order poached eggs and crab cakes. Or maybe the lemon ricotta pancakes with blueberry compote, or the—"

Brodie reached over and touched her hand. "Stop. Don't mention another food item. I'm so hungry I could..."

What had he almost let slip? More than anything, he wanted to nibble on her beautiful, long neck. The way she arched it when she looked out the window made him long to run his tongue from just under her ear down to her collarbone. He stifled his groan. It was a toss-up which he was hungrier for: food or Peyton.

"I'm pretty hungry too," she laughed.

Probably not in the same way he was.

—:—

Over breakfast, Brodie asked her about Cal Poly and told her his brother Naughton had gone there.

"Kade mentioned that a couple of times. I knew him, but didn't really know him, you know what I mean?"

He smiled and nodded.

"Where did you go to school? I'm sure Kade told me at some point, but I don't remember."

"Davis, like Mad did. I started out in enology, but my heart isn't in winemaking the way his is. I worked on the business side of wine in Napa for a few years."

"I thought, for a while, I'd work up there too, but I'm just more comfortable stickin' around home." Would he ask her about her first marriage? Did he even know about it? He must; she had two kids.

"I dated my husband all through college, and once we graduated, he was anxious to get married. It seemed as though I graduated, got married, and had kids before I even figured out what I wanted to do with my life. It all felt too fast, which it obviously was, since it didn't work out."

"I think Naughton might have known him."

"I doubt they were friends. Lang would've been too...uh...*much* for Naughton."

Brodie laughed. "You got that right. *I'm* too much for Naughton. I think everyone is."

"I don't know him very well. I really don't know anyone in your family as well as I should. Kade and I had so little time together that, when we did, we wanted it to be just us and the boys. Kind of selfish, I guess." She and Kade hadn't spent much time with her family either.

"Not selfish. Just in love. You probably would've spent more time with us after you were married."

Married? Where did he get that? She and Kade hadn't talked about getting married...ever, that she could remember, and that's the kind of thing a girl didn't forget.

"Sorry, does it make you uncomfortable to talk about him?"

"No, I like having someone to talk to who knew him. Does it bother you?"

"I feel the same way you do. I can talk to my family about him, but you knew him in a different way than we did. I wish we could've seen more of that side of him."

"See? Selfish."

Brodie reached across the table and rested his hand on hers. "No, Peyton, not selfish. No one thinks that. No one would ever think that. Everyone understands. It took Kade a long, long time to find someone he wanted to be with as much as he wanted to be with you. We were happy for him."

"I loved him." What more could she say? She just told him it didn't make her uncomfortable to talk about Kade, but now she wanted to change the subject.

"How about you? Am I keeping you from something you're supposed to be doing today?"

"Nope. Like you, I have nothing on my schedule. I don't even have anyone I have to pick up after basketball practice."

It was sweet of him to remember she had to pick up her boys. Peyton looked at her watch. Since it was only a little past noon, she still had plenty of time before she had to think about getting back to Cambria. "Feel like driving some more?"

"If you're asking me if I want to drive your car again, baby, I could drive that all day and night."

Peyton felt the heat spread from her neck up through her cheeks. Even her forehead felt as though it was on fire. He hadn't meant it the way she heard it, of course, but damn, she couldn't get the image of him driving *her* all day and night.

"Did I say something wrong?" Brodie asked.

"Not at all. Just a little warm in here. You ready to go?" It wasn't warm at all; in fact, it was chilly. The heat she was feeling had nothing to do with the temperature in the restaurant. She fanned herself for effect.

"Sure, yeah. I'll just take care of the check, and we can be on our way."

"That would be a good idea, wouldn't it?" she laughed. God, she'd completely forgot about the check. Where was her mind? Easy answer—her mind was on Brodie Butler, and as hard as she tried, she couldn't think about anything other than how good it felt to be with him.

"Where to, pretty lady?" Brodie asked when they left Big Sky.

"We could walk around town a little since we aren't in a hurry to get anywhere." She missed being downtown, and all the cute shops she used to visit when she was in college.

Thursdays were the best. That's when most of downtown turned into a giant farmers' market. It wasn't limited to farm stands. There were also booths offering ethnic foods, others sold clothing, and musicians busked on every corner. She couldn't remember the last time she came down for it. The boys would love it.

"You're quiet, but it looks like whatever you're thinking about is something that makes you happy."

"You know what? You're right. I was just thinking I should bring the boys down on Thursday, for the farmers' market. Have you been? It feels more like a street festival."

"I haven't been in years, but I'd love to join you if you wouldn't mind me tagging along."

Oh. Her boys. And Brodie. That wouldn't work. Finn had already asked about Brodie spending time with them.

"Hey, you know, now that I think about it, I wouldn't be able to join you guys this Thursday. Maybe another time though."

"I'm sorry, Brodie. It's just the boys—"

He held up his hand, so she stopped talking. She felt horrible though. He'd been nothing but nice to her. He'd immediately picked up on her discomfort and let her off the hook.

"I know we just ate, but damn, something smells good."

"That's Mama's Meatballs. You can smell their garlic knots from miles around, or at least it seems that way." Once again, being here today reminded Peyton how much she missed it. San Luis Obispo was only a half hour from her place in Cambria. She had no good reason for never coming down here, other than she didn't think about it. She made a promise to herself to start bringing the boys down more often.

"So...maybe...you and I..." he began.

—:—

What would Peyton say? He was about to ask her out to dinner. No way she wouldn't think of it as a date. How badly was he screwing this up? She was his dead brother's girlfriend, and all he could think about was spending every waking moment with her, the sleeping ones too, not that he'd want to sleep if he was with her. He was seriously sick in the head.

"Brodie?"

"I'd really like to have dinner there sometime."

"You should. It's amazing and reasonably priced too."

"Peyton...I...uh, this is just so awkward."

"I know," she sighed.

Did that mean he wasn't losing his mind? Was she feeling what he was feeling? Would she let herself, or was it just too damn weird?

They were quiet on the walk back to the car. When they got close, Brodie wondered if she'd still want to go for a drive or if she'd want to go back to Cambria. He pulled the car's key fob out of his pocket and raised his eyebrows in question.

"Ever been on See Canyon Road?" she asked.

"Not in years. You sure you want to take this baby on a dirt road?"

"Why have an all-wheel-drive car if you never take advantage of it?"

Beautiful and badass. Once again Brodie appreciated why Kade fell in love with Peyton. "Which way should we go?"

"It's only worth it if you drive south to north. Otherwise the views are all behind you."

"You wanna take the wheel?"

"You've got this," she smiled.

Brodie drove through town, to the highway.

"Can we go one more exit?" Peyton asked when they reached San Luis Bay Drive, the turnoff for See Canyon Road. "It's been so long since I've been to Avila, and it'll only take us a couple of miles out of the way."

Brodie couldn't remember the last time he visited Avila Beach either. "I used to stand on the pier while my dad tossed crab nets in the water, imagining, one day, I'd live in the Point San Luis Lighthouse."

"Really? Wow! Were the nets for Dungeness?"

"The seafood feasts we'd have at my grandparents' beach house were epic." Brodie drove through the lush oak valley where most of the spas featuring natural mineral hot springs had been built. He pulled off Front Street and parked her car near Avila Beach Pier. While it was still a commercial fishing pier, every time he visited the little seaside village, it seemed there was another fancy hotel or oceanfront restaurant hogging more of the already small shoreline of the bay. Soon he expected the pier would be overtaken by tourist traps, as so many other piers along the central coast had been.

"We were in Oceano most of the summer. Gramps called their place the Slough House because it sat beside a slough. When we visited Scotland when I was a boy, I realized that the house was almost an exact replica of any you'd find in the fishing villages on the Isle of Barro."

"What happened to that house?"

"Years ago someone who bought it and the house next door, demolished both and built one massive house in place of the two."

Brodie wondered if Kade had told Peyton about their grandparents. Being older, Kade remembered so much more about being there than Brodie did.

"Heard these stories before? Don't wanna bore ya," he smiled.

She shook her head. "I haven't, but I want to."

"We'd arrive from the hot valley on Friday night, and the next morning, two of us boys would go to Pismo Beach with my grandfather. We'd dig for those huge Pismo clams you can't find anymore. The other two boys would come here with our dad. He'd toss the nets, and then we'd drive north to a place that was so secret, I'd never be able to find my way back there." Brodie looked over at Peyton to see if she showed signs of boredom yet.

"Go on. This is fascinating." When she smiled at him, he almost forgot the next part of his story.

"When we were little, we had to wait in the car. Dad would take a crowbar down to the rocks and pry off abalone. Can't find abalone anymore either."

"Mmm, I miss abalone." Peyton closed her eyes and put her hand on her stomach. "Sometimes they have it at the Sea Chest."

"One of my favorite restaurants."

"Mine, too. Sorry to interrupt you, Brodie. This is a great story."

"After the abalone harvest, we'd come back here and raise the crab nets. If we were lucky, they'd be filled with Dungeness."

"You're making me hungry again."

"We'd haul our take back to the house where Gramps, Dad, and all us boys prepared dinner."

"What did your mom and sisters do?"

"Relaxed, which they never got to do at home. Especially my ma. My grandmother loved to talk to her about Scotland. Ma's from a little village close to where Grandma Analise was born. The two would talk 'home' all weekend long, and then the next time we visited, reminisce about the same stuff all over again. Which is why I asked if you'd heard these stories before. I got so I would tune them out."

"Not bored, Brodie."

"There was a huge tree stump in the yard where Gramps would take a rubber mallet to the abalone. While he did that, we'd clean the clams and separate them. Some were used for chowder and the others, we would fry.

"While this was going on, there'd be a big pot of water heating on the grill Gramps built in the yard. It was made of stone, and a giant grate sat on top of it. Have you ever had fresh-caught lobster cooked outside over an oak wood fire? The best lobster I've had in my life."

"I haven't, but I love oak-grilled artichokes."

"Right? Me too."

"I love seafood, no matter how it's prepared."

"I remember hanging out with my friends after being with my grandparents for the weekend, and telling them about our feasts. So many of them turned up their noses. I didn't get it. How could you not like clams and crab and abalone?"

"I could eat fish and other seafood every day of the week. We already know I eat crab cakes for breakfast," she laughed.

"How about your boys, do they like it?"

"Worst mistake I ever made was introducing my two eating machines to sushi. They can go through a hundred bucks of raw fish faster than my car goes from zero to sixty."

"I'm the same way. My ma isn't a big fan, but my brothers, sisters, dad, and I can power through a hundred bucks worth each. It's a lot different now than it was when you could spend a morning going out and finding it for free."

"Don't I know it."

"It was a great childhood. I'm surprised Kade never told you about it."

"Me too, although Kade wasn't big on reminiscing. Maybe he got as tired of hearing the stories as you did."

"Ready to roll?" It was just after two, and it would take them at least an hour to get over the pass and through See Canyon.

"Sure. Know where you're going?"

Brodie smiled and backed the car up. It was a short drive from Avila Beach Drive back to San Luis Bay.

"Did you know Alex's family was one of the first to settle here?"

"I've always wondered if their name was a coincidence."

"They take native Californian to a whole other level."

When they reached the See Canyon turn-off, Peyton hit the audio button on the sound system.

"Who's this?"

"A guy who lives not too far from here, in Ojai. I've been a fan for years. The first time I went on this drive, was the first time I heard his music. It's been the soundtrack since. I thought I'd put an Amos Lee CD in, but I ended up liking this better."

"Does he still perform?"

"Yeah, usually down in Ventura though."

"Not that far. Maybe we could drive down and see him sometime." Brodie's chest got tight when Peyton didn't answer. He kept putting his foot in it, crossing the line from being the brother of her dead boyfriend, and wanting to be her next boyfriend. It was more than that, Brodie wanted to know everything there was to know about Peyton Wolf.

"What's his name?"

"This guy? Syd."

"He's good."

"The music fits, doesn't it?"

Yep, it did. It was perfect. Later, after he got home, he'd download it and try to keep himself from listening to nothing else.

—:—

The beginning of the thirteen-mile drive was deceiving, with the thick canopy of oak trees lining the paved road scattered with apple orchards and vineyards. Five miles in, the trees opened up, and the winding, paved road turned to dirt.

"I can't believe how few people know about this drive," Peyton commented when the only car they'd seen since they began the drive passed, going in the opposite direction.

"You'd think, by now, it would be on every map handed out to tourists."

Peyton rolled down her window and breathed in. "Can't see it yet, but there's no mistaking how close to the ocean we are."

The road switched back and forth through the rolling, golden hills of the coastal mountains, still miraculously untamed by developers.

The blue sky was free of clouds, so the vistas from the summit extended from the miles and miles of unspoiled oceanfront to the west, all the way beyond the hills of Paso Robles to the east. When they were at the very top of the narrow strip of road, Brodie pulled off.

"Everything okay?" Peyton asked.

"There's something I need to talk to you about."

"Did you bring me all the way out here so I didn't have a choice?"

"This drive was your idea, pretty lady," he smiled.

"Right. It was. The words 'something I have to talk to you about' fill me with dread, though." What would Brodie say? Whatever it was, she knew instinctively she didn't want to hear.

"The box."

"That's right, the box." The one she didn't want, filled with things that would bring her pain she didn't want to feel anymore. "Brodie, I—"

"This is the last time I'm going to bring it up. If you don't want it, I'll take it home and stash it away. If there ever comes a time you change your mind, all you have to do is ask me for it."

Peyton opened the door and climbed out of the car. She stood with her hands in her pockets and took in the view of Morro Rock.

Kade would've done the same thing Brodie was doing. He'd always been so easy on her, but he'd known what he was doing. The easier he was on her, the more she wanted to prove to him she could handle whatever he was shielding her from.

Brodie got out of the car and stood next to her.

"You remind me so much of him."

"Thank you. That's high praise. Lots of guys want to be just like their older brother, but for me, that really means something."

"I dream about him all the time, that it was just a mistake. I dream I'm somewhere in town and I see him. That's why I was so freaked out at Louie's yesterday morning. I saw you walk in, and from the back, you look so much like him."

"I'm sorry, Peyton."

She didn't want to cry, but she couldn't stop herself. "In a way, being with you is like being with him. But it's different, too." Peyton walked back to the car and opened the passenger door. "Do you mind if we keep going?"

"Of course not." Brodie got in and started the engine. "I'm struggling, Peyton. As much as I don't want to admit it, I find myself wishing you never knew my brother, that you're just a woman I met on my own, who I'm attracted to. I want to go to the farmers' market with you and your boys, and take you to Mama's Meatballs for dinner, and go see the guy whose music we're listening to."

She felt her chest constrict again. He was being so honest with her, could she be as honest with him?

—:—

Neither spoke on the drive home. When they got back to Los Osos Valley Road, Brodie didn't ask if there was anywhere else she wanted to go, he just got on the highway that would take them back to Cambria.

"I enjoyed our day, Brodie," Peyton said when he pulled her car up next to his truck.

He had, too. He couldn't remember having a day as nice as this one. When he got out of her car, he wouldn't have any excuse to see her again. He'd promised not to mention the box, and that was his only reason for being with her. The thought of not knowing when he'd see her again hurt.

She had his number. He got hers from his mother and had used it to text her this morning.

"You take care of yourself, Peyton. If there's ever anything you need, *anything*, don't hesitate to get in touch with me." Brodie picked up the key fob and handed it to her. Her fingers brushed his when she tried to take it from him, making him want to pull her into his arms and never let go. He held the fob tighter and looked into her eyes. "Peyton…"

"Bye, Brodie."

He let go of the fob and got out of the car. "Bye, Peyton."

4

Peyton went around to the driver's door and waved as Brodie backed his truck up and drove away. She pulled out her phone and saw she had two voicemails and several texts. She hadn't looked at her phone since they left Big Sky Café, and that wasn't like her. It wasn't responsible either. What if her boys needed something? Her heart raced as she checked the texts first. Both were from Alex, saying she was just checking in. If anything had happened to the boys, Alex was her emergency contact; she wouldn't have just "checked in."

She didn't recognize the phone numbers from the voicemails, and they turned out to be sales calls, which irritated her.

"Well, hello there, where on earth have you been?" asked Alex when she answered her cell.

"Wait, what? You didn't want to run."

"Settle down! You're right. I didn't want to run. That doesn't mean I don't want to know where you've been."

"I'll tell you later." Peyton wasn't ready to admit she'd spent the day with Brodie Butler, even to her best friend.

"You've got to be kidding. First you give no clue as to why you canceled something you nag endlessly about, and now, after I haven't talked to you all day, you're still holding out on me?"

"I said I'll tell you later. I have to leave now to pick the boys up from school."

"When will you be home?"

"I don't know, fifteen minutes?"

"I'll see you in twenty, and have a bottle of wine open."

"Okay."

"Are you hungry? I can pick up take-out on my way over."

"I'll ask the boys what they want and call you back."

"Sounds good, and I'll see you soon. I'm warning you though, you'll pay for torturing me like this."

"I'm rolling my eyes."

"As if you wouldn't react the same way if the situations were reversed. You'd be worse, actually."

Peyton laughed and disconnected the call. Alex was right. Peyton would've been relentless if Alex disappeared for an entire day. Unfortunately for her friend, Peyton would be making her wait even longer. There was no way she'd tell her about her day with Brodie if either of her boys were still awake.

"I'm seriously craving seafood," Peyton told Alex when she called back. "Too bad the Sea Chest is closed."

"I'll drive by and see if Stormy is there. If she is, I can probably talk her into letting me have some chowder, maybe even some oysters."

Stormy Blue, her given name, was the manager of the Sea Chest, and had gone to high school with Alex. Peyton crossed her fingers that Stormy was there, because no one else in town compared when it came to clam chowder.

"If not, I'll swing by the market. Can you wait that long?"

"I can wait. I'll just nibble on a piece of the pizza I ordered for the boys."

"Don't forget the wine," Alex teased.

"As if. I have a Skyrider white chilled."

"Perfect. I'm starving and a little wangry. See you soon."

Peyton and Alex knew *wangry* well. It's what they called customers who came in grouchy from their day and barked their order. "Are you a little wangry?" they'd ask and give them an extra heavy pour on their first glass.

"I forgot how much I like this wine," Alex said after her second sip. "Do we have any of it at Stave?"

"No, they're sold out."

"I didn't think we had it. How'd you get it?"

"I know a guy," Peyton grinned.

"Alright, enough with the mystery. What did you do today?"

"Shh," Peyton put her finger in front of her lips. "I'll tell you after they're in bed." Peyton nodded her head in the direction of the family room, where the boys were doing their homework.

Alex got up and walked to where she could see both of them. "Jamison? Finn?"

She walked back and plopped into a chair. "Headphones on, can't hear a thing. Now talk."

"I'd rather wait until I know they're asleep."

"Not a chance. I've been way more patient than you would've been."

"Alright."

Peyton told Alex she spent the day in San Luis Obispo, about having breakfast, and then going to Avila Beach and driving back through See Canyon. She just left out who she was with, which did not go unnoticed by Alex, who was glaring at her with her arms folded.

"I was with Brodie," she whispered and looked in the direction of the family room, hoping her boys still had their headphones on.

"Oh my God."

"Shh," she said again. "The boys were asking about him last night, and I don't want them to get the wrong idea."

"What's the right idea?"

"I don't know. It's weird."

"When are you going to see him again?"

"I'm not. At least not intentionally." She'd already been trying to figure out a way to "bump into him," but so far, hadn't come up with anything plausible.

"Does he want to see you again?"

"Too much."

"What does that mean? What did he say?"

"That he wished he'd met me under different circumstances."

"Do you feel the same way about him?"

If there was anyone she could admit her feelings to, it was Alex, but something made her hold back. Two days ago, she wouldn't have known Brodie Butler if he walked into her house uninvited. She would've known his connection to Kade though; no one could miss it.

She was lonely, and she missed Kade so much. Brodie reminded her of him, but there was more to it. If she'd met him under different circumstances, she would've felt the same attraction. It was too powerful. It wasn't just that he reminded her of Kade. There was more to it.

"What would people think?" she asked out loud, without meaning to.

"Who gives a shit, Peyton? What do you think? That's all that matters."

This wasn't the first time Alex lectured her about caring too much about what other people thought. For the most part, Alex was right. Part of growing up was coming to terms with how little other peoples' opinions mattered. The truth was, people were rarely as critical as most assumed.

"This goes beyond that, Alex."

"Tell me what he said."

"I already told you."

"No, you told me he wished you'd met differently. He must've told you why he felt that way."

"It was a nice day. We enjoyed each other's company. It was easy."

"Tell me more."

"Before I do, tell me what you know about him."

"Brodie?"

"Yeah, Brodie. Duh."

"Okay, okay. No need to get testy. Brodie Butler, hmm. Not a lot, to be honest. It's kind of weird that you were so close to Kade, but you don't know anything about his brother."

"It isn't just Brodie. I don't know much about Kade's whole family. I learned more about them in one day with Brodie than I did in all the time I knew Kade."

"There isn't a single one of the Butler boys that isn't hotter than hot, and terminally single."

"That reminds me, I have something to tell you on that subject, but I want to come back to it."

"O-o-o-kay. I know Maddox better than the rest of them. I feel like I knew Kade, but I never really did. I knew your version of Kade."

"That makes sense, and I know what you mean. I never felt as though Kade was secretive, I just never realized how little I knew about him."

"Mad has always been the charming one. Naughton is all dark and broody Scottish guy. Brodie, well, he never wanted for women, if you know what I mean."

"But not the charming one?"

"I don't think Brodie ever required charm. He's just all that and more, right?"

"I guess...I really don't know."

"You had a nice day. It was easy. Isn't that what you told me? How many people can you say that about?"

"Not many. So, you think that's just how he is?"

"No, I didn't say that. I just think he's easy going, hotter than shit, and very sure of himself. Confidence is pretty damn sexy, don't ya think?"

"Yeah, I do think."

Kade was hot, in a big, tough, teddy bear sort of way. There was sheer power in every step he took. It was weird that Brodie reminded her so much of Kade, because describing the two of them, he was so different.

Brodie was taller than Kade, probably six foot three to Kade's straight up six. He held himself the same way, but when Brodie walked across the room, he sauntered. Kade strode. Kade was attractive, but Brodie was handsome. Kade was dead, but Brodie was alive.

"Here's the problem—I don't know if I will ever stop comparing the two of them." Peyton shook her head. "It doesn't really matter."

"Whoa, whoa, whoa. What just happened?"

"I can't see him again. It's just too much."

"Peyton..."

"Can we change the subject?"

Alex burst out laughing. "To what?"

Peyton laughed too. "Shut up."

—:—

"Hey." Brodie tossed his keys on the kitchen table.

Naughton didn't look up or answer.

Brodie walked over to where his brother sat, looking at nothing. "Did you hear me? What's goin' on?"

"I heard you."

"Okay. Good night, Naughton."

"Where're you going?"

"Upstairs."

"Where were you today?"

"What do you mean?"

"Easy enough question to understand. Where were you?"

"I spent the day with Peyton."

"Why?"

"What's with all the questions?"

"Somebody saw you, told Ma."

"Ma's the reason I was with her."

"No, Ma asked you to give something to her, not spend the day with her."

"Did Ma say something about it?"

"She didn't have to. That why you were asking so many questions about her last night?"

"What the hell?"

"Forget it." Naughton brushed past him, almost knocking him over on his way upstairs.

Instead of following his brother, Brodie put his jacket back on and went outside. When he was younger, he and Kade would take a lot of walks outside after dark.

"See those stars up there?" He'd point at the sky. "No matter where I am in the world, I see the same stars as you. So you come out, talk to these stars, and they'll tell me what you said."

Brodie was twelve or thirteen when he and Kade had had that conversation. He remembered punching his brother's arm and telling him he was too old for that kind of bullshit. They'd laughed about it then. Now, more than ever, he wished it had been true.

"What should I do, Kade?" Brodie questioned the sky. "I can't stop thinking about her. You know what I'm talkin' about, because I know you couldn't either. She's amazing, big brother."

Brodie sat on a tree stump and thought about earlier in the day, when he'd told Peyton about his grandfather pounding the abalone. Her eyes were lit up the whole time he'd talked about his family. It wasn't just Kade she wanted to hear more about; she loved the stories he told about his parents and grandparents.

"So, Kade, didn't you tell her anything about our family? I don't get it." He shook his head.

It was cold again tonight, just as cold as it had been last night. Before he came out, he'd grabbed a jacket, but he should've grabbed a hat too.

He'd asked Kade once why he shaved his head. "I'm gettin' a little thin up top. Decided to shave it instead of fighting it. Chicks like bald heads, brother."

There was something else nagging at him. His whole family knew Kade had intended to propose to Peyton when he came back from his last mission. He even had a ring. Brodie wondered where the ring was now. Did his mother have it?

"Did she know how you felt? Did she know you wanted to marry her?" He had so many questions the stars couldn't answer for him. Only Kade could, and he was gone.

—:—

Alex yawned and stretched her arms over her head. "Better call it a night, girlfriend."

"Do you want to skip our run again tomorrow?"

"No way, Peyton. I plan on grilling you the entire time, until I pry every last detail out of you."

"It isn't that interesting, I promise."

"Brodie-the-booty is very interesting. I assure you."

"Good Lord, do people call him that?"

"Nope, not people. Women."

"See? He's a player. I don't have any interest in players."

"Did he make you feel that way today? Like he was playing you?"

"No, but isn't that what players do?"

"I think you know when you're being played, and you make the conscious decision to play along."

Peyton stood. "Okay, that's enough dating philosophy for one night. See you tomorrow, Alex."

"Get some rest, and I'll see you around nine." Alex hugged her and went out the door.

Peyton checked on both boys, who were sound asleep. She'd tucked in Finn a couple of hours ago, while Alex had a nighttime chat with Jamison.

"He informed me he's too old to be tucked in," Alex had told her when they met back in the living room. They were growing up too fast.

With the lights off in the rest of the house, Peyton closed her bedroom door and picked up the remote for the TV. She never went to sleep without it on. It was too quiet, and she'd spend too much time in her head. She also heard every noise the old house made, and then her imagination ran amok, and she couldn't sleep. She hadn't had a decent night's sleep since the night before Kade left for the last time.

Alex had invited the boys over for a slumber party so she and Kade could be alone. Together, they made dinner, which neither ate. Their hunger for each other had been stronger. They'd made love again and again, until Peyton fell into a coma-like sleep.

When she got into bed tonight and closed her eyes, she expected to see Kade, like she did every other night.

Except, this time, she saw Brodie. Brodie-the-booty, that's what Alex said women called him. Understandable, given how amazingly he rocked a pair of jeans. The barn jacket he wore had covered his "booty" most of the day, but when they were at Big Sky, he'd taken it off. When he left the table to use the restroom, her eyes had followed the back of him the whole way. Between his saunter and perfect ass, Peyton's mind wandered, wondering if the rest of him was as perfect as his backside. She'd never know, because she had no intention of seeing him again, let alone his naked body.

She woke up when her phone, sitting beside her on the nightstand, vibrated. She looked at the clock that sat near the television. It was after one in the morning. Worried it was something with her mom or dad, Peyton picked up the phone. It was hard to focus, so she picked up the reading glasses that sat near the phone, on the nightstand. Kade's reading glasses.

The text was from Brodie, and in it, he apologized if she thought he was an asshole, but he wanted to see her again. He told her he had to go out of town tomorrow, but wanted to know what she was doing Thursday.

Peyton sat up and read his message over and over again. After an hour of not being able to go back to sleep, she picked up her phone again.

I'll be at Stave in the afternoon, she wrote. Now that it was after two, she doubted he'd respond, but he did.

I'll be in.

Peyton studied the words and wondered what in the hell she thought she was doing. And what was Brodie thinking?

She set the phone back on the nightstand, hoping, now, she'd be able to go back to sleep. It vibrated again.

I can't stop thinking about you, Brodie wrote.

He couldn't? She couldn't stop thinking about him either. *Jesus.* They were both out of their minds.

5

Every time Peyton heard the tasting room door open, she vacillated between hoping it was Brodie and praying it wasn't. She checked her phone every five minutes to see if there was a text from him, saying he needed to cancel.

Soon Alex would be back from the bank run, and Peyton would have to tell her. She couldn't act like it was a surprise when Brodie showed up. She also needed to explain why she was hanging out so late on her day off.

It wasn't unusual for Peyton to come in Thursday morning to help Alex get the tasting room organized for the weekend. She was usually out of there by one or two at the latest, and it was getting close to two. The only thing she had left to do today was put together the list of the ten wines they'd serve tomorrow during happy hour.

Every Friday, between four and six, Stave offered a new release tasting. The place would be packed, and wine sales would be good. It was also the most fun night to be at Stave, outside of the nights when they hosted the wine dinners.

If they knew their wines were being served, winemakers often came, which gave them the opportunity to see firsthand what customers thought about the new release. Peyton closed the door of the wine chiller, and was about to take case inventory for the wines she chose, when she heard the back door open and close.

"I'm back," Alex shouted from their office.

"Hey," Peyton answered.

"How's it goin'? Can I see what you chose?"

Peyton handed her notes to Alex and looked out the front window.

"This looks good. I see you've got a new one on here from Butler Ranch."

Maddox had sent an email over a week ago, before her run-in with Brodie at Louie's Market, listing Butler Ranch releases for the next ninety days. Peyton had decided then that she'd add their first, a Sauvignon Blanc, to the tasting this Friday.

She'd stayed away from Butler Ranch wines since Kade died, but as a member of the collaborative, her excluding them wasn't fair. They deserved to have their wine featured as much as any other winery in the group. She didn't need to explain her reason for choosing it. Alex would know it had nothing to do with Brodie.

"So, by the way, I heard from Brodie Tuesday night. He said he would stop in today."

Alex raised her eyebrows.

"I need you to not give me shit about this, Alex. I'm giving myself plenty on my own."

"I'm glad you said that, because you're right. The other night, I told you that you shouldn't give a crap what anyone else thought, and that includes me. Although whether you want to know what I think or not, I'm going to tell you. I think it's great. Kade died over a year ago, Peyton. You didn't know Brodie when you were with Kade. You didn't even spend time with their family. So, I say go for it."

"Maybe he's stopping in to tell me he's thought it over and changed his mind about wanting to see me."

"Yeah, you're right. He's stopping by to see you to tell you he doesn't want to see you." Alex rolled her eyes.

"Shut up. And do you realize how often you roll your eyes at things I say?"

Alex laughed and set the tasting notes down on the bar. "I'll make myself scarce when he gets here."

"By scarce do you mean you'll hide in the back and listen to every word we say, or will you leave?"

"Tell you what—you make yourself scarce instead. It's *your* day off."

"Okay, but you gotta start going easier on me, Alex. I'm freaking out."

"I heard you, and I will. I'm now the captain of team Peydie, or should it be Broton?"

—:—

Brodie walked toward his 918 Porsche Cayman after a productive meeting at San Ysidro Ranch. Their restaurant, the Stone House, had recently been named the most romantic restaurant in Santa Barbara, and Butler Ranch wines were heavy on their *Wine Spectator* award-winning list.

In the last two days, everywhere he went, everything he saw, he thought about sharing with Peyton, including the cottages here at the ranch where Laurence Olivier had married Vivian Leigh. This place was straight out of a romance book, or so he'd heard. It wasn't as though he'd actually read any.

Brodie imagined spending a weekend here with Peyton in one of the ocean view cottages. They'd have dinner at the Stone House, or share a chef-prepared meal alone in their cottage. After dinner, they'd sit by the stone fireplace found in every one of the ranch's cottages, and then later, he'd show her exactly how much pleasure he could bring her body. He adjusted the trousers of his suit as he opened the passenger door to put his briefcase inside the car.

The weather was warmer, so before getting back on the highway, Brodie put the top down. He couldn't wait to see her face when he drove up in his lava orange "baby." Her beamer was fun to drive, no question, but he wondered how she'd like driving this car.

He found the playlist he'd made two nights ago, and the music they'd listened to on their See Canyon drive began to play.

He checked his phone one last time before putting the car in gear. There weren't any messages from her, a good sign since he expected her to send him a text asking him not to come. It was a little after noon, which would put him at Stave by two-thirty or three.

At three on the dot, Brodie pulled up in front of Stave. There were several people sitting on the patio, and when he looked inside, the tasting bar looked full.

He went inside and perused the wine racks. He recognized every label. The wine was made by people he knew from school, celebrated the crush with, and with whom he shared life's most important events. Butler Ranch wines sat next to the ones made by the Avila family at their Los Caballeros winery, and to those made by Wolf Family Vintners, among others.

It was hard to believe he and Peyton hadn't met until this week, since they were so close in age. He knew she'd gone to Mission Classical Academy, not to the high school he and Alex had graduated from, although back then, the Butlers weren't on speaking terms with the Avilas.

Then, right out of high school, Brodie left for UC Davis, and once he graduated, he went to work in Napa. He remembered when Kade had asked Brodie if he knew her. He told him he'd heard of the winery but didn't know the family. Although now he knew that if he'd met her first, she wouldn't have been available when she met Kade.

Alex approached him first, nudging him. "Hey, booty-man."

"Give me a break, Alex." Brodie looked in Peyton's direction to see if she was paying attention.

"She's heard it before, Brode."

Brodie led Alex out to the patio. "How's she doing?"

"What do you mean?"

"Come on, Alex, you know what I mean."

"Did you just roll your eyes at me? That's hysterical. Peyton made me promise to stop rolling my eyes when she talks about you."

"She talks about me?"

"Brodie, Brodie, Brodie. Yes, she's been talking about you." Alex's demeanor went from playful to serious. "Don't play with her though, Brodie. That bastard Lang Becker did a number on her, and then Kade goes and gets himself killed. She's closed up pretty tight, but she likes you, and if you're not into her as much as I'm afraid she's into you, you'll devastate her."

Brodie surveyed the patio. "I can't stay away, Alex."

"This isn't some f'd up thing with your brother, is it?"

"She's all I think about. Alex, I don't have a choice about this. I'm obsessed."

"That doesn't reassure me."

"Alright, how about this? You've got it backwards—I'm more into her than she is into me."

—:—

Peyton watched Brodie and Alex from behind the bar. She was surprised when they walked outside, but from the looks of it, Alex was lecturing him, no doubt about her.

She almost didn't recognize Brodie when he'd walked in earlier. He was wearing a suit and tie, and damn if he didn't look fine. He exuded the confidence of a man who knew who he was and what he wanted out of life. It probably served him well, both in the business of wine and with other women.

He looked in her direction, but Peyton wasn't sure if he could see her staring at him through the glare of the windows. When he smiled and waved, she knew he could. He pulled his phone out of his pocket, held it to his ear, and then excused himself from his conversation with Alex. When he did, she came back inside.

Alex took the glass Peyton had been drying for the last several minutes out of her friend's hand. "You're relieved. Go get him."

"He's on the phone."

"Yeah? So?"

"Maybe it's a private conversation."

"It's Maddox. I overheard the beginning of their conversation."

"I'll still wait in here until he's finished."

Brodie walked back inside, grasping the back of his neck with his hand, the way Kade used to. When he did, it usually meant he had a lot on his mind. Peyton wondered if it meant the same thing with Brodie.

She untied her apron, hung it on the office door, and walked out to where he waited.

"Hi."

Brodie leaned in, almost as though he was going to kiss her. Without thinking, Peyton jumped back.

"God, Peyton, I'm sorry," he whispered.

"It's okay."

"It isn't, or you wouldn't have reacted the way you did."

Peyton looked around the tasting room. Too many eyes were on them. "Do you mind if we leave?"

"Not at all. Alex is okay with it?"

"Yeah, today's my day off, actually." Peyton looked over at the clock. "She has help that should be here any minute." The back door opened and two women walked in. "Oh, here they are now. Do you know Addy and Sam?"

"Abbey?"

"No, Addy, with a 'd.'"

"I don't think so. Who are they?"

"They work here, but they don't come from wine families. Addy's aunt owns the Ollalieberry Diner, and Sam's parents live over on Windsor Drive."

—:—

Brodie was listening to Peyton, but wasn't really paying attention to what she was saying. Instead, he watched the way her eyes danced when she smiled, and how she talked faster than she had yesterday, as though she was nervous. He understood. He was nervous too. If she weren't doing all the talking, he might embarrass himself again, like he did when he'd leaned forward to kiss her. He hadn't been thinking. It just felt natural to want to kiss her hello.

"Where should we go?" Brodie walked over to where his Porsche was parked.

"Is this yours?" Peyton gasped.

"Yes, ma'am." He tossed her the key fob. "Wanna drive?"

"I'm so embarrassed."

"Why?" he chuckled. "I wanted to drive your car as much as I'm guessing you want to drive mine."

"Who does the truck belong to? I know it isn't Kade's."

"No, it's mine too."

The wineries in the Paso Robles region were successful and growing all the time, especially the ones where the land had belonged to the family for many years. Brodie and his brothers all owned more than one car, motorcycles too. He wondered if Kade told her about the helicopter, or if he ever brought her to the ranch to see the horse stables.

"Where to?" she asked once she was behind the wheel.

"Piedras Blancas?"

"You have a thing for lighthouses."

"I'm fascinated by them." As fascinated as he was with her, although he couldn't tell her that.

"Why?"

He thought about why they held such allure, while she drove along the Cabrillo Highway. They drove through San Simeon, past the entrance to Hearst Castle, where his grandparents met, and by Arroyo del Corral, the secluded cove where the elephant seals made their home. Peyton slowed the car as they approached the entrance to the lighthouse station. There were several buildings, one housing a gift shop, as well as a replica of the station's original water tower.

"Did you know you can stay here?" he asked.

"I didn't. Have you ever?"

"I haven't, but I want to." *With you*, he wanted to add.

"So, you haven't told me why you have a thing for lighthouses."

"I thought about it, and I don't really know. It started when we'd go to Avila Beach with my dad. And maybe it's just that simple, that when I see them, it reminds me of a happy time."

They walked through the gift shop, and Peyton picked up a lodging brochure. A tour had left several minutes ago, but the girl behind the cash register told them they were welcome to try to catch up with it.

"I'd rather just walk around. Is that okay with you, Peyton?"

"Yes, definitely." Peyton thanked the gift shop cashier, and they went back outside.

"Piedras Blancas was added to the California Coastal National Monument this year," Brodie began.

"Most of the Cambria shoreline was, too," Peyton added.

"That's right, I remember hearing about that."

"I'm a walking, talking Central Coast guidebook," she laughed. "A lot of tourists come into Stave, and most of them are looking for ideas of other things they can do while they're in town."

"The tasting room is certainly a boon to the Westside Collaborative. It's a good thing you've got going there."

"I usually give the credit to Alex—"

"I know you do."

Peyton laughed again. "But I'm proud of it. When I took over, we sold a few cases a month, of my dad's wines, but it never generated a profit. Now it does, and at the same time, helps spread the word about wineries that aren't on the beaten path, Butler Ranch included."

"It's been a good thing for us, Peyton, and not just here on the Central Coast. Down south, Paso Robles is as well-known as Napa Valley and Sonoma. We may not have the same prestige worldwide, at least not yet, but with every sales trip I go on, more and more of the customers I call on know about our wines before I get there. And not just ours, like you said, many of the region's wineries are growing in acclaim."

"Is that where you were, on a sales trip?" As soon as she asked, Peyton wished she hadn't. What if that wasn't why he was gone? She closed her eyes in an effort to curb her speculation.

Brodie laughed. "What's wrong?"

"Nothing. I just realized I was being really nosy."

He reached over and rubbed her shoulder. "That's where I was, and I like that you want to know, Peyton. Believe me, I'm not going to hesitate asking. I want to know everything you did while I was gone."

"It isn't that interesting. I ran errands, made dinner for the boys and me, did some laundry. Fascinating stuff. Of course I was exhausted yesterday after being up so late the night before. I wondered if you had the luxury of sleeping in."

—:—

"Oh, yeah?" Brodie moved closer to her and whispered, "Were you imagining me in bed, Peyton?"

She laughed and pushed him away, but she didn't freak out. A good sign.

"I was envious, especially when I had to pry my eyes open at seven to get the boys ready for school."

"Nope, no sleeping in for me either. I left early yesterday, before dawn, and timed it so I hit LA after the morning traffic. I spent yesterday afternoon and evening there, and then this morning, I drove back for a meeting in Santa Barbara."

"Nice car to be in for that much driving," she smiled.

"Yours is pretty nice too, Peyton."

"I like it, and so do the boys..."

Brodie studied her face. There were lines on her forehead, and near her eyes, that he'd noticed before, when she talked about Kade. He wondered if his brother had anything to do with her buying her BMW.

"Speaking of the boys, do they have basketball practice again today?" He pulled out his phone to check the time, and she peeked over at it.

"They do. We better get on the road."

"Would you like to drive back?"

"No, I had my fun. I kind of like being a passenger."

The lines on her face were gone. In their place were happier ones, smile lines.

"I like seeing you smile, Peyton." Brodie reached over and touched her face. "I like seeing you happy. You're beautiful, Peyton."

"Thank you, Brodie." She looked away from him, but her smile remained.

"And I hate seeing you sad," he added.

"It can't always be avoided. It's just there sometimes, as much as I don't want it to be, things remind me..."

"Like the car?"

"Kade talked me into it. I was looking at the X5, a far more practical vehicle, but he convinced me I didn't need a 'mom-car' anymore. The boys aren't that old, but he was right, it isn't like I'm lugging around strollers and diaper bags."

There were so many things he could ask, like how Kade had been with her boys, or if they ever talked about having kids of their own, but he didn't. He didn't want to know, and he didn't want to picture Peyton with his brother.

—:—

When Brodie held the passenger door open for her, she breathed in the scent of him. He didn't wear much cologne, if it even was cologne. He smelled good, like the salty air and the pines that grew so predominantly in this area.

"I wish we didn't have to go back yet," Brodie murmured, leaning in closer to her.

If she turned her head just slightly, she'd be close enough to kiss him. Instead, she bent down and got into the car.

Peyton looked out at the sea on their drive back, thinking about how different she felt with Brodie than she had with either Lang or Kade. It had taken months before she'd go out with either of them. With Lang, she thought he was flirting with her like he did with everyone else—she didn't believe he was really interested in her.

Kade was her friend a long time before he became her lover, and it was even longer before she introduced him to her boys. If he hadn't sent her the email, asking her out, she never would've realized he wanted to be more than friends.

With Brodie, his interest was out in the open. There was no pretense. When she and Alex had talked about Brodie being a player, she mentally compared him to her ex-husband. If she hadn't held out on Lang so long, she doubted he would've asked her to marry him. When he did and she hesitated, he'd pressured her. Even then she felt as though she was Lang's conquest more than a woman he was in love with.

The other day, Brodie had mentioned something about how she would've gotten to know his family better after she and Kade were married. They weren't together long enough for either of them to be thinking about marriage.

In both cases, with Lang and Kade, she'd been cautious. In hindsight, she must've sensed both of them would break her heart. With Lang it was intentional, with Kade it wasn't. But why had he pursued her, knowing the danger he was in each time he left on a mission? Worse, why had she allowed her boys to get so close to him? She'd been aware that every time he left, there was a chance he wouldn't come back.

She often wondered, if she had to do it over again, would she let herself fall in love with him?

"You're very quiet over there, Ms. Wolf. Which reminds me, do you go by Wolf or Becker?"

"I go by Wolf-Becker officially, although I only keep Lang's name for the boys' sake, since they're Beckers."

She studied him for a while, wondering how he felt about kids. "I thought about asking him to give up his parental rights, since he hasn't seen the boys in years and has no desire to. If he did, I could legally change their last name to Wolf, but now that Jamison is ten, I think it's too late."

He didn't say anything, but Peyton could see the tightness in his jaw and his hands gripping the steering wheel harder than necessary.

"Brodie?"

"I never met him, and I never want to. I don't understand how a man can leave his kids."

"When he left, he told me he realized he'd never really wanted children. He was a big kid himself, and I should've recognized it before I married him. I see that now, and I blame myself as much as I blame him."

"That's not right, Peyton. He made the choice to become a father—you have no blame in this."

"I'm sorry, Brodie. It's a tough subject. It was for Kade, too."

"Was he going to adopt them?"

"Who? Kade? No. We never talked about it." Peyton looked back out at the sea. "We weren't as close as you think we were. I loved him, and I thought about a future with him, but I had doubts. Mainly about what he did."

"Did he tell you he was going to retire?"

"Not specifically. I knew he would eventually, just given his age, but we didn't discuss it."

"I don't know what I should say and what I shouldn't."

"What do you mean?"

"About Kade, and what he was thinking."

"What was he thinking, Brodie?"

"I knew what his plans were, so did the rest of our family. Before he left, he told us it would be his last mission, and that when he got back, he was going to retire."

"Are you sure?"

"Absolutely. He asked our mother to start planning the ceremony."

Peyton closed her eyes and leaned back into the headrest.

—:—

Brodie pulled the car over and took her hand in his. "Peyton, I'm sorry."

"It's okay, Brodie. I'm just...I don't know what to say."

He gripped the steering wheel with his other hand. How could Kade have kept so much from her? She kept saying they weren't as close as he thought they were. He was beginning to see she was right. It didn't make sense. How could Kade be planning to propose when he hadn't even discussed his retirement with her?

"Listen, Brodie, I realize how hard this is, for both of us. I think it would be best if we didn't—"

Brodie took his hand off the steering wheel, leaned over, and gripped the back of her neck. "Don't say it, Peyton. Don't say it would be best if we didn't see each other. Please."

Without waiting for her to answer, Brodie covered her lips with his and tangled his fingers in her hair. He felt her resistance for a second, and then she relaxed into their kiss.

Her hand came up and rested on his chest, and her lips opened to his. His tongue explored her mouth, battling with hers, and her breath quickened. He pressed harder, then slowed and softened. He nipped at her lower lip and kissed across the side of her face, down her neck. Her hand grasped the front of his shirt.

"Brodie," she groaned. "Stop."

He did and looked into her eyes. "Stop? Am I wrong about this?"

She leaned her head back and closed her eyes. "The question should be, is this wrong?"

"No, Peyton, it isn't. I don't understand your relationship with my brother, and honestly, I don't want to know any more about it. I'm angry, because I can't understand why he didn't tell you the things he told us." Brodie took a deep breath. "Peyton, please look at me."

She opened her eyes and looked into his.

"What I feel for you has nothing to do with Kade. Am I wrong? Tell me. Can you say you aren't feeling the same way I am?"

"No," she whispered. "I can't, but, Brodie..."

"But what, Peyton?"

"We need to slow down. My boys..."

"I get it, but that doesn't mean I'm going to be able to stop thinking about you. I can't sleep. I walk around outside in the middle of the night, asking the sky what the hell I should do. I've never felt this way, and I don't know how to handle it."

Peyton pulled her phone out of her pocket to check the time. "I'm sorry, Brodie, but we have to go. I have to pick up the boys."

6

"Hi," Alex answered her cell.

Peyton had picked up the boys, brought them home, helped them with their homework, and then called Alex.

"Hi," she answered through her tears.

"Peyton, what's wrong?" Alex gasped.

"Where are you?"

"I'm home, why? Where are you?"

"Can you come over?"

"Of course. I'll be there in ten. Anything you want me to bring?"

"N-o-o-o," Peyton hiccuped through her tears.

"Shit, Peyton, what happened?"

"B-r-o-o-o-d-i-e."

"That son of a bitch. I'll be right there, honey."

"Tell me what happened. What did he do?" Alex asked when Peyton answered the door.

She hadn't stopped crying since they hung up.

"It's Kade, and Brodie, and I don't know where to start." Peyton took a tissue out of the box she had tucked up against her and blew her nose.

Alex swept past her into the kitchen and opened the bottle of wine she'd brought in with her, pulled two glasses out of the cupboard, and filled them halfway. She came back out, to where Peyton sat on the couch, and handed her a glass.

Before she sat down, Alex checked on Jamison and Finn, who appeared oblivious to their mother's cry-fest. She came back, sat down, and put her arm around Peyton's shoulders. Peyton rested her head against Alex and cried harder.

"Should I shoot the son-of-a-bitch?" Alex asked after several minutes.

"It isn't him," Peyton eked out. "It's Kade."

"What about Kade?"

Peyton took several deep breaths, blew her nose again, and wiped her remaining tears away. "There's so much he didn't tell me, and Brodie is pissed, and we kissed, and I don't know what to do, Alex." Peyton started crying again, harder than she was when Alex came in the front door.

"Let's break this down into sections, okay, sweetie?"

Peyton nodded her head.

"First, you say you feel as though you didn't know Kade at all. Why?"

"Brodie said there were things Kade told them that he never told me."

"Like what?"

"That he was retiring. He wasn't going back."

Alex took her own deep breath. "And he didn't tell you?"

"No. I had no idea."

"Okay, let's set that aside for a minute. What else? You kissed?"

"He kissed me, but I kissed him back. Alex, I don't know what to do." Peyton buried her head back into Alex's shoulder.

"Okay, you kissed. What else?"

"Nothing. Isn't that enough?"

"Peyton," Alex began slowly, "can you tell me why you're crying?"

"No...I...don't...know," she cried harder.

"Okay. What happened after you left Stave?" Alex waited while Peyton took another series of deep breaths and then blew her nose again.

"We went to the lighthouse. I drove his car."

"Then what happened?"

"He asked me about Lang, and then he told me that Kade was going to retire. That his last mission was supposed to be...his...last...mission." Peyton turned and buried her head in the pillow on the sofa. Her body shook with sobs.

"What does Lang have to do with Kade's last mission, sweetheart?" Alex waited again while Peyton tried to stop crying.

"He asked me if K-k-k-ade was going to adopt the boys."

"And then what happened?"

"I told him we weren't as serious as he thought, and then he got mad."

"At who? You?"

"*No!*" Peyton shouted. "*At Kade!*"

"How did you end things?"

Peyton's tears subsided. She blew her nose again and tossed the tissue into the pile forming on her living room floor. "He's going to call me later, after the boys are in bed."

Alex tapped her fingers on the edge of the sofa. "Can I tell you something?"

"Of course."

"But you have to promise me two things."

"What?"

"First that you won't start crying again, and second that you won't get mad at me."

Peyton took more deep breaths. "I can't promise I won't cry, but I can that I won't get mad at you."

Alex stood and paced in front of the sofa.

"What?" Peyton prodded.

"I'm trying to decide whether to tell you or not."

—:—

Brodie wanted to rip open the cab door of his truck and throw the box Kade wanted Peyton to have down the hillside, but more, he wanted to understand why Kade hadn't told Peyton he was retiring. And why didn't she have any idea that Kade was going to propose?

There were also things she'd said that he didn't understand. Twice she'd told him that she and Kade weren't as close as he thought they were. Yet, more than a year later, she said she still wasn't over him.

The only thing he knew for sure was that Peyton Wolf was more to him than his dead brother's girlfriend, and no matter what had gone down between her and Kade, he wasn't going to give her up. He would pursue Peyton until she was his. *His, not Kade's. His.*

He was about to go inside when Maddox pulled up and parked next to his truck.

"What's up, little brother?" Maddox asked.

"Just trying to figure out the *shitstorm* our brother left in his wake."

"Come on," Maddox put his arm around Brodie's shoulders. "Let's go have a drink."

Maddox drove them into the village of Paso Robles and pulled up in front of the Pine Street Saloon. "Think we need somethin' a little stronger than wine tonight, don't you?"

Brodie nodded his head, following Maddox inside.

"Two Angel's Envy, neat," he told the bartender. "And keep 'em comin'."

"You got a ride home, Butler?"

"Yeah, Naughton's on his way."

"What the f…"

"Settle down, little brother. Naughton may have been a jackass to you, last night, but now he's worried about you."

Brodie shook his head. Was this really happening, or was it all a weird-ass dream?

"You see Peyton again today?" Mad asked after they downed their second shot.

"Yep, sure did. Got somethin' to say about it?"

"Hell, no," Maddox laughed.

Brodie glared at him and signaled the bartender to pour him another round. "You in?"

Mad nodded his head.

"You're gonna think I've lost my damn mind."

"Oh, yeah? Then you're thinkin' I believed you had a mind to begin with."

Brodie lowered his head and shook it. "I think I'm fallin' in love with her. I've known her four days, and I'm fallin' in love with her. How crazy is that, Mad?"

"Pretty damn crazy if you ask me, but I don't know if I've ever been in love, little brother, so I'm not a good judge."

"What's wrong with us? Kade couldn't tell the woman he loved that he wanted to marry her. I fall in love with the same damn woman in a hot minute, and you and Naught don't know your asses from your hearts." Brodie's head felt heavy. When was the last time he ate? This morning? Too much hard liquor on an empty stomach wasn't going to end well.

"I need food, Mad."

"You got it. Hey, Jimmy, fire up that grill. Three steak sandwiches with all the fixin's."

"Medium rare?"

"All three."

"Food's on its way. Now tell me what's goin' on with Peyton."

Brodie told Mad everything that had happened in the past four days, including the kiss he and Peyton had shared. He expected his brother to give him shit about it, but Mad didn't. He just listened.

"What can I get ya?" Jimmy asked when Naughton sat down at the bar, next to Brodie.

"Better make it a coke. How many have these jackalopes had so far?"

"Lost count," Jimmy laughed.

"Shit."

"They ordered steak sandwiches though. One for you too."

Naughton nudged Brodie's shoulder with his. "Sorry I was such a dick last night."

"Nothin' new," Brodie bumped back.

"Peyton got you all twisted up?"

"How'd you know?"

Once he had food in his stomach, Brodie asked Jimmy to give him what Naughton was drinking, as long as there wasn't any alcohol in it. Maddox raised his hand, "I'm done too."

"Damn wine-drinkin' lightweights," Jimmy sputtered and slid their tab over to Naughton. "You're the only one sober enough to give me a decent tip."

Maddox stood behind Naughton and Brodie. "You gotta follow your heart, Brode. Kade isn't here anymore, and whatever happened between them stopped mattering the night he died."

Brodie looked at Naughton. "How do you feel about it?"

"I don't know, to be honest. Sometimes I think it's really f'd up. And then I think about Peyton and her boys, and I find myself hoping you mean the things you're saying about her."

"I mean every word, Naught. I'm just afraid I'm scarin' the shit outa her. By the way, what did I say?"

"Nothin'. It's more a feeling I get."

"Yeah, I get that." Brodie's head was spinning. "You better get me home."

"Good idea. Where'd you park, Naught?"

"Over by the park."

"The park? What the hell? Jimmy got a family reunion that pulled up since we got here?"

"Figured you both could use a long walk in the fresh night air. Might sober you up some."

Maddox pulled his cell phone out of his pocket when they'd walked halfway to where Naughton parked.

"Yeah?" Maddox answered.

"Hell if I know," they heard him say, but didn't hear the rest of the conversation.

Brodie and Naughton kept walking while Maddox argued with whoever had called him. He caught up with them after he hung up.

"Who was that?" Brodie asked.

"Alex Avila."

"What did she want?"

"Mainly what I knew about what was goin' on with you and Peyton."

"Mainly? What else?"

Maddox put his hand on Brodie's shoulder. "You think you're the only one who's got a pretty girl wrappin' you around her finger?"

"Really? You and Alex? When did that start up?"

Maddox hung his head, but then raised his eyes and grinned. "Where you been, little brother?"

Brodie looked at Naughton. "What's he talkin' about?"

"High school. Pretty sure that's when he started chasin' her around like some ol' bull after a heifer."

"You watch it, Naught. Alex will kick the shit out of you if she hears you call her a heifer."

Alex hung up her cell and waited for Peyton to come out of the bathroom. When she did, Alex would have no choice but to tell her exactly what she thought about Kade Butler, and how long she'd thought it.

"Alright," Peyton said when she sat back down on the sofa. "Tell me whatever it is you have to tell me."

"If you told me you and Kade were going to get married, I would've done everything in my power to talk you out of it."

"Why?" Peyton was stunned.

"Because he wasn't the man you thought he was."

7

Alex convinced Peyton to come in late the next day, and get some rest. Peyton didn't argue. After everything that happened in the last few days, she needed sleep.

"I'm gonna crash in the spare bedroom and take the boys to school in the morning. At what God-awful hour do I have to wake them up?"

"You don't have to do that."

"Yeah, I do. What time?"

"Seven."

"Jeez, why do teachers have to be so cruel?"

"I think the teachers would prefer a later start time. Blame the administrators."

Peyton went into the bedroom and fell across the bed. As tired as she felt, she wasn't sure she'd even turn the television on. She heard Alex bumping around the bathroom in the hall, and fell sound asleep.

When she woke the next morning and looked at the clock, Peyton wondered if Alex had slipped something into her wine. It was after nine, and she was still in her clothes from last night. She hadn't heard the boys get up, or get ready, or leave the house.

She slowly made her way to the kitchen and found a note from Alex, telling her all she had to do was turn the coffeemaker on. "God bless Alex," she muttered on her way back to the bathroom. Peyton found her phone sitting on the counter when she came back into the kitchen. No wonder she hadn't woken up. She didn't remember leaving it out here, but once she hit the bed last night, she didn't remember anything.

She picked it up and punched in her security code. There were several text alerts. One from Alex, telling her to go back to bed, which made her laugh. There was one from Jamison, saying that he and Finn loved her and hoped she felt better soon. The last was from Brodie.

Call me when you get this, it said.

After stopping herself from throwing the phone across the kitchen, Peyton poured a cup of coffee. She jumped when she heard a noise coming from the living room.

"You up already?" Alex said, joining her.

"You scared the crap out of me." Peyton had one hand on her heart, the other on her forehead.

"You'll forgive me when you hear what I brought you."

"What?"

"Warm ollalieberry and cream cheese muffins from the Ollalieberry Diner."

"I love you so much right now."

"See?"

"How were the boys this morning?"

"Absolutely fine."

"I'll go take a shower, and meet you at Stave in an hour."

"Uh, nope. I don't need you to come in until later this afternoon."

"It's new release night, Alex. It'll be nuts."

"My mom and your mom are coming down around noon. They'll help me set up, pick the boys up from school, and take them to the movies."

Jamison and Finn stayed on the ranch with her parents Friday and Saturday nights. Her dad would bring them back Sunday afternoon and would stay until Peyton got home from Stave. If it was a slow weekend, she'd leave early or not go in at all.

When Kade was still alive and home on leave, he'd be at her house with the boys Saturday nights. It was their "guy time," he'd tell her.

"Are you sure your mom doesn't mind?"

"She's just as much their *abuela* as your mom is. She loves those boys."

"Your mom is a saint. So are my parents, if you think about it."

"I'm just glad she has your boys to spoil, so she isn't on my back to get married and have kids as much as she used to be. My brothers thank you too."

"What is it with your family?"

"In no hurry to get married." Alex grabbed her coat off the chair in the dining room. "I'm leaving. Go back to bed and get some rest. You look like shit, Peyton."

"Thanks, Alex. Brutal honesty is my favorite."

"Hey, I meant to tell you, Jamison asked me about Brodie this morning."

"Oh, God. What did he say?"

"That he hoped you liked each other."

"Get out of here! He didn't really say that."

"Yeah, he did. He also said that he and Finn talked about it, and they wouldn't mind hanging out with him too."

"Oh, good. Just in case I was afraid I would lose my 'worst mother of the year' plaque, I can now rest assured I'll be hanging on to it for a while."

"Don't worry. I told Jamison you were just friends."

"I hope they're not waiting around for me to find my happily ever after. With my luck with men, they'll be waiting for that bus until I'm old and gray."

"What do they know of the yin and yang of dating? To them, it's as simple as you like someone, you hang out, you get married, and bam—happily ever after."

"I'm a colossal failure at happily ever after, Alex."

"Third time's a charm, girlfriend. Hey, uh, are you sure you're not mad about what I told you about Kade?"

"No, I'm not mad. I'm confused, but not mad. I need some time to process though, okay?"

"Of course. Alrighty then, need anything else? If not, I gotta get to Stave and start prepping food for tonight."

"I'm good, but seriously, I can come in this morning. You don't have to do everything yourself."

"Pretty sure I owe you about a hundred get-well days. You've covered for me so many times I lost count."

—:—

Brodie checked his phone again and rolled back over. He felt as though he ate a thousand cotton balls the night before and there was a marching band practicing inside his head.

Just like the twenty other times he checked, there was no message from Peyton. He knew he needed to give her time, but it didn't make it any easier to wait for her call. If he felt better, he might even be tempted to get in his car and drive over the hills into Cambria.

He'd never been impulsive. It wasn't part of his personality. He had great self-restraint and nothing much rattled him. It was different with Peyton, though. He had no self-control where she was concerned.

Other than losing his oldest brother, Brodie had little to complain about in life. His family loved him; they were all healthy; the wine business was booming, and he, Mad, and Naughton were all doing jobs they loved. They'd each found their niche.

Naughton managed the vineyards, which had been certified organic several years ago. Maddox made the wine, and Brodie sold it. His sister Skye was a happily-married stay-at-home mom, and Ainsley, the academic in the family, was at Stanford, pursuing an endless number of degrees that Brodie had lost track of long ago.

Even Kade had been happy before he died. He loved what he did, in spite of the danger, or maybe because of it.

"I can't picture myself getting old," Brodie had overheard Kade tell Maddox once. "I just don't see it in my head." Maddox asked Kade if he thought it meant something. "I don't know," Kade answered. "I don't think I'm going to live long enough to find out."

Had Kade shared the same concerns with Peyton? Was that why she had doubts about their relationship? She said it was because of what he did.

Kade told their father that, while he was retiring from the military, he wasn't going to quit what he was doing. He'd been interviewing with the CIA, known in Kade's circle simply as "the agency." If they accepted him, he would have more control over when and how much he traveled, and his pay would quadruple. Brodie doubted Kade had cared much about the money—it was the adrenaline rush, the danger, that would have been hard for him to give up. He couldn't imagine his older brother sitting behind a desk forty hours a week. He also couldn't imagine him working the vineyards, or in the winery. Even the ranch hadn't held much interest for him. If it had, Kade never would've joined the military.

Education was important to their parents, but if any of them had decided against going to college, they would've had a built-in, life-long job on the ranch. There was a vast amount of positions they could choose from too. Just managing the barns and livestock took three full-time employees.

When Kade was "home" he didn't spend much time there. Before he met Peyton, he'd come home on leave, rest, spend some time with the family, and then disappear for a few days on his motorcycle. After Peyton, he spent almost all his time with her and her boys.

Maybe it had been wishful thinking on his parents' part that Peyton would be the person Kade stuck around for. She may have recognized his wanderlust on her own, and Kade's restless spirit was the reason she doubted him.

Brodie reached over and picked up his cell phone. He must've fallen asleep. Still no call from Peyton. He had missed a call from Maddox, though.

"What's up?"

"I need your help with something. Feel good enough to handle some wine business with me tonight?"

That *was* his job, and while he didn't feel great now, if he showered and ate, he'd probably feel better.

"Of course. What are we doing?"

"Meet me in the barrel room around four, and I'll tell you then."

This sounded promising. Barrel tastings meant something special was going on. He just hoped Peyton called before it was time for him to leave.

—:—

"She isn't going to like this," Peyton overheard Alex say when she walked in the back door of Stave. Alex was on the phone, and turned to wave when she heard the door close.

"Alright, gotta go now."

"What was that all about?"

"Nothing important."

"If you're telling me it's nothing important, then whatever it is must be *very* important." When Alex deflected, Peyton knew to be on high alert.

"This time it isn't. I swear."

Swearing. Another bad sign. "Tell me what's going on."

"No."

"What do you mean 'no'? Alex, what the hell?"

"I knew this wasn't going to work. I told him it wasn't. "

"Who?"

"Maddox."

"Oh, no."

"He offered to do a barrel tasting tonight. He'll be here with it around five."

"And Brodie is coming with him, am I right?"

"Yep."

Peyton walked out of the office and into the tasting room. The bar and tables were full inside, and the patio looked just as crowded.

"Hey," Alex said, coming up behind her. "You want me to call him and tell him not to come? We haven't promoted it."

"No, it's okay. You should've called me though, with as busy as it is."

"That's what we have employees for, Peyton. And it isn't that busy."

"You're right, we don't have any open seats, but it isn't that busy."

"You're turning into quite the eye-roller, missy."

Peyton smiled and walked over to put her apron on.

"Not mad?"

"Why would I be mad?"

"So you're happy Brodie is coming with Maddox."

"I wouldn't go that far."

"But you're smiling."

"Yes, Alex, I'm smiling. But before I get too wrapped up in serving wine, I have a phone call to make."

—:—

His cell was ringing when Brodie got out of the shower. Normally he'd let it go to voicemail, but if it was Peyton, he didn't want to miss her call. He grabbed the phone and pressed the accept button.

"Brodie here."

"Hi, Brodie. It's Peyton."

"Peyton, it's good to hear your voice."

"Did I get you at a bad time? You sound out of breath."

"Not at all. I was climbing out of the shower when you called, so the only rush was to get to the phone before you hung up."

"Do you want to call me back?"

"No, no. It's fine. I'll just put you on speaker for a sec while I grab a towel."

He pulled one off the bar and wrapped it around his waist, picked up the phone, and took it off speaker. "I'm back. You still there?"

"I'm still here."

"You sound like you're smiling. Are you, Peyton?"

"You can hear smiling? I wasn't aware you had that particular superpower."

"Oh, baby, you have no idea how many superpowers I've yet to show you."

She laughed. He loved the sound of her laugh.

"Thanks for calling, Peyton. I wanted to apologize." He rolled his eyes. That wasn't what he wanted to do at all. He wanted to see her again, that's why he'd asked her to call him.

"There's nothing to apologize for, Brodie. We both got caught up in the moment."

"It wasn't a moment for me."

"I don't know what that means."

"I want to see you. Soon."

"I think you've got that covered, Brodie. Alex said you and Maddox will be here around five."

"Wait. What?" Shit. That's where they were going for the barrel tasting?

"Don't pretend like you don't know anything about it," she laughed.

"But I don't. Mad asked me to help him with a tasting tonight, but he didn't say where."

"Oh. You don't have to come if you don't want to."

"Are you kidding? Of course I want to."

"Then I'll see you later, Brodie."

"Peyton…"

"Yeah, Brodie?"

"Are you happy I'm coming?" He waited, but she didn't answer right away. He was just about to let her off the hook when she sighed.

"Yes, Brodie. I am very happy you're coming."

"Very? Well, that's even better. See ya, Peyton."

—:—

She disconnected the call, put her cell phone in the pocket of her apron, and then pulled it back out. She opened her photos and studied the last one Kade had sent her. He was at the base in Afghanistan. She recognized the palm trees and the outdoor walled-off area from other photos he'd sent. He was wearing sunglasses and had on a greenish-tan Yankee baseball hat. The front pockets of his protective tactical vest were full, and beneath it, he wore a black, short-sleeve shirt. When she woke up the morning after he'd sent the photo, she got a call from one of the guys he served with, telling her he'd been killed.

She'd asked him once how'd she know if anything happened to him. "Either Paps or Razor will get in touch with you." She recognized both names. The call came from Razor, that morning, and she knew, without him having to say it.

For a long time, it didn't feel real. There were times it still didn't. That's what she'd told Brodie. She'd dream it was a mistake, and in her dream, Kade would walk into the tasting room, like he did before they started dating. He'd smile and say hello, and she'd walk over and welcome him home.

What would Kade think about this thing between her and Brodie? If she had to guess, she'd say he'd be happy about it. He was protective of her and the boys. He'd want her to be happy and cared for, especially by someone he trusted. He never said, but she sensed he had something to do with Lang getting caught up with the boys' child support.

Alex peeked her head into the office door. "Everything okay?"

"Yep, on my way back out now." Peyton stuffed her phone back in the pocket of her apron. "What's with the subterfuge between you and Maddox?"

Alex smiled, but didn't answer. Peyton followed her back out to the bar and lost track of time, waiting on customers and talking about wine.

She heard the knock on the back door and looked at the clock. They were right on time. "You want me to go?" she asked Alex, who was talking to one of their regular customers.

Alex nodded.

When Peyton opened the door, she saw Maddox and Brodie loading the barrel onto a dolly. She shielded her eyes from the afternoon sun and held the door.

"Hey, Peyton," Maddox said as he wheeled the barrel in the door.

"Hi, Maddox. Thanks for doing this. We love barrel tastings around here, and most of the wineries think it's too much trouble to lug them down here."

"No trouble at all," Maddox smiled as she watched him walk inside.

Maddox looked more like Kade than Brodie did. She hadn't realized it until now, but then, she didn't see him very often. He kept his head shaved, like Kade used to. Instead of a goatee, Maddox had a full, dark beard. His deep blue eyes were the same color as Kade's and Brodie's, and most of the time, Maddox looked as though he was smirking. He was taller than Kade, like Brodie was, but built more like his older brother. He probably could've swung two wine barrels on his shoulders and carried them both inside without a problem.

"Mmm, that man is *fine*," Alex gushed when she passed Maddox in the hallway. "Do they need any help?"

Brodie was unloading cases of wine from the back of Maddox's truck, but if they were anything like their older brother, they would never allow her or Alex to help carry them in. Brodie stacked one on top of the other and hefted them up on his shoulder. "Hey, pretty lady," he said, noticing her holding the door.

"Hi, Brodie," she grinned, shaking her head.

"What?"

"You're such a flirt."

"Only with you, Peyton," he smiled. As he walked through the door, he leaned over and kissed her cheek. "Hi," he murmured. He stayed close and looked into her eyes. "How are you, Peyton?"

"I'm fine, Brodie," she laughed. "How are you?"

"Better now. I missed your pretty face."

When she groaned, he laughed out loud and took the cases into the tasting room.

Peyton came back inside and saw that Alex directed Maddox and Brodie to set up near the front of the room. On the left side, there was a double-wide garage door that opened out to the patio. It was a brilliant idea to have them set up there. Any woman over the age of twenty-one, and under one hundred, would definitely come into Stave, if only to flirt with the two hot men offering wine tastes.

She kept busy, writing orders and signing customers up for wine club memberships, but every few minutes, she'd sneak a look at Brodie. He smiled and talked to customers about their wine but glanced over at her as much as she did at him. When he caught her looking first, he'd wink, and his smile would come through his eyes.

"He is too," Alex whispered and nudged her.

"Yep, he sure is." He was fine, and hot, and sweet, and he seemed genuinely into her. Could she go forward with this? Would Brodie want to have sex with her, knowing his brother had? How weird would that be? And what about her boys? They already knew who he was. Should she let him meet them? Or should she wait?

"Quit chewing the inside of your cheek. You look like a chipmunk." It was a bad habit, one which Alex gladly gave her shit about.

The new release tasting usually wrapped up at six, but with the Butler brothers' barrel show still going strong, she and Alex continued handing out copies of that night's tasting notes and opened more bottles of the other wines.

—:—

By nine most of the customers had left. Peyton and Alex, along with their two servers, were busy washing wine glasses.

"Can I help?" Brodie offered.

"No, thanks," Peyton answered at the same time Alex said yes. They both laughed and tossed Brodie a towel.

"You can dry, but be careful," Alex instructed him.

"I've run my own tasting room," he informed her. "With glasses at least as expensive as these."

"You don't have to stay," Peyton began. "You and Maddox can take off any time."

Brodie leaned forward so Alex couldn't hear him. "Maddox isn't any more ready to leave than I am," he winked.

"I kind of noticed something passing between the two of them. Wonder how long that's been going on?"

"According to Naughton, since high school."

"Uh, so, I guess you have to wait for him to leave. By the looks of it, it may be a while."

Alex left the bar and was talking to Maddox as quietly as Peyton and Brodie had been.

"I drove down, too."

"Oh?" Peyton's forehead creased just slightly.

"Before you start accusing me of anything, it was Mad's idea."

"I wasn't going to accuse you of anything."

Brodie reached over and ran his finger across her forehead. "Oh, yeah?"

"I guess you can leave whenever you want to, then."

"You kickin' me out?"

"No."

"Hey, I was wondering earlier—where do your boys hang out when you're here at night."

Peyton looked away from him before she answered. "They spend Friday nights at my parents' ranch. Sometimes Saturday too."

"You up for a nightcap once you're done here?"

She threw her towel on the bar and motioned for Brodie to follow her out the back door.

"Listen, I was thinking about this, earlier today, and I think it might be too weird, Brodie."

"Weird? Not the word I expected you to use."

"I was *involved* with your brother. Doesn't that bother you?"

He was catching on. By involved, she meant intimacy. It crossed his mind for a split second, and that quick, he got over it. There were things that bothered him more about her relationship with Kade than them sleeping together. "It doesn't bother me, Peyton. Does it bother you?"

"Yes, it kind of does."

"Let's do this. Let's go back inside, finish up, and then really talk about this. Not just you and Kade having sex, but all of it."

"I don't know..."

"I do. I'm not taking no for an answer."

Peyton raised her eyebrows and burst out laughing.

"Yeah, that was pretty stupid, wasn't it?"

"Really stupid," she laughed.

"Let me try putting it a different way." Brodie cleared his throat. "*Please,* Peyton. Pretty please."

"Stop, Brodie. Whining is worse, way worse."

"You still haven't answered me."

"We can talk, Brodie. But that's it. Just talk, no kissing."

"Yeah, no kissing. Got it," he smirked.

"I mean it."

"Yes, ma'am." Brodie held the door open and followed her back inside. When she got to the end of the hallway that led into the main tasting room, she came to a stop.

"What—"

"Shh," Peyton turned around and pushed him back toward the door.

"What's goin' on?" he whispered.

"I didn't want to interrupt."

"Interrupt what?"

"Unlike us, they *are* kissing."

"I can fix that." Brodie swooped in before she could argue. He held her face in his hands and brought his lips to hers. "Peyton," he groaned when she pulled away. "I've been thinking about that all day. All night, too. Can't I have just a little bit more? Please?"

She put her hands on his shoulders and reached up, kissing his cheek instead of his lips.

"Uh uh, that isn't gonna do it, sugar."

Peyton twisted away from him and went out the back door. When he followed, he heard her laughing.

"Come on, Peyton. Give a guy a break."

She pulled her key fob out of her pocket and unlocked her car, which was parked on the other side of Mad's truck.

"Where're you parked, cowboy?"

"'Bout a block down, on the street."

"Hop in."

"You got it." Brodie ran over and climbed in the passenger seat.

Peyton started the engine and put the car in reverse.

"Do you need to let Alex know you're leaving?"

"Nope. If you get caught kissing in the tasting room, you have to finish closing up by yourself."

"Is that a rule?"

"Is now."

8

"Where are we going?"

"It's a surprise."

"Oh, I like this." Brodie reclined his seat just a little and settled back into it.

"Are you comfortable?"

"You know it, baby."

Peyton shook her head. She liked how playful Brodie was. Kade had sometimes been too, but not very often. He was sweet and considerate, and protective, and conversational, but *not* playful. Lang had been, but with him, it was *all* play. Brodie balanced fun and seriousness well, and she liked that.

"Whatcha' thinkin' about?"

"You."

"Now there's an answer I like. What about me?"

"Hmm. Should I tell you, or would a little mystery be better in this instance?"

"You should definitely tell me."

"A little mystery it is."

"Oh, man. You got me. Since I have three brothers, I should've seen that coming."

Two. He only had two older brothers, but she knew what he meant.

"Come on, Peyton." He touched the side of her face with his fingertips. "Don't lose that smile I've been watching all night long."

She looked over at him and couldn't help but smile. In Alex's words, damn, but he was fine.

"There it is. Her smile is back, ladies and gentlemen, and I think that means she likes me."

Peyton drove south on Highway One until she came to Green Valley Road. She took a left, away from the ocean, toward Paso Robles.

"You giving me a lift home?"

"Patience, Brodie." She heard her mom's voice in her own. "Sorry, didn't mean to turn into your mother."

"I like it. But can we pretend you're my teacher instead?"

"Huh?"

"You know, teacher-student fantasy."

"Ew."

"Guess that's a no."

"Relax and enjoy the ride, Brodie." Peyton turned up the music, and Brodie closed his eyes.

About a mile in, she turned off on to a dirt road and parked where the hill they were on crested. "I love this view," she murmured.

"Me too, especially when there are no clouds and the full moon lights up Morro Bay."

Brodie opened his door when she did.

"You wanna take a walk?" he asked.

"No, not really." She walked behind the car and popped the trunk. She reached inside and pulled out a heavy fleece blanket. "Mind if we sit?"

Brodie took the blanket from her and spread it out on the grass. She sat down, and he saw her shiver. "Are you cold?"

"A little. There's another blanket in the trunk."

When she started to get up, he put his hand on her shoulder. "I'll get it."

Peyton pulled the fob out of her pocket and used it to pop the trunk. "Thanks, Brodie."

He brought the blanket over and put it around her shoulders.

"Aren't you cold?" she asked in return.

"Nah, I'm okay."

"Liar," she laughed and held the blanket out so he could sit next to her.

"This I like, Peyton."

—:—

He waited to see if she'd start their conversation. After a few minutes, she rested her head on his shoulder.

"What's running through your pretty head, Peyton?"

"I don't want to keep comparing you and Kade. You know?"

"Not sure. Am I coming out ahead or behind?"

That made her laugh. "It's a toss-up."

"Ouch! Woman, that was not nice."

"I do it all the time. But it isn't just Kade. I compare you to Lang, too."

"I know I come out ahead of him."

"Brodie, Kade and Lang are the only two men I've been with, and I took things pretty slow with both of them."

"I can do slow."

"That isn't really what I mean. It took Lang a long time to win me over, and ultimately, I think that's all it was. Two babies later, he realized he missed the chase."

"He's a douche, Peyton. Forgive my language."

She laughed again. "It's okay. I've called him far worse."

"What about Kade? Did it take him a long time to win you over?"

"It was different with Kade. We were friends. I had no idea he was interested in more than that. He kind of sneaked up on me."

"And me?"

"What's today? Friday? I have known you five days, Brodie, and I'm sharing a blanket with you. That isn't slow."

"Are you telling me you want me to back off a little?" Keyword little. He had no intention of backing off completely.

"No, not necessarily."

"Good answer."

"Slow hasn't worked out all that well for me. As hard as I tried to avoid being hurt, in both cases, I was. And not just hurt, more like devastated." She leaned forward so she could see his face. "Scaring you away yet?"

"Not even close."

"You're so easy to talk to. That's part of it. It doesn't feel like five days."

"For me either."

"You aren't saying much."

"I'm listening."

"I'd like to hear what you're thinking."

"I'm not sure you do, Peyton." Talk about being scared off. If he told her what he was thinking, she might get in her car and drive away, leaving him sitting here. Everything he knew about Peyton Wolf, he liked. When he learned something new, he liked that too.

"Brodie?"

"I really like you, Peyton. If I told you all the thoughts that ran through my head just now, you'd think I was nuts."

"Maybe I said too much."

"That isn't it at all. And you didn't. But I'm worried I'm going to."

"This was your idea, Brodie. You're the one who said we should talk, not just about my sex life with Kade, but all of it. Isn't that what you said?"

Brodie took a deep breath, and then blew it out. "It is. So here goes. You ready?"

She nodded.

"When I said I wanted to talk, I didn't mean we should talk about Kade, or your relationship with him. I want to talk about you and me, separate from him."

"Okay."

"You asked me if I thought it was too weird, that you had been with my brother. I guess if I let myself think about it, it might be. But I don't let myself think about it. I don't think it's any different than me not thinking about anyone you were in a relationship with. That was then, and them, and this is now, and us."

"I get that."

"What about you, Peyton? Do you think about me and other relationships I've been in?"

"Not relationships."

"Ah. So you think about me having sex with other women."

"I didn't say that either."

"What do you think about?"

"Lang was such a player—"

He started to argue, but she asked him to let her finish.

"Alex and I talked about this the other night. I asked her how well she knew you. Her answer makes a lot more sense after tonight."

"How so?"

"She talked more about Maddox than you. She said he was 'charming.'"

"What did she say about me?"

"We just talked about whether you were, you know, a player."

"I'm not crazy about where this conversation is going."

"You should be, because I don't see you that way. There is, however, a little voice deep inside, screaming at me to be careful, take it slow, and not be so quick to trust you."

"I like being with you, Peyton. When I'm not, I want to be. If I had my way, I'd be with you all the time. Every minute. It's like I can't get enough of you."

"Are you always like this?"

"Never have been before. So Peyton, would it be okay if we stopped talking now?"

"I guess so."

She moved the blanket off her shoulder, as though she was going to get up. Instead, Brodie eased it off his shoulder too and pulled her down on top of it with him.

"No talking now, just kissing."

Peyton wrapped her arms around him and pulled him closer. He cushioned her head from the hard, cold ground under them. He held her tight and rolled so she was stretched out on top of him.

"That's better," he said against her lips.

His hands fisted her hair; his mouth devoured hers. He loved the feel of her on top of him. Her curves melded into his body, as though she was made for him. Brodie put both his hands on her ass and pulled her closer. If he ripped her clothes away, he could slide into her warmth so easily. She shifted, rubbing against him. There was no mistaking she was feeling him the same way he felt her.

He brought his hands back up to her hair and held her still. "Peyton, I don't think I've ever wanted someone the way I want you."

She slid lower, so her head rested on his chest. Her arms were tucked close to her sides, and her breasts were pushed into him. He could feel her pebbled nipples rubbing back and forth against him.

"Come on," he said. "Let's go." He sat up and flipped her over, so her back was to his front, and then he stood, holding her in his arms.

"How did you do that?" Her arms were around his neck, holding on, but he had her, she didn't have to worry. No matter what, he had her.

Brodie carried her to the passenger side of the car, released the arm that held her legs, and slid her down his body. When her feet hit the ground, he turned her around and pushed her up against the door. He wrapped his hands under the back of her thighs and brought them up to his hips. When he pushed his clothed body against her sex, she moved back and forth, rubbing against him. His mouth captured hers, and her thighs tightened against his splayed hands.

He held her there, trapped between his body and her car, and looked into her eyes. "This isn't slow, Peyton, and it won't be. It'll be hard and fast. Do you understand?"

Her breathing hitched, and she nodded her head.

"Is this what you want, Peyton?"

She nodded her head again, a stifled groan escaping her lips as she pushed herself against him harder.

"Say it. I need to hear you say it," he demanded.

"Yes, Brodie, I want this."

"What, Peyton? What do you want?"

"I want you."

"That's my girl." Brodie released her thighs and captured her mouth with his, probing, pushing as hard as his body was pressed against hers. "Let's go home, Peyton."

—:—

Home. What did that mean? Her home? Peyton's eyes drifted over to the man driving her car. His light touch on the steering wheel defied the hardness of biceps so toned and powerful they strained the sleeves of his shirt. The glow from her car's dash illuminated his hard, angled jaw and the slash of his cheekbones. His tightened muscles held untold promises of the pleasure just his kissing her had brought. When he looked her way, she saw the light dance in his deep blue eyes, his grin, and the dimples that cut into his beautiful face when he smiled at her.

His hand came over and rested on her leg. His powerful fingers squeezed as they slowly moved closer to the heat radiating from between her legs.

His eyes drooped, and his breath caught as his calloused fingers sought the peak of her beaded nipple. "I want my mouth on you, Peyton. Everywhere." He pinched her hardened flesh. "Here." He slid his hand down and palmed her sex. "And here."

She was in too deep already, allowing herself to be drawn into the sensual spell he weaved around her. Logic and restraint fled. She could not deny the pleasure she sensed he could give her. It had been so long since she'd been taken that she could barely remember how it felt to have her body stretched, her flesh penetrated.

The lustful look burning through his eyes, the dominance she felt in his hands, was assurance that, once he had her, his touch would be one she'd never forget. His heat would sear into her memory and leave a mark that no amount of time would heal. His pull was so magnetic, she felt herself move toward him with no resistance.

Was she ready for this? Could she let herself go and open her body to him? There was no way she could fight it. In five short days, Brodie Butler had claimed her. He owned her body, her mind, and soon he would own her heart.

9

Peyton whimpered softly as Brodie's tongue slid in, tangling with hers. Hot, pulsating pleasure spread down his body. He had her pinned between himself and her kitchen counter, nuzzling the soft skin on her neck and breathing her in. "You smell so good." He crashed his mouth into hers again and fisted his hand in her long, blonde hair. Even if he climbed inside of her, he still wouldn't be close enough.

He lifted her until her behind rested on the counter, and trapped her legs between his. Both hands splayed over her breasts. His hands were big, but not enough that he could hold all of their fullness.

"Let's take this off." He pulled her shirt out from where it was tucked into her jeans. "Unbutton it." If she didn't hurry, he was going to rip it open, sending buttons flying across the kitchen.

She shimmied out of it and started to unfasten her bra.

"Hands on me, Peyton." She rested her palms on his arms. "That's my girl."

Brodie left her bra fastened, but pulled the front down, so her breasts fell over the cups. Back and forth he went, kissing, nibbling, sucking, laving. It was the little nips that took her breath away. Her fingers dug into his arms, and then relaxed when he soothed her with his tongue.

"Brodie, you're torturing me."

In between nips, he kissed and licked, going from one shoulder to the other. "You wanted me to go slow, baby. Isn't that what you wanted?"

"No, God, not anymore. Please, Brodie."

More kissing, more nipping. "Please what, Peyton?"

"More, Brodie. I need more."

"More what?"

"Of you," she whimpered. "God, I'm begging you."

"Alright, sweetheart. Let's see if Brodie can take care of whatever it is you need."

His hands went under her, pulling her to the edge of the counter. "Wrap your legs around me, Peyton."

Her legs went around his hips, her arms around his neck. "I'm not little, Brodie."

"I'm not sure what you mean, Peyton. But I can tell you this, I'm not little either."

"I'm heavy."

"You're kidding, right?" He carried her in front of him. "Tell me where, Peyton."

"Down the hall. Last door on the right."

Brodie rested her on the edge of the bed. "Lie back for me, baby."

He unfastened her belt, unzipped her jeans, and pulled them off in one tug. Her eyes closed, then opened. He watched as her breath caught, her body flushed with need.

"Open your legs for me, Peyton." He lifted her knees and knelt between them, resting her legs over his spread thighs.

"You have too many clothes on," she whined.

"I'm takin' it slow, Peyton. Just like you wanted," he teased.

He pulled her body forward. Her hips tilted then, and the hardness trapped inside his jeans kissed her sex. He could feel her wetness, and groaned as pleasure shot through his body.

Her black, lace bra was the only thing left on her beautiful body, and he intended to leave it there. He ran his hands from her still-beaded nipples, down her taut abdomen, and back to her knees. He lifted her just slightly, so he could kiss the tender skin on the back of her knee. He ran his tongue from there, up the inside of her thigh. When he reached her warmth, he pulled away and kissed the soft backside of her other knee.

Peyton writhed and whimpered, but nothing she did would change his course. Tonight was about making her his. Every inch of her body would learn the touch of his hands, his mouth, his body.

Her green eyes glowed in the moonlight streaming in through her bedroom window, and sweat glistened on her bare skin. He'd never seen anything more beautiful than the woman spread before him.

He rose and reached behind him to pull his shirt over his head and, at the same time, toed off his boots. When she sat up and reached for his belt, he grasped both her wrists with one hand and held her still.

"I want to help," she pouted.

"Not yet, Peyton." With his other hand, he unfastened his belt and tore at the button on his jeans. He clenched his jaw and took a deep breath. He wasn't going to rush this. They had all night, and he planned to make good use of it.

She gasped when his jeans slid down his legs and he knelt back between her thighs. "You still want it slow, Peyton?"

"No, Brodie. I never wanted it slow."

He laughed and reached over to where he'd tossed his jeans. He pulled a condom out of his wallet and breathed a sigh of relief. He hadn't been sure he had one with him. He looked into her eyes and saw heat, and need, and longing. His body rested close to hers. As much as she wanted him to hurry, he couldn't allow it.

"Oh, God," she tried to tighten her thighs, pull him in closer, but he wouldn't relent.

"Look at me, Peyton. I want to see your eyes the minute we come together. I'm going to make you mine, Peyton. Do you understand?"

She nodded and whimpered as he eased in and back with maddening slowness. He was mesmerized by the need he saw as he entered her. He stopped and let the feeling of her warmth spread over him. And then he came undone.

His restraint was lost as he took her harder, his fingers digging into the flesh of her hips as he held her as close to him as he could.

"That's it, baby," he breathed as she clenched and jerked against him. He wanted to enjoy watching her pleasure spread over her flushed skin, to savor her. He fought to regain his control, but when she tightened around him, he exploded in a sea of sharp, intense, overwhelming pleasure.

Peyton stiffened beneath him and gripped his shoulders. "Come with me, baby. Right now." Her fingers dug into his skin as he watched her unravel beneath him.

He held himself above her, watching as she came down from the heights of pleasure she hadn't known existed.

"Look at me," he murmured, and she did.

She stared into eyes that had haunted her only a handful of days ago, but now whatever other memories they may have evoked, were gone. Shattered. The eyes she looked into were Brodie's, and if she never saw another set of eyes boring into hers the way his were, it wouldn't matter. All that mattered now was the man who lowered himself against her and kissed the dewy wetness on her neck, her shoulder, and in the soft groove between her breasts.

"I liked it slow, Peyton. Very much." He brought his lips to hers and tangled her tongue with his. "But next time, we do it fast. Fast and hard. Okay, baby?"

"Brodie..." She had no words, other than to say his name again and again, in something she could only describe as reverence.

He slid away into the bathroom, dragging his fingers over her body as he went. A chill spread over her, and she reached for the blanket.

"No," he pulled the cover away from her as he came back to bed. He rested his body next to hers. "I'll keep you warm, Peyton. I've got you. Always. Do you understand?"

She let her heavy eyelids close and snuggled into his heat.

—:—

She stirred, her body entwined with Brodie's. He moved against her slowly, every inch of his body pulsating.

"I want you again, Peyton," he moaned.

As if her arm had free will, she opened the drawer of the nightstand, her fingers feeling the way until they touched on what they sought. She pulled the condom packet out, closed the drawer with the back of her hand, and rested it between them.

True to his word, he took her fast and hard. They came together, pulling at one another, hands grasping, looks searching, until they exploded, landing in a heap of tangled limbs. She'd never be cold when she slept with Brodie. His body knew nothing but heat.

He pulled her close to him and spooned her body, his powerful hands and arms covering more of her than a blanket could.

"Sleep, baby," he whispered, and she did.

—:—

He should let her sleep, but was powerless against the overwhelming need to take her again. Reaching to the nightstand, he gently pulled the drawer open and felt another foil packet. He snatched it up, tore it open, and sheathed himself. Peyton's breathing was still even, and she hadn't moved a muscle.

Slowly he eased himself inside her wetness and held himself still as she came awake.

"Oh my God, Brodie, you feel *so* good," she groaned and moved her hips back and forth.

He put his hand on her hip and stilled her. Slowly, slowly, he began again, easing in and out of her. His hands came up and held her breasts as he ran his tongue from her shoulder to the back of her neck, where he rained soft kisses up and down. Taking her from behind, he couldn't see her eyes, but he could hear her soft mewls as he rotated his hips. He slid his hand down and cupped her, holding her still, so only he could control their movement.

"Mmm," she whimpered.

"Shh." He stilled her again. He felt every part of her skin heat against him and forced himself to focus on how good it felt to have her wrapped around him. He never wanted to lose this feeling. When he dreamed of her, this is what he wanted his body to remember.

This time when their wave of pleasure crested, he stayed where he was, allowing himself and her to sleep with their bodies joined.

—:—

Peyton opened her eyes to the morning light casting a soft glow on her body. Brodie's arms held her tight, one leg bent over hers, trapping her against him.

"Good morning, my beautiful Peyton." His lips kissed across her neck, as they had the night before.

Her need for him had not diminished. If it wasn't for the exhaustion that came with the release he gave her body, she would want him again, only moments after their bodies came apart. Her legs were stiff from sleeping so soundly in one position, and her arms felt too heavy to lift.

"I want to see your eyes," he said as he managed to turn her body around to face him.

His hand cradled the side of her face, and he brought his lips to hers. His kiss was soft, not hard, as it had been last night.

"When do you have to be at Stave?"

"Later," she grinned. "Why do you ask?" She squirmed against him, but he held her still.

"Breakfast, baby."

Brodie was standing and pulling her out of bed before her lips could form a pout. "But—"

"Breakfast," he whispered as though it was the most sensual word in the English language. "Let's see, what would Peyton want after a night of full-throttle, mad, crazy, passionate, all-out lovemaking? Hmm. Let me guess. Honey pancakes with an ollalieberry drizzle? Or maybe a Dungeness crab omelet with shrimp and mushrooms and swiss cheese?"

"Stop," she swatted at him. "I'm suddenly ravenous."

"Not sudden, baby. You've been ravenous all night long." His dimples creased his face as he smiled at her.

Peyton brought her fingers to his lips and caressed his cheek in the same way he'd done to her so many times last night. "Brodie, last night was..."

"Was...go on..."

"I'm searching for words."

"How about if I help? Spectacular. The best sex of my life." He grinned.

"Without question." She sauntered into the bathroom, reached in, and turned on the shower.

Brodie came up behind her and wrapped his arm around her waist. "Those were my words, Peyton. Tell me yours."

"Mind-blowing. Other-worldly. Sweet, sensual, loving."

"I like your words, Peyton."

"I like you, Brodie."

—:—

He followed her into the shower and took the bottle of shampoo from her hand. "Let me." He drizzled it into his hands and rubbed his fingers into her scalp.

"I didn't realize how long your hair is. It's always up. I like it, especially when I can run my fingers through it."

She moaned as he massaged her scalp, kneading it with his powerful hands. That sound, so like the ones he'd heard from her the night before, made him want her again.

"Rinse, sweetheart."

Peyton closed her eyes as the water washed the scent of him away.

When she turned and picked up the soap, he caught her wrist. "Breakfast," he growled.

"But—"

"No, Peyton. Breakfast."

She pouted at him and rubbed her body against his as she got out of the shower.

"You'll pay for that, darlin'." He followed, swatting her bottom as she ran into the bedroom.

"Breakfast, Brodie." Peyton stuck her tongue out at him.

He laughed, throwing his head back, marveling at how, in such a short time, she had him wrapped around her finger, and his heart beating out of his chest.

—:—

Peyton's phone vibrated in the bag resting near her feet. She pulled it out and reached over to turn down the music wafting from her car's sound system.

"Hi, sweetie, good morning," she answered, seeing Jamison's name flash on the screen.

"Hey, Mom."

"How was your night with Grandma and Grandpa?"

"Good. Abuela Lucia stayed and watched movies with us until it was so late, Grandpa said he didn't feel comfortable letting her drive home, so he drove her."

She loved that Alex's mom was so close to her parents. The friendship between Lucia and Peyton's mom reminded her of her own friendship with Alex. When Alfonso died, Peyton's mom brought Lucia into their family in the same way Lucia would've had, had Peyton's father died. Alex said that her mom was as much the boys' *abuela* as her mother was, and she was right. Her boys were well-loved by their two grandmothers.

"Hey, Mom, is it okay if Finn and I stay here again tonight? Grandpa said he'd take us to the stables and we could ride in the morning."

"Of course, sweetie, but I'll talk to you again later, okay?"

"Yeah, bye. Love you, Mom."

"I love you too, Jamison."

She disconnected her call and looked over at Brodie, whose smile, once again, brought out his dimples.

"How are they?"

"They're good. They love their time with my parents, and even though I miss them like crazy, I'm happy they get to be with them as much as they do."

"Did I hear Jamison say something about riding?"

"My dad keeps horses at Los Caballeros. He and my mom love to ride, and take the boys every chance they can."

"We have stables too." He grinned.

"I know you do." She grinned back.

"Do you ride, Peyton?"

"Please, Brodie. Ride? I was born on the back of a horse."

—:—

He reached over and stroked her cheek with his finger. "Beautiful and badass."

"Huh?" she laughed.

"Every time I look at you, that's what comes to mind. You're breathtakingly beautiful and so badass that I wonder, sometimes, if I'll be able to keep up with you."

Peyton laughed again and looked out at the waves crashing on Moonstone Beach. "Do you surf, Brodie?"

"Surf? Please. I was born on a surfboard."

He stopped the car in front of the Ollalieberry Diner, climbed out, and came around to open her door. He loved that she waited for him, loved that she let him do that for her.

Brodie's phone vibrated in his pocket, but he ignored it. Whoever it was, he'd call back later. When it vibrated again between the car and the front door of the restaurant, he decided he better answer it.

"Excuse me for a minute," he said to Peyton, looking at the screen on his cell.

Naughton was calling.

"What's up, brother? House on fire?"

Naughton's words sent a chill down Brodie's spine. "It's Ma, Brodie. Took her by helicopter to Twin Cities Hospital. It's her heart."

"I'll be right there."

Peyton was standing in front of him, concern etched into her face. "What is it?"

"My ma. I'm sorry, Peyton, but I've gotta go."

"It's okay, I'll take you to your car."

10

Ten minutes earlier Peyton had been starving. Now the thought of eating made her nauseous. Instead of going home, she drove to Stave. They'd be opening in an hour, and there was no telling what kind of shape Alex left the place in last night.

Alex's car was in the parking lot when she pulled in, but that didn't mean much. After the night she'd had, who knew what might have gone on between Alex and Maddox.

"Well, good morning, sunshine," Alex beamed when Peyton walked in the back door.

"Hey, Alex."

"Wait, you're not smiling like the sun. What's wrong?"

"They took Mrs. Butler to the hospital by helicopter this morning. Her heart—"

Alex's hand went to her mouth, and she ran to the office before Peyton finished her sentence.

She came back out a minute later, holding her cell. "It went to voicemail," she explained.

"Maddox?"

"Yeah."

"My dad—" Alex's eyes filled with tears.

Peyton walked over and hugged her. "I know, sweetie."

Alfonso Avila had died too young, of a massive heart attack. Brodie's mom being taken by helicopter hit too close to home. Alex's dad had been too, but was dead before it touched down.

Alex hit the buttons on her phone again, waited, and then hung up.

"You can go if you want to," Peyton offered.

"No. I don't want to intrude."

"Alex, that's the last thing they'd think. You've known the Butlers your whole life."

"I'll wait." Alex walked to the front of the tasting room and opened the garage door. "The weather is so beautiful. We should take advantage of it."

Peyton noticed the way Alex's hands shook when she hit the opener. Her skin had gone pale, and her eyes were filled with tears.

"Go. Please. If you're okay to drive. Please go."

"I don't know."

"Go and see if they need anything. I'll be fine here."

"Call Addy?"

"Yep, I'll see if she can come in early. If not, I'll try Sam."

"Okay. You're sure?"

"I'm sure."

Peyton was as worried as Alex was, but it wouldn't be appropriate for her to go to the hospital. Maddox knew about her and Brodie, but what about the rest of their family? What would they think of her? And after last night—she wasn't proud of herself at the moment.

There wasn't anything for her to do to get Stave ready to open. Alex appeared to have been there a while. The floor was swept and mopped, the counters had been scoured, and the wine chillers were full. Peyton went into the kitchen to see if any food needed to be prepped, but that had been done too. She walked over to the coffeemaker and brewed a fresh pot.

She was worried about Mrs. Butler, but knew Alex would call and give her an update as soon as she knew anything.

With a full cup of coffee, Peyton walked out front and sat at one of the tables on the patio. The sun, beating down from the east, felt warm on her face. She breathed in the aroma of the strong coffee and closed her eyes.

She opened them just as a man walked in the store across the street. She held her breath. From the back, he looked so much like Kade. This time she knew it wasn't one of his brothers. What she didn't know was whether she had imagined him or not. Would he ever stop haunting her?

She put her feet on the chair across from her, and set her coffee on the table, letting her mind drift wherever it wanted to go.

"Peyton, wake up." The gravelly voice she knew so well, startled her.

She opened her eyes and blinked, trying to focus. Kade was sitting at the table, in the chair opposite hers.

"Kade?" she gasped. "What—"

He held up his hand, and she stopped talking.

"She's going to be okay."

"Your mom?"

"It was a mild one, more of a warning. They'll keep her a couple of days, for observation, and then let her go home."

"But—"

"Everything will be okay, Peyton. She'll be okay, and so will you."

"Peyton?" When she opened her eyes, Addy was shaking her shoulder.

"Where did he go?" She shot up and looked around the patio.

"Who?"

"Kade! He was just here. Where did he go?"

"Peyton...you were dreaming..."

"No, Addy," she barked. "He was just here. He told me his mom was going to be okay."

"That's why I came out looking for you." Addy handed Peyton her cell that she'd left on the desk in her office. "Alex is trying to get in touch with you."

Peyton walked to the front of the patio and looked up and down the street. No one was out yet this morning. She looked across the street and saw a closed sign in the window of the store she'd, only moments ago, thought she saw Kade walk into.

"I'm sorry, Peyton." Addy stood next to her.

"I need to find him." Out of the corner of her eye, Peyton saw Addy shake her head as she walked away.

Instead of calling Alex, Peyton went to her favorite's screen and punched the icon for Kade.

The phone rang and rang, but he didn't pick up, and it didn't go to voicemail. That was odd. As soon as she set the phone down on the table, it rang. Peyton grabbed it. It was Alex.

"Hi."

"Hey, Peyton. I'm not at the hospital yet, but Maddox called. Their mom is going to be okay. It was a mild heart attack."

"I know. They're going to keep her at the hospital for observation."

"Yes. How did you know? Did you call the hospital?"

"No, Alex. Kade told me. He was just here. I've got to go, though. I closed my eyes, and he was gone. I've got to find him."

"Wait, wait, wait, honey. What's going on?"

"I've got to go, Alex. I have to find him."

Peyton disconnected the call and shoved the phone into her back pocket. He couldn't have gotten far. He was just here. Why did he leave? Where was he?

She walked all the way from the west village to the east. No stores were open yet, except the market. Maybe Louie had seen him. She pulled open the front door and went inside.

"Good morning, Peyton," Louie greeted her. "What can I get you? Coffee?"

"No, Louie, but thanks. Have you seen Kade?"

"Kade? Do you mean Brodie?"

"No, Louie. Kade. He was at Stave, and then he was gone. I need to find him."

Louie came out from around the counter. "Peyton, sit down." He pressed her shoulder, guiding her to one of the chairs near the bakery counter. He pulled another chair around and sat down in front of her, taking her hands in his. "Peyton." He looked into her eyes. "Tell me what this is all about."

She jerked her hands away. "I saw him, Louie. He told me his mom was going to be okay. He told me everything Alex said. I already knew. He's here somewhere, and I need to find him."

Peyton got up and went out the front door of the market, glad that Louie didn't follow her. She searched both sides of the street again, wishing she'd drove instead of walked. A few minutes later, Alex pulled up just as Peyton was about to cross the street.

"Get in," she shouted.

"No, Alex. I need to find him." Peyton started to cry, and covered her face with her hands. "He was here, Alex. He told me about his mom. He was here," she sobbed.

Alex got out of the car and walked around to where Peyton stood.

"He was here, Alex. I swear," Peyton cried.

Alex put her arm around Peyton's shoulders and guided her into the car. Once Peyton started to cry, she couldn't stop. She looked up when Alex turned a corner. "Where are we going?"

"Home."

"Home? I don't want to go home, Alex."

Alex pulled the car off the side of the road. She took Peyton's hands in hers and looked into her eyes. "Kade is dead, Peyton. He wasn't here. He didn't tell you about his mother."

"But—"

"No, Peyton. *Kade is dead.*"

She rolled over and sat up. It was dark in her bedroom. Peyton remembered Alex drove her home and guided her inside. Alex had brought her into the bedroom and sat on the side of the bed while Peyton sobbed. Her body felt spent from being wracked with sobs, and from lack of sleep the night before.

"She's sleeping now," she heard Alex say from the other room. "I don't know. I have no idea what brought it on. She was fine when I saw her earlier. Better than I was actually." Alex paused. "I'm going to stay with her." Another pause. "That would be great. I appreciate it so much." Pause. "No, I think it would be best if I was with her."

Alex peeked around the corner. "You're awake."

"I'm awake. Who were you talking to?"

"Your dad. He's going to help out at Stave today. I'm sure Addy and Sam would be fine, but if it gets busy, it'll be better if he's there."

"This is crazy." Peyton started to get up, but Alex pushed her back on the bed.

"You and I are going to stay here, Peyton. You need some rest, and maybe I do too."

"Alex, I need—"

"Peyton," she shouted. "Don't say it again. *Kade was not here.* You can't find him, because he wasn't here. Stop this."

What was wrong with her? She knew Kade was dead. She knew it, but it had been so real. How many times had she imagined that she saw him? But this was different. He'd talked to her, and he'd told her his mother was going to be okay.

"How would I know about their mom if Kade didn't tell me?"

"I don't know, honey. Premonition?"

"But it seemed so real. He seemed so real. I couldn't have been dreaming, Alex."

"I don't know, Peyton. All I know for sure is that Kade is dead, and you didn't see him this morning. Now, please, try to get some rest."

Peyton rolled back over and closed her eyes. A few minutes later, Alex got up and walked out of the bedroom. Peyton rolled to her back and looked up at the ceiling. She wasn't *crazy*. She knew it was nuts to think she saw Kade, to think that he talked to her. But it had seemed so real that she couldn't shake it. Maybe Alex was right. She and Brodie had hardly slept at all. Between the stress of something happening to his mom, and him having to leave, and the weirdness of it all, her mind played tricks on her, as it had so many times before.

Alex was talking to someone again, but Peyton couldn't hear what she was saying. She reached over and looked at her phone. It couldn't be afternoon already. Had she really slept that long? She sat up and felt dizzy. She grasped the edge of the bed and waited for her head to stop spinning. She was just about to stand up when she heard Alex's footsteps coming down the hallway.

"I'll check." She heard Alex say. When she came around the corner, she spoke into the phone again. "I don't think it's a good idea, but I'll see. Hold on."

Peyton watched Alex press the mute button on her phone. "It's Brodie."

Peyton shook her head and walked into the bathroom.

"She's still sleeping, Brodie. I'll tell her you called when she wakes up."

Peyton came back out of the bathroom and pushed past Alex.

"How are you feeling?"

"Fine."

"You slept a long time."

"I guess I was pretty tired."

"Peyton?"

"Don't say it, Alex. I feel stupid, okay? Really stupid."

"Don't be so hard on yourself."

"The whole town probably knows by now. 'Peyton Wolf was out wandering the streets this morning, saying she saw Kade's ghost.'"

"No one is saying that. The only person who saw you, other than Addy, was Louie, and you know he'd never say a word."

"How do you know I saw Louie?"

"He called Stave and asked Addy if you were okay. She called and told me, so I called him back."

"Great."

"Come on, Peyton. It isn't that big of a deal."

"How's Mrs. Butler?"

"She's fine. Like we talked about earlier, they're keeping her for a couple of days, but otherwise, they aren't concerned."

Peyton wouldn't say it out loud, one because she knew it sounded like she'd lost her mind, and two, Alex would get angry with her. But she couldn't shake the feeling that she *saw* Kade this morning, and that he talked to her. Her chest felt tight, making it hard to breathe, and the sick feeling that had settled in her stomach hadn't left.

The last thing she'd heard him say was, "She'll be okay, and so will you." What did that mean, she'd be okay?

"Brodie wants to come by."

Peyton knew he would, given the way he left this morning. "Does he know?"

"No. I told you that the only people who know are Addy and Louie."

"My parents."

"They aren't going to tell Brodie, or anyone else, sweetie."

"Maddox?"

"Give me a break. What did I just say? I said no one else. And jeez, do you really think I'd tell *Maddox?*"

"No. I had to make sure."

"Back to Brodie. He wants to see you. Unless you tell him, he's not going to understand."

Peyton nodded her head. "I'll call him."

"Good."

"You can leave now. I'm okay. My momentary lapse into madness is over."

"If you're sure."

"I'm fine, Alex. I'm not coming in tonight, but I'm fine."

"If you said you were going to, I wouldn't let you."

"My car..."

"I'll have your dad or Addy follow me over. I'll do that now, before it gets busy with the Saturday night crowd."

"Thanks, Alex. For all of it. As much of a bitch as I've been, I want you to know I appreciate everything you did for me today."

"Yeah, if I suddenly went bonkers and started seeing the ghost of my father, you'd do the same for me."

Peyton laughed out loud. "Yeah, I would."

She waited until Alex drove off before she picked up her cell to call Brodie. He answered before she even heard it ring.

"Hi, I've been worried about you."

"I'm fine, just really tired. How's your mom?"

"She'll be fine. It was only—"

"Alex told me." Peyton didn't want to hear the same words Kade had spoken to her earlier from Brodie.

"Alex said you slept most of the morning. Are you feeling okay?"

"Not really."

"What's going on with you, Peyton? You're not smiling."

That made her smile. *Hearing* her smile was one of his superpowers. And maybe Kade's superpower was coming back from the dead.

"Can I come over?"

"No, Brodie. That isn't a good idea."

"Why not?"

"I need some space. Last night was..."

"Mind-blowing. Other-worldly. That's what you said earlier."

"It was a mistake, Brodie. I was in love with your brother, and that isn't something I can just shut off. I'm sorry, but we can't do that again."

"Don't go there, Peyton. Don't let his memory come between us. Kade is gone, and I'm here, and this thing we have is something special. I feel it everywhere—my head, my heart, and the rest of my body."

"It's wrong, and I can't do it. Bye, Brodie."

Peyton disconnected the call and went back in the bedroom. She made the bed, and then decided she should wash the sheets instead. It was another warm day, so even though it was five in the afternoon, it was still warm enough to open some windows and air her room out.

Once the sheets were in the washer, she decided to clean the bathroom and the kitchen. As long as she was stuck here, she might as well make good use of the time.

She heard the garage door open, and went out to thank her dad and Alex for bringing her car.

"How's my girl?" her dad asked, wrapping her in a big hug.

"Nuts, but okay."

"I can't tell you I've ever had anything like that happen to me, but I understand, sweetheart. You'll mourn Kade's loss for the rest of your life, in some way. The pain is less now than it was a year ago, and five years from now, it'll lessen more. There may even come a day, and I hope it's soon, that you'll find love again. You deserve it, sweetheart."

"Thanks, Dad." Peyton pulled away from him. He meant the best with his words, but they cut into her nonetheless. She couldn't think about finding love again. She wasn't ready, and maybe she never would be.

"How's business?" she asked Alex.

"Swamped. Sorry, but we need to get back."

"I can come in—"

Both Alex and her father said "no," at the same time.

"Okay, okay," she held up her hands. "I'll be in tomorrow, though."

"I wouldn't expect anything else. See you then." Alex waved and climbed into the passenger seat of Peyton's father's truck.

"See you, Dad. Give those boys a big hug from me when you get home later, and tell them I'll see them tomorrow."

"Love you, Peyton."

"I love you too, Dad."

Peyton went back inside to finish cleaning. Maybe she'd clean the boys' bedrooms too while she was at it.

An hour later, she heard a knock at the door. There was only one person it could be, and she didn't want him here.

11

She heard the knock again, only louder. Since most of the windows in her house were open, she couldn't hide. Besides, anyone standing at the front door could hear music playing.

"Peyton, open the door," Brodie called out.

She wiped her hands on her jeans and slowly walked into the foyer. She didn't want to see him, and she didn't appreciate his lack of respect for not honoring what she told him. She swung the door open, intending to tell him exactly what was on her mind, but the haunted look in his eyes stopped her cold.

"Brodie, what's wrong? Did something happen with your mom?"

"We need to talk." He pushed past her and stood in her living room with his arms folded in front of him.

"I already told you—"

"There's something I need to tell you, Peyton. It's important, and I'm asking you to listen to me."

She didn't appreciate the tone of his voice any more than his lack of respect for her wishes. It was only his appearance that kept her still. He looked like hell, and still hadn't told her what was wrong.

"Something happened."

Peyton gasped. "With your mom?"

"No. Yes. With my mom, but not in the way you're thinking."

"What happened, Brodie?"

"She told us she talked to Kade."

Peyton grasped the closest chair. She was lightheaded and knew the color had drained from her face. "What did she say?"

"He told her it wasn't her time, and that we needed her. Especially me. He told her that I needed her to help me with what I'm going through."

Peyton sat in the chair she'd been holding onto.

"She said he told her something else, Peyton."

She didn't want to know. Whatever it was, was too much. She closed her eyes, hoping he wouldn't go on.

"He told her that the family needed to accept that you needed me."

"No, Brodie."

"How would she know, Peyton?"

"Maybe your brothers told her."

"They were as shocked as I was."

"Then it was a premonition."

"She was rattled, Peyton. And that wasn't all."

Peyton wanted to put her hands over her ears. She wanted to unhear what he'd already told her, and she didn't want to hear anything else.

"She said he talked to you, too."

"Brodie..."

"So he didn't? You didn't dream about him talking to you?"

Taking in a deep breath, she needed time to decide whether to lie to Brodie, or tell him the truth.

"You did. I can see it in your face."

"Another superpower, Brodie?"

"Don't give me that, Peyton. Tell me."

"No." It wasn't any of his business. And whether she'd dreamed about Kade or not, he hadn't said a word about Brodie.

He walked forward and knelt in front of her, reaching up to touch her cheek.

"Don't, Brodie."

"Peyton—"

She pushed past him and stood behind the kitchen island. "When we spoke earlier, I told you that I don't want to see you again. I'm sorry if I made you believe there was something more between us. There isn't. The sex was great, I'll concede that, but that's all it was. Sex.

I'm confident it wasn't your first one-night stand, nor will it be the last."

"That isn't necessary."

"It is, Brodie. You're not listening to me. I don't want you, not in my bed, not in my house, not in my life. Please leave."

He held the back of his neck, the same way Kade always had. She'd seen him do it so many times before. It meant something was troubling him, and was typically followed by action. With Brodie, it was no different. He strode over to her, as though he was on the attack.

She went around to the other side of the kitchen island. "I said no, Brodie, and I meant it. *Do not touch me.*"

Those four words did it. Brodie backed off. His eyes darted back and forth, and his hand went back to rubbing his neck. "Peyton, please—"

"*No!* How many times do I have to say it? No, Brodie. *No*. Now go." Peyton walked to the front door and held it open.

Brodie slowly walked over to where she stood.

"This isn't over, Peyton. I'll give you some space, time even, but it isn't over."

"You're wrong. No matter how much time passes or space you give me, I'm not going to change my mind. Bye, Brodie."

Once he was out the door, she closed it behind him, locked it, and rested her back against it. She needed to get the hell out of this house, but everywhere she thought to go, would be a place she'd gone with him. If she drove north, she'd pass Piedras Blancas. If she went south, she wouldn't be able to think of anything other than her day with him. Same thing if she went east, but her boys were east. That's what she needed, time with her boys.

There was a bag in her closet, packed and ready for when she decided to stay out at her parents' guest house. She did it often enough. She grabbed it, went out the door to the garage, and got in her car.

When she passed the turnoff to where she and Brodie had gone the night before, she accelerated. When she reached the turnoff for Adelaida Trail, she contemplated going a different way around so she didn't have to pass the gates of Butler Ranch, but that was silly. She could drive by. It wouldn't affect her.

—:—

Brodie gave his horse a hard nudge, and she knew what it meant. His sweet little chestnut Morgan loved to run as much as he did. He'd named her Baroness when he bought her, and only Brodie would call her little. She was just over sixteen hands, with a compact build and strong-as-hell hindquarters.

He took her over the hills, and out to the pasture near the front gates of the ranch. He looked up and saw the little black BMW fly by, and the long blonde hair of the woman driving it. The car had to be going seventy, at least. A car like that could handle the curves of the road at those speeds without any problem, but he still didn't like her driving that fast. He had half a mind to take Baroness back to the barn, hop in his car, and follow her. He knew she was headed to the sanctuary of her parents' ranch.

Instead, he slowed his horse and took a leisurely ride back. Last night had been the best sex of his life, and that was saying something. It was more, though. When he'd told Peyton she was his, he'd meant it.

Something had spooked her. Regardless of what it was, he wouldn't allow her to keep her distance very long. The connection between them was real. It was powerful and undeniable.

"Wish you'd come to me, older brother," Brodie said to the sky. "I've never needed your advice more than I do right now. As much as you may think she needs me, I need her more."

—:—

"Mom!" Finn raced over and jumped into her arms, wrapping his legs around her waist and linking his feet behind her back. "You're here! Grandpa's at Stave, working 'cause you're sick. Are you feeling better?"

"I am feeling better, now that I'm here." She tousled his hair. "I missed you, kiddo."

"Missed you too, Mom." He let go, and his feet hit the ground beneath him. "You stayin' for dinner? It's almost ready."

"Sure am." Peyton could smell the aroma of her mom's Santa Maria-style tri-tip.

"Hi, darling girl. Are you feeling better?"

Peyton walked into her mother's arms and rested her head on her mom's shoulder. Peyton got her height from both her parents, along with their long, thin, Germanic facial features. Her high cheekbones, and long wavy hair, she got from her mom alone.

A few years ago, her mother had let it go gray, but kept it long. It fell in cascading waves down past the middle of her back. And in her early sixties, her mom still rocked a pair of jeans like a supermodel. She stayed fit, doing yoga at least five days a week. She ran, and rode, and spent as much time out in the vineyards as her dad did, so she was tan even though she lathered her skin with sunscreen and always wore a hat.

Her name was August, for the month of her birth, and Peyton couldn't imagine a more fitting name for her mom. Jamison was named after her dad, and while Lang chose Finn's name, Peyton loved it too.

"I'm okay. Weird dreams."

Her mom wrapped Peyton's arm inside the crook of hers, and walked her in the opposite direction of the house. "Tell me what's going on, Peyton. I know it's more than a weird dream."

"I've been spending time with Brodie Butler."

"I see."

"What does that mean?"

Her mom smiled. "Nothing."

"It's so weird."

"What makes you say that?"

"Come on, Mom. It's weird."

Her mom walked further, without speaking, until they came to the prettiest spot on the ranch. The view of the valley never failed to take Peyton's breath away.

"I'm going to tell you something you may not like."

"Okay..."

"I wasn't crazy about Kade Butler."

This was news. Never before had her mother said a negative word about Kade, or Lang. Even when he left her and the boys, her mother didn't defend him, but she didn't disparage him either.

"This isn't like you, Mom."

"I know it isn't. I've always believed that you were capable of making your own decisions, for your own reasons. I can't pretend to know how you feel inside."

"Why didn't you like Kade?"

"It should be obvious, Peyton."

"Well, it isn't," she snapped, tired of her mom's cat and mouse game.

"We rarely saw you when you were with him, sweetheart. That's a red flag. There were others. I don't know if he was always honest with you."

"Alex said the same thing the other day. Only she said he wasn't the man I thought he was."

"Did she elaborate?"

"Yes." She wasn't ready to tell her mom what Alex had told her about Kade. It really didn't make him seem any different in Peyton's eyes. It hadn't changed the way she saw him. Maybe because she'd sensed it about him.

"Peyton?"

"She told me he was going to work for the agency, the CIA."

"I know what the agency is, sweetheart."

"She said he kept it from me. He was afraid I wouldn't like it."

"And did he?"

"He didn't discuss it with me, but I don't think he intentionally kept it from me."

"He discussed it with your dad."

"What? Seriously? Why didn't Dad say anything to me about it?" And why did Kade think it was okay to talk to her dad about something he hadn't shared with her?

"Kade asked him not to."

"Then Dad isn't any better than Kade was."

"Peyton!"

"I'm tired of men keeping me in the dark about things that affect my life. Lying, sneaking around, cheating—I'm sick of it."

"Your father didn't do any of those things."

"He didn't tell me Kade spoke to him about things I was unaware of. That's lying."

"No, it's waiting. Kade asked him to wait."

"For what?"

"He was going to ask you to marry him."

Peyton sat down on the ground and put her elbows on her raised knees. "It would've been important for me to know that before I gave him my answer."

"Yes, and your father would've told you, but then Kade was killed, and there was no reason to."

"We never discussed marriage, Mom. Never. Brodie said something about how things might have been different after we were married. That I'd get to know the rest of his family better. I told him that Kade and I weren't as close as he seemed to think we were."

"Maybe you didn't think so, but Kade believed you were."

There were so many things she didn't know about him, not just about his new job. The more she heard, the more it sounded as though Kade had assumed things, took things for granted, or believed he knew how she felt without discussing it with her.

"I don't think I would've married him, Mom. I had a lot of doubts, even about the relationship continuing. He swept me up. I loved him, but that little voice inside me that I refused to listen to before I married Lang, wasn't keeping quiet."

"I'm happy to hear you're paying more attention to your intuition."

"I had a dream about Kade this morning. I was at Stave, sitting in the sun, and I must've dozed off. I dreamed he was sitting at the table, across from me. He told me his mom was going to be okay."

"Alex told us it left you quite shaken."

"Worse. I went looking for him."

"Oh, sweetheart." Her mom knelt down and put her arm around Peyton's shoulders.

"I'm mortified about it now. Addy's probably going to quit since, now, she works for a madwoman."

"Don't be ridiculous. Addy is fine. She's worried about you, but otherwise fine."

"Worried about my madness."

"No, Peyton, just worried about you. Don't make more of this than it was."

"You sound like Alex."

"I've always loved that girl." She smiled. "Peyton, talk to me about Brodie."

And say what? They had crazy sex last night? That she spent a day with him and he swept her off her feet, just like Kade had?

"I don't know what he wants from me."

"Maybe he just wants to get to know you."

"Why? Aren't there other single women in the valley the Butler boys can chase after? Or maybe they've already gone through all of them."

"Peyton!"

"What? Have you seen them? They're Adonises. Every one of them. Kade was. Maddox looks just like him, except taller. Naughton is...what did Alex say? All broody Scottish guy, but no less godlike. And then there's Brodie with his gorgeous blue eyes and his eight-pack abs, and, and that..." Ass. She was going to say ass. That incredible ass, and his powerful legs, and his mouth. His mouth was magical.

Her mom was fanning her face. "Your father always made me feel the way Brodie makes you feel."

"Brodie doesn't make me feel anything, Mom."

"Now who's the liar?"

"That isn't very nice."

"Neither is lying."

Peyton's cell phone rang. "This is probably Brodie calling, and I don't want to talk to him."

She took her phone out of her pocket and looked at the screen. It was Jamison.

"Hey, Jamie. What's up?"

"Where are you and Grandma? We're starving."

"Sorry, honey. We went for a walk. We'll come back up now."

"Boys are starving," she said to her mom.

"We'll finish this conversation later."

"No, Mom, we won't. There's nothing more to say on the Butler subject."

—:—

"Where have you been?" Naughton asked when Brodie walked into the house.

"First I went and saw Peyton, then I came back and went for a ride, and then I drove over to the hospital again to see Ma."

"How is she?"

"She's fine, although she begged me to bring her home. Says the walls are closing in on her."

Naughton laughed.

"She said you were with her."

"She and I were in the vineyard, talking about the old vine Zins, and she said she didn't feel well. The way she was holding herself, where she said she had pain, I knew it was her heart."

"I'm glad you were there."

"Me too, since neither of my brothers bothered to come home last night."

"Mad didn't either? Interesting."

"I can't believe you didn't know about him and Alex."

"Not a clue."

"He's more in love with her than you are with Peyton."

"I'm not in love with Peyton." Although he could be, very easily. If she'd let him.

"You tell her that Ma dreamed she saw Kade?"

"Yeah."

"What'd she say?"

"That she never wants to see me again."

Naughton laughed again, but Brodie didn't find it funny. "Wait until you're where I am, brother. Some girl getting you all tied up in knots."

"Who says I'm not?"

Brodie raised his eyebrows. "Then how come you were home last night?"

Naughton returned to chuckling, and Brodie went upstairs. He was exhausted, between waking Peyton up over and over again last night, Ma's heart attack, and then this shit with Kade, he needed sleep. When he woke up tomorrow, maybe he'd know what to do about Peyton.

—:—

"You guys want to go home tonight or stay here with Grandma and Grandpa?" her mother asked. She had cookies baking in the oven, what were her boys going to say?

"Can we ride tomorrow?"

"Of course we can."

"Mom, will you go with us?"

"I think I can do that. Although Alex may think I've abandoned Stave completely."

"Call her. I'm sure she'll be fine with it. I know your dad enjoys spending some time there. Maybe he'd like to fill in for you again tomorrow."

"I don't want to ask him to do that."

"He loves it. It's been a while since he got to interact with customers and listen as they tell him how fabulous his wine is. It's good for his ego."

"If you think so."

"I'll talk to him when he gets home later, but I'd wager I'm right."

After dinner, Peyton walked down to the guest house. The boys wanted to sleep in the main house again tonight, and she didn't mind. At least she was with them for dinner, a rare occurrence on a Saturday night. She'd be with them again tomorrow, if her dad agreed to cover for her.

She'd spent a lot of time in this little house right after Kade died. Her pillow could tell stories about how she cried into it night after night. She found comfort being so close to her mom and dad, particularly since her mom would often walk down and check on her.

She was their only child. After she was born, they tried to have more children, but her mom miscarried enough times that her dad said he couldn't stand to watch her go through it again. They talked about adoption, but the process was long and complex, and soon they gave up on that too.

Peyton often wished for a brother or sister, but once she became friends with Alex, she realized how overwhelming a big family could be. Alex had six brothers, and she was right in the middle of the pack. She'd beg to spend the night at Peyton's house just to get away from the madness of it.

Her phone vibrated, and she saw a text alert. She guessed it was Brodie, and she was right. It would be so easy to give in and answer him, but she couldn't. It was better to cut ties now, before either of them got in any deeper. She didn't care what Kade's ghost had told their mother.

—:—

He should've anticipated Peyton wouldn't answer. She'd made herself clear this afternoon. It wasn't as though she was the first woman to break things off with him, if you could call what they had enough to break off. With her, though, Brodie couldn't accept it. He couldn't shrug his shoulders and walk away. He was used to letting go, knowing another woman was waiting in the wings, probably someone he wanted more anyway. This time, he didn't want another woman.

He wanted Peyton, and no one else. It was crazy. He knew that. A week ago, he hadn't met her, and now he felt as though he couldn't live without her. He was obsessed, and that went against who he'd believed himself to be all his life.

After an hour, he got up. He couldn't sleep, and he couldn't lie there letting his mind wander. He checked the time. It was just after midnight. How many nights had he gone out for a midnight stroll? Too many, and this one, just like the others, was all because of Kade.

If Kade was going to talk to anyone in a dream, why couldn't it have been him? Brodie needed his advice, counsel, and guidance so much right now.

Telling their mother that Peyton needed him didn't help one bit. If it had even happened. It could've just been his mother's mental state, whatever medication they had her on. But then how did she know about him and Peyton? As far as she knew, he was just delivering Kade's box of stuff.

Kade's box of stuff. Maybe there'd be something in it that would help him figure out what to do about Peyton.

12

"If you're sure you don't mind, I could use another day out here with my boys and Mom."

Her dad kissed Peyton's cheek. "I don't mind at all. I'm enjoying myself. As long as I know it's temporary, I love it. The idea of running the tasting room full-time never appealed to me, which is why I hired you thirteen years ago."

Her father couldn't stand the idea of being trapped inside anywhere. Weathered by the sun, his face was tan year round, and if it wasn't for his full head of wavy hair, he'd look older than he was. It was still almost completely blond, with very little gray, if any. He kept himself fit, in the same way her mom did. They were a beautiful couple. Strikingly so.

His eyesight wasn't as good as it once was, so he wore square-shaped tortoiseshell glasses, which made him look more like a professor than a farmer.

"Winemakers are farmers," he'd say. "At least those of us who manage our own vineyards."

Peyton supposed there was truth to it. It didn't matter what their crops consisted of; farmers needed to educate themselves on how best to maximize their production. Grapes or corn. It was essentially the same.

"Are you going to Los Cab?"

"We are. I haven't ridden in so long. I need it."

"You used to ride every day when you were a teenager. Your mom and I hardly saw you, between that and surfing."

Peyton loved both, and hadn't made enough time for either. It was the reason she and Alex set up Stave's schedule the way they had. They both had three days off in a row. Alex was off Monday, Stave was closed Tuesday and Wednesday, and Peyton was off Thursday. Instead of taking advantage of it, both of them spent too much time in the tasting room on their days off. The last few months especially.

They'd talked about hiring a manager, but it seemed silly. With a four-day work week, they should've been able to balance their personal and professional lives with little effort.

"Ready, Mom?"

The boys were climbing into her mom's Range Rover while her parents said goodbye. Peyton watched them. What they had is what she'd always wanted. They respected and admired each other. Dad was Mom's biggest fan and vice versa. They didn't agree on everything, but they found a way to discuss their differences without anger. When her dad gripped her mother's neck and kissed her, Peyton looked away. It reminded her too much of Brodie, and how he'd done the same thing.

"I'm so happy you're with us today, Mom." Finn snuggled up to her, and Peyton melted.

Had she been absent in their lives lately? She prided herself on the time she spent with them, but obviously, something was off. Starting right this minute, that was going to change. Her boys were her number one priority, and had been since the day they were born.

"Me too, kiddo."

Jamison was looking out the window, lost in thought. "What's up, Jamie?"

"Nothin'."

"It's somethin'. Tell me."

"I just want you to be happy, Mama."

Peyton eyes filled with tears, and she turned and looked out the front window so her boys didn't see. Jamison never called her "mama," unless he was feeling sick, or sad, or he was worried about her.

"I'm happy when I'm with you guys."

"You know what I mean."

She almost laughed, and would've if her heart wasn't splitting in two. Sometimes she thought Jamison was the wisest person she knew. How a ten-year-old could have the sensitivity and insight he had, was a mystery.

"Riding makes me happy." Peyton turned around and looked at him.

He smiled and rolled his eyes. Yep, he was her boy.

—:—

The box sat on the kitchen table all night, and was still there when Brodie went downstairs the next morning.

"You takin' that over to her?" Naught asked before he left for the vineyard.

"I told her I wouldn't, unless she asked me for it."

"Why's it on our table, then?"

"I'm thinkin' about looking inside."

Naughton shook his head, but didn't say anything.

"Would it be wrong?"

"Can't answer that."

"What would you do?"

"Doesn't matter. What are you gonna do?"

"I don't know. I thought if I did, I might find something that would help me figure out what to do about Peyton."

Naughton slapped him on the back and walked out the back door. "Good luck," he shouted before he climbed in his truck.

He needed it. He needed her. What the hell was he thinking, and why couldn't he just *stop*? All of this was so unlike him. It would've been unlike Kade, too. Both of them could walk away, not think twice. Ultimatums never worked with him or his brothers, not that Brodie could see Peyton ever issuing one. It was likely one reason none of them were married. No one had been important enough to stay with when things got messy, or uncomfortable, or a woman wanted more than they were ready to give.

But Peyton? It was as though two atoms had collided when they met, and instead of bouncing off each other and spinning in different directions, they fused. They formed a new particle, and it was impermeable.

Brodie heard music playing in the other room, coming from the wireless speaker. He checked his phone, but it wasn't connected. What was that? Where was the music coming from?

He recognized the song and the band. He shook his head, laughed, and looked up at the ceiling. "You tryin' to tell me somethin' Kade?"

You're the one, the only one, the only one
that's just right just for me
For that I say,
I will come, and I will stand, and I will live my
life beside you
I'm a proud, a proud man, but all the same
I'm just a fool, I'm a fool for you
I'm a fool, I'm a fool for you

The band was Kade's favorite. He'd paid them to play at the vineyard one year in May, during the Paso Robles Wine Festival. Even the first line of the song playing was what he'd just been thinking.

Two atoms they collide, you and I make them
a child
What lovely creatures they are, something right
from the stars
And I helped you bring them forth
I offered a safe place to land
An overflow of love, falling right into my hands

How could he not believe this was Kade talking to him? Brodie didn't need to look inside the box. His brother had finally answered him. Now it was up to him to figure out how to convince Peyton that they were meant to be together. He'd told her he was going to make her his when their bodies fused together.

Look at me, Peyton, he'd said. *I want to see your eyes the minute we come together. I'm going to make you mine, Peyton. You're mine. Do you understand?*

Her eyes had told him that she understood. So had her body.

—:—

"Isn't this weather wonderful?" her mom rode up beside her. "Hard to believe it's the beginning of March and it's this warm. Good for the vines."

In the last few weeks, the parched valley had received sorely-needed, blessed rain. Lake Nacimiento was at more than ninety-six percent of its capacity, and other lakes in the region were as close or over capacity. The region was still in what was considered a moderate drought, but after years of below-average rainfall, they'd finally gotten some relief. Hot summers meant the grapes would produce bigger, bolder juice, but lack of water put more strain on the vines than they could handle.

They rode past rows and rows of grapes laid perfectly on the rolling hills of the Los Caballeros ranch. Some of the best wine in the world came from these vineyards. Alfonso Avila was renowned for coaxing the best from his vines, and then masterfully blending what they produced. Alex's oldest brother, Gabe, was the head winemaker now, and he'd learned everything he knew from his father.

Her father made really good wine, but the Avilas made great wine. He didn't begrudge them though. Alfonso had taught her father the kinds of things you could only learn in the vineyard, from a master.

Butler Ranch wines were on par with Los Cabelleros. It was part of the feud that went on for years between

Alfonso and Brodie's father, Laird. When Alfonso died, Laird Butler took over the Avila's harvest and crush, when the family wouldn't have been able to handle it. Gabe Avila was vocally appreciative throughout the valley, and word spread the feud was over.

"Slow down," Peyton shouted to her boys. They were getting farther away than she was comfortable with. "I'm going to catch up with them, Mom."

Her mother nodded, and Peyton was off.

All too soon, she saw why there were riding in the direction they were. In front of her sat Brodie Butler, on one of the most beautiful Morgans she'd ever seen. A powerful horse for a powerful man. He sat regally, yet comfortably, in the saddle. Brodie was a beautiful man, as though God handcrafted him to be the perfect specimen.

"*Finn!*" Peyton heard Jamison scream.

She couldn't see either of them, but took off in the direction of their voices. Brodie must have heard it and was riding toward them too.

Peyton jumped off her horse when she reached her little boy, on the ground, but being held in Brodie's arms.

"He's okay," Brodie looked up at her. "I think his leg might be broken, but otherwise, I don't see any sign of head trauma. You're good, right, partner?"

Finn nodded his head and reached for Peyton when she fell on her knees in front of him. Jamison was standing over them, trying to wipe his tears away.

She reached up and squeezed his hand. "It's okay, Jamie. He's going to be fine. We'll just get him to the hospital for an x-ray. Okay?"

Brodie was on the phone, telling someone their GPS coordinates, and asking them to get down here as soon as possible. "Call the hospital and see if I can land," she heard him say.

"Brodie?"

"I'll fly him over, Peyton." He motioned with his head to Finn's leg.

She could see bone protruding near Brodie's hand. The break was bad, and her little boy had to be in a tremendous amount of pain.

"Peyton! What happened?" Her mother rode up, jumped off her horse, and ran over to where Brodie still held Finn in his arms. "Brodie, hello." She was out of breath, concern etched on her forehead. That's where Peyton's worry showed too. Her mom held her hand and squeezed.

"Someone is coming to get Finn, and Brodie is going to fly him to the hospital!" Jamison announced.

"Well, he's quite a hero, isn't he? And so is Finn." Her mother smiled at them. "And you too, Jamison. I bet you're the one who called for help."

Jamison's chest puffed out at his grandmother's words.

"There's Naught," Brodie told her. "I'll get him in the backseat. You get in the front."

"Mrs. Wolf, could you and Jamison take our horses, get back to the house, and meet us at the hospital?"

Jamison nodded and climbed back on his horse. "Ready, Grandma?"

"Are you sure?" Peyton looked at Brodie.

"Yes. Whatever it is, yes, I'm sure. I've never been more sure of anything in my life."

"I meant—"

"I know what you meant, Peyton. And you know what I meant too."

"We good?" he said to Naughton.

"Yep. Mad's on it."

"I get to fly in a helicopter?" Finn winced, but Brodie held him close.

"You sure do. Your mom will be my co-pilot. Naughton here is going too. Do you know Naughton?"

"No, but I don't know you either."

Brodie laughed, doing his best not to jostle Finn's little body. "I'm Brodie, Finn. We'll shake later, okie-dokey?"

"Oh, *you're* Brodie." Finn looked over at his mother and smiled. "He's nice, Mom, and he flies helicopters and rides, too. And he owns a vineyard."

"The vineyard isn't technically mine, only partially. Some of it belongs to Naught, and our other brother, Maddox, and our sisters. But really, the ranch belongs to our parents."

"So it used to be Kade's too, right?"

Brodie flinched, but not enough that anyone would notice. Peyton wouldn't have noticed if she hadn't been staring at him.

"Sure did. Bet you miss Kade, don't ya?"

"Yeah," Finn said softly. "Bet you do too."

"You got that right."

Brodie slid Finn into Naughton's arms and climbed in the back seat of the Suburban. Once he was in, Naughton handed Finn to him. Brodie sat just off the center of the seat so he could get Finn's leg positioned as comfortably as possible.

"Hey, Finn, did you know that the guys used to call Kade 'Doc'?"

"No, why?" came Finn's little voice.

Peyton was so proud of his bravery.

"He was what you call a physician's assistant," Brodie explained. "So if a doctor wasn't there, Kade could help if someone got injured."

"He helped when doctors were there, too," Naughton added. He looked over at her, and his eyebrows came together. "You okay, Peyton?"

"I'm fine, Naughton. Thank you. And thank you for coming out to get Finn, and helping us." She looked back at Brodie holding her son. "I don't know what we would've done if you hadn't been out there. Thank you, Brodie."

"It's what family does, right, Naught?"

"That's right."

Peyton faced forward and, for the second time that afternoon, hid her tears from her son.

Naughton maneuvered the truck over the terrain, doing his best to minimize jarring bumps. Peyton turned in her seat and watched as Brodie absorbed what Naughton couldn't avoid, keeping Finn as still as he could. The ten minutes it took to get to the landing pad seemed so much longer. However, if Brodie hadn't been out, riding, Peyton couldn't fathom how they would've transported Finn to the hospital.

Naughton got out of the truck and climbed into the back of the helicopter. Brodie eased Finn onto a small stretcher not quite long enough for him. Naughton fastened a harness around her boy, being as gentle as he could, and then did the same for Peyton.

He leaned forward, reached for the harness, and brought it over her head. His forehead briefly rested against hers. "You okay?"

"I will be. Again, I can't thank you enough, Brodie."

His lips brushed against hers for an instant as he backed away and shut her in.

—:—

"How's he doing?" Brodie asked when Peyton came out to the waiting room.

"They're taking him in to surgery in a few minutes." Peyton hesitated, taking a deep breath. "He asked to see you first."

"Oh, uh, is that okay with you?" Brodie wasn't sure how to navigate this situation. Was it a good thing Finn wanted to see him, or was Peyton unhappy about it? He couldn't tell.

"Of course it's okay, Brodie," she smiled at him like his ma would've.

"Okay, so, where is he?"

"I'll take you back."

"I'll hang out here and let your mom know what's goin' on when she gets here," Naughton offered.

Peyton approached him. He was standing near the window, his hands in his pockets. Brodie watched as she rested her hand on his arm, reached up, and kissed his cheek.

"Thank you, Naughton," he heard her say. Then she walked back over and motioned for Brodie to follow her. "He's back this way."

Brodie followed, looking left and right into the small partitioned areas of the emergency room. Finally they reached the one all the way in the back, where a nurse was talking to Finn.

"I'll get the doctor," she told Peyton. "He needs to talk to you before we take him back. Better yet, if you could come with me, I have some forms for you to fill out."

Peyton looked at Brodie.

"Go," he told her. "We'll be okay. We'll wait right here. Won't we, Finn?"

Finn nodded, and Brodie watched as Peyton blew him a kiss, which Finn pretended to catch in his palm.

"Tell me the truth," he said to Finn once Peyton was out of earshot. "How are you really doin'? I know you're being brave for your mama."

"It doesn't hurt as bad anymore. They put something in this thing." Finn pointed to his IV.

"Oh, gotcha. Yeah, you're probably feelin' pretty good right about now."

Finn smiled, but it didn't reach his eyes. "She's gonna be *super* worried the whole time. Will you stay with her?"

"Of course." Brodie saw the concern in Peyton's son's eyes. "Look at me, Finn."

Finn turned his head.

"I'm not going anywhere. You got it? Nowhere. I'll stay right with her and help her not worry so much."

"That'd be good. Thanks, Brodie."

—:—

Peyton pulled the curtain back and joined them. "All set." She took Finn's hand. "You ready for this, kiddo? I know you'll be brave, and before you know it, you'll be right back here, and you won't remember a single thing."

"I'm ready, Mom. Oh, and, Mom? Brodie is going to stay with you. And he's not going anywhere, right, Brodie?"

"That's right, buddy." Brodie leaned over and kissed Finn's forehead. "I'll take care of her while they take care of you."

"Thanks, Brodie."

Peyton leaned over and kissed Finn too, and hugged him as best she could. When he tried to sit up, she bent down further so he wouldn't try to move too much. She was such a good mother. Both her boys were well-loved, and loved her back equal measure.

The orderly wheeled Finn away while Peyton stood in the hallway, tears streaming down her face.

"Come here." Brodie wrapped his arms around her, and Peyton's head fell against his shoulder.

"You were so good with him, Brodie. I really don't know how to thank you."

He had some ideas, starting with her letting him be a part of their lives, but that was something they'd talk about later.

When they walked back through the waiting room doors, Jamison, Peyton's mom, and Alex came running toward her. Jamison landed first, wrapping his arms around his mother's waist. Her mom and Alex hugged Peyton at the same time, standing over Jamison.

"They just took him in to surgery."

Peyton knelt down and looked into Jamison's eyes. "His leg is broken in a couple of places, and they need to operate so it heals properly. Do you have any questions?"

"How long will it take?"

"I'm not sure, maybe a couple of hours, maybe longer. Do you want to go back to the house with Grandma and wait there?"

"Can I stay?"

"Of course you can, sweetheart."

Peyton took his hand and led him over to a chair. She sat next to him and cuddled him closer to her.

"I was so scared," Brodie heard him say.

"So was I," she answered.

"She's something, isn't she?" Alex whispered to Brodie. "She's such a good mom. Almost makes me not want children. I think I'd have a hard time measuring up."

"You'll be a great mom too, Alex." Brodie put his arm around her and pulled her close.

Peyton's father walked in, went straight to his wife, and put his arm around her. "How's Finn?"

"He's in surgery." She led her husband away from where they waited.

Brodie couldn't hear what else she said to him. A few minutes later, they walked back, and Mr. Wolf knelt down and talked to Peyton and Jamison. She rested her head on her father's shoulder and whispered something.

Mr. Wolf stood and approached him. "I understand you saved the day." He shook Brodie's hand. "Thank you, son." He walked over to the window. "You too, Naughton," he shook Naught's hand.

"You're welcome, sir," Naughton answered.

"Who's at Stave?" Peyton asked Alex, who laughed.

"We're closed. Out of business, in fact. It all went to hell with you gone. Sorry, Peyton. I did my best."

Peyton smiled. "Shut up."

It was great to see her smile.

"Seriously though, we're closed. It was deader than dead. So your dad and I made an executive decision to stop worrying from so far away, and drive over here."

Peyton shook her head, but was still smiling. Brodie couldn't take his eyes off her.

"Your love is showing," Alex whispered.

"Good. I hope she can see it."

"Oh yeah, impossible to miss."

"Hey, Brodie," Naughton called over to him. "Mad wants to know if he should come get us."

Brodie couldn't leave. He'd made a promise to Finn that he'd take care of his mother.

"Actually, he'll leave the truck, and we'll fly ol' Betty back."

"That's a better idea. Thanks, Naught."

Brodie walked over and sat next to Peyton.

"Betty?"

"Don't ask me. Naught's weird sometimes." Brodie leaned forward. "How are you doin', big guy? Is there anything you need? Hungry? I don't know how good hospital food is, but I saw a vending machine with candy bars."

Jamison looked over at his mom, who smiled and nodded.

"Thanks," she mouthed to Brodie.

"My mom is still upstairs. We should probably go say hello."

"Oh," Peyton gasped, "I'm so sorry, Brodie. I completely forgot she was here. Go. We'll be fine. I can take Jamison to get a candy bar too. God, I'm so sorry."

"Stop." He leaned in close to her. "I'm going to take Jamison to get a candy bar. Several in fact, and then I'm coming back here with him. When I do, you and I are going to zip upstairs, say hello to my ma, and then zip right back down."

"Brodie—"

"Please, Peyton. Naught told her we were here and what was going on. She's worried about you. A couple of minutes will be all it will take to ease her mind. It isn't good for her to worry about anything right now." Brodie was embellishing the truth a little. His ma was worried about Peyton, but she was also stronger than his Morgan.

"Of course, I'm sorry. Of course, we can go say hello to your mother."

Good. Guilt worked. He'd try not to use it too often.

Brodie returned with several candy bars and some chips. He and Jamison went around the waiting room, offering food to their family and friends. Naughton came in a few seconds later, carrying water bottles.

He walked over to Peyton first. "Figured you'd skin me if I offered your boy soda, so it's water for everybody."

Brodie watched Peyton interact with his brother. It was such a shame Kade hadn't brought her around more. She fit with them, and it was obvious Naught adored her.

She caught him looking and smiled. "Ready?"

"We're gonna go see Ma. If you're not here when I get back, tell Mad I owe him." Brodie looked over at Alex, and since she was hanging on his every word, he winked and said. "Hey, Alex, your love is showing."

"Shut up, Brodie," Alex laughed.

Jamison walked up to Alex and held out his hand.

"What?"

"Shut up is a bad word, Alex. You owe me a buck."

Alex laughed, reached into her pocket, and pulled out a five. "I'm covering your mom too, kiddo. I think I heard her say it at least four times, to me, of course."

"Alex!" Peyton shouted at the same time Jamison shouted, "Mom!"

Peyton walked over to Alex. "By the way, when this is over and Finn is home and healing, you have a lot of explaining to do."

"What?"

"Maddox? Since high school?"

"Yeah, yeah. Not that much to tell."

"As if I believe you. By the way, I understand he didn't come home last night."

"Don't you mean *either?*" Alex smiled.

Brodie grasped Peyton's hand, hoping she wouldn't pull away from him. She didn't. Instead, she held tight, and came closer, resting her head on his shoulder.

"You don't have to thank me again, Peyton. Your head on my shoulder is more thanks than I could ask for."

"I will though. I keep imagining us out there alone, with Finn's leg broken. I honestly don't know what I would've done."

"Now you know. Any time, any reason, you need anything at all—call me. If you can't reach me, call Naught. After Naught, call Maddox. We'll take care of you, Peyton."

"Thanks, Brodie." Peyton leaned into him again, so close that her breast brushed against his arm. He managed not to groan, but it took every ounce of strength he had to squelch it.

Peyton stopped when they rounded the corner to the elevator.

"What's wrong?"

She pulled him closer to her and wiggled her finger for him to lean down. When he did, she covered his lips with hers. She was between him and the wall, and leaned back against it. Brodie leaned down farther, kissing her back. Her hands went to his arms, and she held tight.

Brodie looked into her eyes. "Was that part of my thanks?"

"No, Brodie. That was just because I wanted to kiss you." She pressed the button for the elevator. "What floor?"

"You gotta give me a sec, baby. After that kiss, I don't remember my own name."

She slipped in the elevator door. When it closed behind him and they were the only two inside, he pushed her against the back wall. Brodie leaned into her, plundering her mouth with his.

He pulled back. "Peyton?"

"Don't ask questions, Brodie. For now, please, just kiss me."

"Gladly."

She pulled back from him and smiled. "Remember yet?"

"Remember what?"

"What floor your mother's on?"

As much as he wanted to stay alone with her in the elevator, they had to get upstairs to see his mother, and then back to the waiting room in case there was word about Finn.

"Six," he grumbled.

13

Brodie's mom was filled with questions about how Finn was doing. She even offered to come downstairs with them, to wait while he was in surgery.

"You're just angling for someone to sneak you outta here, Ma," Brodie teased her. He promised to come back up later, give her an update on Finn, and tuck her into bed.

His mother beamed at him and smiled at Peyton. "He's a good one."

When Brodie told her they had to get back downstairs, she wiggled her finger at Peyton.

"Come here, sweetheart."

Mrs. Butler took her hand and held it tight. "You let my boy take care of you. You need him, Peyton."

Peyton nodded her head. Brodie stepped forward, but his mother told him to go wait in the hall.

Even with her back to him, Peyton could feel his discomfort. "It's okay," she told him.

"Sit down for a minute." She pointed to the chair next to her bed.

"Mrs. Butler—"

"Call me Sorcha, lass." She patted Peyton's hand. "There have been many times I wished we knew you better, but now I see why we didn't. You weren't ready to become a part of our family then, it wasn't right. But now, you are."

"I don't know what to say. This is all so—"

"Just let it happen, Peyton. Kade wants this for you both."

Peyton's eyes filled with tears. "It seems wrong," she whispered.

"Wrong? Love is never wrong, lass. Sometimes we love the wrong person at the wrong time, but it isn't ever the love itself."

—:—

Brodie was pacing when Peyton came out into the hallway. He came over and took her hand. "I'm sorry about my ma."

"Don't be. She's very sweet."

"And a meddler."

"She cares about you."

"You too."

"She comforted me, Brodie."

"You look as though you've been crying."

"Haven't I been all day?" She laughed. "This time was different. They were good tears."

"Ready to go back downstairs?"

"Yes, I should. Listen, Brodie, you don't have to stay. My parents will, and I doubt Alex will leave either."

"I promised Finn that I'd stay with you, and I won't break it, no matter what you say." He smiled.

"Okay, but—"

"I'm staying."

Peyton laughed. "You're pretty bossy sometimes."

"Sometimes? Always, sweetheart. It's part of what makes me so lovable."

As ironic as it was, Peyton agreed. It did make him lovable, and sexy as all get-out.

Peyton's parents took Jamison home after Finn was out of the surgical recovery room, and in a room on the pediatric floor of the hospital. Since it was customary for parents to stay overnight, the room had two recliners, making for relatively comfortable sleeping.

When she tried again to tell Brodie he could leave, he reminded her that he said he was staying, and he meant it.

"But Finn's out of surgery now. We'll be fine."

He didn't answer. He'd inherited his father's scowl, and knew how to use it. He only wished he could be closer to her, hold her, comfort her. The recliners were good sized, but certainly not big enough for two. He moved them closer together, so he could reach over and hold her hand until she fell asleep.

Brodie dozed off and on, but the slightest noise woke him. The nurses came and checked on Finn several times, and while they tried to be as quiet as possible, he stirred whenever they came in the room.

Finn slept soundly through the night, but Peyton was restless. She talked in her sleep, and while Brodie couldn't decipher her words, it was obvious her dreams were troubling. Around three in the morning, she sat straight up and looked around the room. "Kade?"

"No, sweetheart. I'm here, what do you need?"

"Brodie?"

"Yes?"

She rested in the recliner and went back to sleep. He wondered if she'd remember it later.

The doctor came in before seven, checked Finn over, asked what he wanted for breakfast, and then asked if Peyton could meet him in the hall.

"I'll wait here," Brodie offered.

"Would you mind joining us? Would it be okay with you, Finn?"

Finn nodded, so Brodie followed Peyton.

"He's doing well enough that I think he can go home after lunch. I want to see how he tolerates food after going under anesthesia," the doctor told Peyton, who thanked him before he went over to the nurses station to update Finn's chart.

"What a relief. He'll feel better in his own bed, and honestly, so will I."

"You were dreaming last night. Do you remember what about?"

"Same thing I always dream about, Brodie," she sighed. "Although my dreams have been different in the last few days."

"How so?"

"I used to dream about Kade."

"And now?"

"I dream about you more."

"Based on how restless you were last night, I don't know whether that's good or bad."

"I dreamed about both of you last night."

"Do you want to tell me about it?"

"I think so, but not right now. Okay?"

"Of course."

"Mom, I'm starving, and I want to go home."

"You sound like my ma," Brodie laughed. "She's upstairs, and she wants to go home too."

"Did she break her leg?"

"It was a little more complicated. She had a problem with her heart, although she didn't have surgery like you did."

He should probably go upstairs and check on her, as much as he didn't want to leave Peyton's side. If Finn went home this afternoon, he'd have to anyway, and then there was no telling when she might want to see him again.

"It's okay, Brodie. Go see her. We'll be fine."

Brodie went to Finn's bedside and tousled his hair. "I shouldn't be gone too long. Take care of your mom, okay?"

When Finn smiled and nodded, Brodie knelt down and kissed his forehead. Finn's arms went around Brodie's neck, and he held on.

"Finn," Peyton began.

"It's okay," Brodie whispered.

When Finn let go, Peyton walked Brodie out of the room.

"I'm sorry if I'm getting too…I don't know…familiar, Peyton."

"I don't want him to get hurt."

"I understand," he said, but as Brodie walked away, he was more worried that he was the one who was going to get hurt, not Finn.

"There he is." Maddox stood when Brodie walked into his mom's room. "How's the little guy?"

"He's good. Hey, Ma." Brodie knelt down and kissed her cheek. "They're saying he can go home this afternoon."

"That makes two of us."

Brodie looked at his father, who nodded.

"They're filling out her paperwork now, so my guess is an hour or so and we'll be able to go home."

"Blessed Father." Sorcha put her hands together and looked at the ceiling.

"The nurses are probably thanking the Holy Father more than you, Ma."

"Mind your tongue, Maddox Butler. I can still tweak your ear."

"Is the Suburban still here?" Brodie wanted to be the one to take Peyton and Finn home. That way, he'd be able to spend a few more hours with her.

"Left it yesterday. Da and I drove down to get Ma."

"You take care of Peyton, Brodie. Are you understanding me?"

If she'd let him, that was his plan. "Yes, Ma."

He waited until they brought the wheelchair, and then walked with his brother and father down to the hospital entrance.

"We'll see you when we see you." His mother waved from the open window of his father's car. "Remember what I said."

"Yes, Ma." He smiled and waved.

Once the car pulled away, Brodie went back up to Finn's room.

—:—

"I was worried you weren't coming back," Finn whined when Brodie walked in.

"Finn Becker, you mind your manners," Peyton scolded. "Brodie has other responsibilities." She was standing near the window, but walked over to him. "How's your mom?"

"On her way home, I'm happy to report."

"Oh, if you need to leave, it's okay."

"And if I leave, how will Finn get home?"

"My parents—"

"Peyton, please, let me take you and Finn home."

He looked sad, as though he expected she'd walk away from him, or push him away like she had before. "We've taken so much of your time already."

He turned his back to Finn, motioning for her to come closer. "If you don't want me here, you're going to have to say so directly. Otherwise, there is nowhere else I need, or want, to be."

Peyton looked over at Finn, whose hopeful look mirrored Brodie's. "We want you here, Brodie. We just don't want to be a burden."

"How was breakfast, kiddo?" Brodie turned his attention to Finn.

"It was great. I had eggs and bacon and pancakes and orange juice."

Brodie groaned at the same time Peyton did. "I'm starving," he muttered. "Did you get anything?"

"Not yet. I haven't wanted to leave."

"Hey, Finn-man, will you be okay if I go get your mom and me some breakfast?"

Peyton knew immediately that Finn wanted to ask Brodie not to leave, but was proud of him when he nodded his head.

"What would you like?"

"Anything will be fine, thanks."

"I think I know your taste in breakfast foods," he whispered.

"Mmm hmm," she smiled.

Peyton got Finn settled in his bed at home. "Are you sure there's nothing else I can get you, sweetie?"

"No, Mom. I've got a hundred books, Jamie's phone to play games on, and I had two milkshakes."

"Okay, but I'm just down the hall if you change your mind."

Finn rolled his eyes at her, which made her laugh. "You crack me up, kiddo."

"Same." He sounded so much like Jamison. God really did bless her when he gave her these two boys to raise. She couldn't have asked for better, more thoughtful, caring, loving young men.

Before going back out to the living room, Peyton slipped into her bedroom and looked in the bathroom mirror. The last couple of days showed on her face. So many highs and lows, she was a little nauseous. She splashed cold water on her face, and then gave her cheeks a little pinch, although Brodie wouldn't care how she looked. He wasn't stingy with his compliments, whether it was how good of a mom she was, or how he loved to see her smile, or how good he said she smelled.

"I didn't remember how red your mom's hair is," she said, walking back out to the kitchen.

"It's natural—she wants everyone to know it, too."

"Can I get you anything? Glass of wine?" She opened the refrigerator. "I have beer in here, if you'd prefer that."

"Peyton, I'm fine. Come and sit down." Brodie patted the cushion next to him on the couch. "You've had a long day."

When she walked over, he pulled her down in front of him and rubbed her shoulders.

"God, that feels good," she moaned.

His hands moved to her neck and continued kneading her tired muscles, then to her hair. She was almost asleep when he stopped.

"Come on, let's get you to bed." He tugged at her hand to help her stand up.

"Brodie, the boys—"

"Peyton, I'm going to tuck you in, and then I'm going to say goodnight."

"Oh."

"Sweetheart, you're killing me. Don't pout. You stick that lower lip out, and I'm a goner. I'm a goner anyway when I'm with you. Listen, I know it's not right for me to stay with your boys here. I get that. Okay?"

"Okay. Thanks for understanding, Brodie."

"I'll call you in the morning, okay? Stave is closed, right?"

How did he know just exactly what she needed from him? "Yes, I'll be able to stay home with Finn tomorrow. Oh, wait. Crap. Jamison."

"What about Jamison?"

"I need to take him to school. Alex is not a morning person. I can't ask my parents. They took him this morning. Maybe I'll just let him stay home with us tomorrow." A friend whose son was Jamison's age had dropped him off this afternoon, but it was too late now to call and ask if she could pick him up in the morning.

"There's another solution, Peyton."

"No, Brodie. I can't ask you to do it either. He has to be there at seven-thirty. By the time you got home, you'd have to turn around and come back."

He pushed her toward the bedroom. "Go get in bed."

As they walked by the hall closet, he opened the door. "Extra pillows, extra blankets. I'm good."

"Brodie?"

"I'm going to crash out right over there." He pointed back to the sofa in the living room. "Tomorrow morning, I'll take Jamison to school, and then, if there isn't anything else I can do for you, I'll give you some space."

She was so tired, and it would be so easy to let him, but she couldn't. Could she? "I can't. You can't. You haven't slept in a proper bed—"

"Let me do this, sweetheart. Why make it so hard on yourself when the solution is so easy?"

"Okay, but, Brodie?"

"Yeah, Peyton?"

"I can't remember what I was going to say."

"Then say goodnight, and go get into bed. I'll see you in the morning." He nudged her into the room, and she let him.

—:—

He heard her get up in the middle of the night, and then he heard Finn, crying. He shot off the couch and rushed down the hallway. He looked inside Finn's room and saw Peyton, sitting on Finn's bed, rocking him back and forth.

"Shh," she murmured as she rocked. "Shh."

Lullaby, and good night, in the skies stars are
bright.
May the moon's silvery beams bring you sweet
dreams.
Close your eyes now and rest, may these hours
be blessed.
'Til the sky's bright with dawn, when you
wake with a yawn.

Brodie could stand outside Finn's door and listen to her sing to her son all night long, but he was intruding on a private moment between her and Finn.

He walked back to the living room and sat on the couch. He was about to lie down when Peyton walked down the hall.

He sat back up. "Everything okay?"

"He has some pain, but he's back to sleep now. I hope we didn't wake you. I mean, obviously we did. I'm sorry."

"Stop it. Come sit down for a minute."

"Will you rub my shoulders again?"

"Do you want me to?"

"Yes," she whispered.

"Come here, baby." He sat with his back to the end of the couch, and brought her down between his legs. "Lean back, sweetheart."

He started with her neck. Earlier he'd kneaded her sore muscles. Now she needed to relax enough to fall back to sleep. He kept his stroke feathery as he hummed the lullaby he had heard her sing to Finn. Moments later Peyton's head fell back against his shoulder. She was sound asleep.

Brodie eased back as gently as he could, and propped a pillow behind his head. With Peyton wrapped in his arms, he let his heavy eyelids close.

14

"Mom, wake up. Mom..." Jamison was shaking her arm.

Peyton opened her eyes and realized she'd fallen asleep on the couch with Brodie, who woke up too.

"Hey, sweetie," she said, climbing off the couch. "Is everything okay?"

"I have to leave now, Mom."

Peyton looked her son up and down, realized he was dressed, and looked at the clock on the stove in the kitchen. Jamison was right. It was a little after seven, and they needed to leave if he was going to get to school on time.

"Come on, partner." Brodie put his arm around Jamison's shoulders. "I'll give you a lift."

Peyton watched as Brodie stepped into his boots, grabbed his jacket, and opened the front door. Jamison came over and kissed her goodbye, and then walked out.

"I'll be right back." Brodie closed the front door behind them.

The scene was so *familial.* Was it because Brodie reminded the boys of Kade, or were they just comfortable around him already? Jamie hadn't seemed bothered that she was essentially sleeping in Brodie's arms when he woke her. Both he and Brodie acted as though this was an average morning at home.

Peyton went into the kitchen and started a pot of coffee before checking on Finn, who was still sound asleep. Even Finn had assumed Brodie would stay with them at the hospital, and then when they came home yesterday, he made sure Brodie was staying for dinner. He'd done more than stay. He'd made dinner while Peyton fussed over her little boy.

When Jamison came home from school, Brodie helped him with his homework, and then after they ate, took him outside to shoot some hoops.

She could at least offer to make him breakfast, after all he'd done to help her.

Jamison's school was only a few minutes away, so Brodie was back shortly after she took eggs and bacon out of the refrigerator. He walked in the front door without knocking, and then stopped just inside.

"I guess that was presumptuous of me."

"What? Just walking in? Don't be silly."

He walked over and turned her away from the counter, so she faced him. "Peyton, I think we should talk."

She knew he was right, but it would be so much easier to just keep pretending all this was normal. As soon as they talked, they'd have to decide what "this" was, and how they intended to proceed. Shortly after that, Brodie would leave, and her house and life would go back to being too quiet and lonely.

"Can we have breakfast first?" She stood on her tiptoes and kissed his cheek.

"Woman, sometimes I think you're heaven-sent." He cringed. "That was probably the wrong thing to say, wasn't it?"

"No, Brodie. It was a sweet thing to say."

"This is what we need to talk about, Peyton." Brodie put his hands on her waist and brought her close to him.

She rested her head against him and put her arms around his neck. If they could just keep pretending a little while longer, she wouldn't have to think about letting him go so soon.

Brodie put his finger underneath her chin and gently covered her lips with his. Was it only two or three days ago they were in this same kitchen, him kissing her, and then carrying her into the bedroom where they'd had the best sex of her life?

"What are you thinking about?" he murmured.

"You, me, you know."

"No, don't know."

"Brodie..."

"Oh, you mean, you, me, your bed."

"Yes."

"That's what I was thinking about too."

"But, Brodie, we can't."

"I know, sugar, but we sure can think about it."

Peyton pushed away from him. "I'm making breakfast, not thinking about bed," she grinned.

"Hey, uh, would you mind if I took a quick shower?"

"I'm so sorry, Brodie. If you want to go home, I completely understand. You haven't been home. You've been in the same clothes...wait you're not."

"Maddox brought me a bag."

"I didn't even notice."

"You've had a lot on your mind, Peyton."

"Brodie, I don't—"

"Stop, sweetheart. I'm going to shower, and then we'll have breakfast. After that, we'll talk, okay?"

"I should, too."

"Shower?"

"Uh, yes. I'll, um, wait."

"Honey, you're killing me. I am the last person you need to be so nervous around."

"I'm just so...oh, no..." She was crying. "What is wrong with me?"

"Come here." Brodie took her by the hand and walked over to the sofa. He sat down, pulling her with him. "My ma had her hands full when we were all little, as you can imagine."

"Yeah?"

"I can't speak for my brothers and sisters, but what she did always seemed to work for me."

"What was that?"

"She'd tell me to close my eyes, take five slow, deep breaths, and then open my eyes and tell her what was wrong. If I couldn't, I'd close my eyes again, take five more deep breaths, and so on. Sometimes it took two or three rounds of deep breaths, but it almost always worked. Wanna try?"

"Not really."

Brodie laughed. "Okay."

"But I will." Peyton closed her eyes and took five deep breaths.

"Can you tell me what's bothering you?"

"Yes, but I don't want to."

"Five more breaths, then. We'll keep going until you're ready." This time Brodie breathed in and out with her.

"Better?"

She closed her eyes tight. "I don't want this to end, but..."

"I see. What you'd like is for me to go home, and we go back to life as it was before Finn's accident."

"I'm sorry, Brodie."

"Because you want to be with me? Sweetheart, that is the last thing you need to apologize for. If I could have my way, I'd never leave."

"Really?"

"Really. I'm hoping you aren't gonna kick me out."

"I'm just so...tired, Brodie." She sniffled. "And I can't stop crying."

"Honey, I wish you'd just let me take care of you."

"But you have your own life, and I know that, and I know you need to leave."

Brodie stood and pulled her up from the couch. "Come with me."

Peyton followed him down the hallway. When they were near her bedroom door, she stopped.

"Trust me."

She followed him in, and into her bathroom, where he turned the shower on. "You're going first. I'll keep an ear out for Finn, and I'll make breakfast. We'll eat. I'll take a shower, and then, sweetheart, one of two things is going to happen. Either you'll come back in here and go to sleep, alone, while I hang out with Finn. Or, if you're up to it, we'll talk until Finn wakes up, and then we'll both hang with him. Now scoot." Brodie tapped her bottom, turned around, and closed the bathroom door behind him.

Peyton let the warm water rain over her. Every part of her hurt from first sleeping in a chair at the hospital, and then falling asleep on the couch with Brodie. On top of that, she was exhausted, mentally, physically, and emotionally. The best thing would be if Brodie went home, and she got some sleep. She knew this. She wasn't the whiny complainer that just cried on Brodie's shoulder. She'd weathered far worse than this in the last ten years, and was a strong, independent woman in the aftermath of her divorce and Kade's death.

There were times, though, when it was nice to chuck the strong independence out the window and let someone else take care of her for a change. It didn't make her weak—Kade used to tell her it made her human.

The aroma of bacon wafted into the bathroom, and Peyton shut off the water in the shower. Now that she was clean, she was more hungry than tired.

—:—

Finn was on the sofa, watching cartoons, and chowing down his breakfast of bacon and scrambled eggs. Brodie had just tossed the chopped vegetables in the skillet for the omelet he was making to share with Peyton, when she came out of the bedroom in a white cotton sweater and comfy-looking jeans. Her damp hair hung in long strands down her back, her face was pink from the warm water, and she smelled like spring rain.

"Hungry?"

"Starving. I see Finn is a happy camper. Hey, buddy, how are you this morning?" Peyton sat down on the floor next to where Finn was stretched out.

"Brodie made me scrambled eggs and bacon."

"I see that. Whatcha' watchin'?"

"Teen Titans."

Peyton sneaked a piece of bacon from Finn's plate.

"Hey!" He laughed. "It's okay, Mom. You're probably more starving than me."

"Sure am, but it looks like my breakfast may be ready. Need anything before I eat?"

"No, Mom. Jeez. How long are you gonna be like this? Brodie helped me get out of bed, but I made it to the bathroom, and out here on my own." He pointed to his crutches.

"Okay, tough guy. You're officially on your own."

"Thanks, Mom."

Brodie set two plates on the kitchen island and pulled out a stool for her. "Feel better?"

"Immensely. Thank you for making breakfast, although I wish you would've let me cook for you this morning. You've done so much for me."

"Dinner."

"When?"

"Tonight."

"Okay," she laughed. "Any requests?"

Brodie looked over at Finn, who was engrossed in cartoons, so he leaned forward, kissed right under her ear, and inhaled. "God, you smell good."

"Brodie, we were talking about dinner tonight." She smiled and kissed his cheek.

"I can't think when you're this close and smell this good."

"Okay, never mind. I'll figure it on my own. Anything I should stay away from? Food allergies? Hate green beans? Anything like that?"

"I'm okay with green beans, but I hate lima beans."

"*Ew,* lima beans. They're disgusting," Finn added.

"When have I ever made lima beans?"

"They have 'em at school, and when they do, everybody pukes."

"Finn! We're eating."

"So? It's true."

"Okay, so no lima beans. Anything else?"

He wasn't kidding when he said he couldn't think. With Peyton this close, the only appetite he had was for her.

"Yoo-hoo, Brodie."

"I don't care. I'd even eat lima beans if you made them for me."

When they finished breakfast, Peyton insisted she clean up while he showered. She asked him again if he'd be more comfortable going home, but dropped it when he raised one eyebrow.

He went out to Naughton's Suburban and grabbed his bag. After he showered, he'd call Naught and make sure he didn't need his vehicle any time soon. If he did, he'd see if Peyton and Finn wanted to go to the ranch with him, to get out of the house for a bit. That wasn't the real reason he wanted them to go with him. Like he told her, if he could be with her every minute from now on, he wouldn't complain.

—:—

Peyton washed the breakfast dishes and started a load of laundry. While Brodie showered, she called to check in with Alex. They'd talked yesterday when Alex called to see how Finn was, and then again when Peyton called on their way home from the hospital.

"Good morning," Alex yawned.

"Am I calling too early?" Peyton looked over at the clock. It was after ten. "You weren't seriously still sleeping."

"No, miss morning glory, I wasn't, but I haven't been awake all that long."

"Was it busy yesterday afternoon?"

"Heck, no. I closed at five."

"And?"

"And what?"

"Why were you still asleep at ten in the morning?"

"It's really none of your beeswax, but if you must know, I'm not home."

"Where are you?"

"Hanging out on Adelaida Trail, where I happen to know Brodie is *not* hanging out."

"No, he's still here. In the shower at the moment. What's the deal with you and Maddox? And seriously, why don't I know anything about it? I'm a little hurt, honestly."

"Don't be. There was nothing to know for a really, really long time. We talked a few times after all the weirdness with you and Brodie, and then when he came to Stave Friday night, things just sorta, you know, happened. And here I am. Although whenever this has happened in the past, after about a week, we're ready to scratch each other's eyes out. I figure I've got three or four days of amazing sex left, and then we'll hate each other again."

"I feel as though I keep repeating myself, but Alex, how do I not know any of this?"

"I don't know. It's too...can't think of the word. Raw, maybe?"

"I actually get it. I'm feeling that way right now about Brodie."

"I can't believe you let him spend the night with the boys there. That's not like you."

"I keep looking in the mirror to make sure I'm still me. That's how much I'm not like me right now."

"That's great. I'm gonna steal it. I keep looking in the mirror to make sure I'm still me. Classic Peyton."

"Oh, before I forget, did you cancel with Peter yesterday?"

"I did. Didn't he call you?"

"I don't think so, but I'll check after we hang up. Why would he have?"

"He wanted to talk to you about a little somethin' somethin' would be my guess."

"Oh, Alex. This isn't good. I wish you hadn't encouraged him. It's going to be so awkward at the wine dinner."

"Just call him and tell him you're not interested."

"Let me check something. Hold on." Peyton set the phone on the kitchen counter, counted to five, and then picked it back up. "Just checked. I am still me, which means I'm not you. You make those kinds of phone calls. I just avoid people until they get the message."

"Handle it your way, sista. Only, my way is far more effective. Gotta go. I think the Mad-man might've just come back to ravage me again."

"Talk to you later, Alex."

"Buh-bye."

Peyton saw there was one voicemail from a number she didn't recognize. She put it on speaker to listen.

"Hi, Peyton. Uh, this is Peter Wells calling. I'm, um, sorry to hear about your son. So, I was wondering if you'd like to reschedule. I could come up next Monday, and then maybe after we finalize the menu, we could have dinner somewhere. Give me a call when you get this message, and we can figure it out. I'm, uh, looking forward to seeing you, Peyton."

"Not if I have anything to say about it."

"Brodie! God, you startled me. How long have you been standing behind me?"

"Only long enough to hear the tail-end of that message."

"It isn't polite to eavesdrop," Finn shouted from the couch.

"Who's eavesdropping?" Peyton shouted back. "This doesn't concern you, Finn, any more than my message concerns you, Brodie."

Brodie sat down at the counter next to her.

"What?"

"It does concern me, Peyton."

"It doesn't. That was a private message from a guest chef who we have a wine dinner planned with."

Brodie shook his head. "That message had nothing to do with your wine dinner, Peyton. You're definitely not having dinner with him."

"Brodie!"

"What, Peyton? It's time for us to talk." He looked over at Finn. "Let's go outside."

Finn got up and steadied himself on his crutches. "I'm going to my room now, parental units. I'll be putting my headphones on in order to refrain from eavesdropping."

Peyton laughed as he passed them by, but would need to discuss his "parental units," remark with him later.

"Let it go."

"Let what go?"

"Parental units. The less attention you draw to it, the less often he'll do it."

Peyton took a deep breath. Did he really just tell her how to handle her son? First he tells her she's *not* having dinner with someone, and then he tells her to let something go with her own son.

"I had a lot I wanted to say to you, Brodie, but I've forgotten all of it, so I'll just say this. Don't think for one minute that you know one iota more about my little boy than I do. You may think you've got me all figured out, but you don't. And you sure as hell don't know my son better than I do."

Peyton stood and opened the front door. "It's time for you to leave, Brodie. I appreciate everything you've done for me and my family in the last few days. As I said, I don't know what I would've done without you."

"Peyton, I'm sorry. I didn't mean—"

"But you did, and that's the problem. You've known Finn for what? Three days? I'm 2,931 days ahead of you."

"I'm sorry. I won't ever make that mistake again. Believe me, I absolutely do not think I know your son better than you do. It was a stupid thing to say."

"Tell you what. When you can give me that speech and actually mean it, give me a call and maybe we'll talk. Bye, Brodie."

"Peyton—"

"In the last few minutes, I saw a side of you that I'm not crazy about. You eavesdropped on a private message and then called me out on it. You actually told me that I wasn't having dinner with someone. *Wasn't.* Then you told me how to handle a situation with my son when I did not ask for your advice. I let you take charge of certain things in the past couple of days because I was exhausted, and I trusted you. Don't abuse my trust,

Brodie, by thinking you can waltz in here and take over everything, especially my relationship with my boys."

"That isn't what I was doing."

"No?" Peyton walked back over to the counter. "There's this thing I do with *my* boys kind of like the thing your mom did with you. When I know they aren't being honest with me or with themselves, I make them take a time out. I tell them that when they're ready to take an honest look at the situation, I'll be happy to discuss it with them. Until then, I'm not interested. So Brodie, right now, I'm not interested."

Brodie stood and went down the hall. He went into the guest bathroom and grabbed his bag, and then stopped at the door to Finn's room and waved.

"Hey, Brodie, wait!" she heard Finn call out.

"I gotta go, but I'll see you soon, okay? Take it easy on that leg."

Brodie stopped in front of her, and for a minute, Peyton thought he was going to continue arguing with her, but he didn't.

"I'll see ya, Peyton."

She probably should've stopped him before he walked out, and thanked him again for all he'd done to help her and the boys, but hadn't she already thanked him a hundred times? Instead, she sent a text to Alex.

Call me when you're done on the trail, she wrote. *Need to talk.*

I think I might've just f'd things up, she added a few seconds later.

—:—

"Hey, brother. You're back."

Brodie handed Naughton the key fob to the Suburban. "Not for long. I'm takin' off again this afternoon."

"Goin' back to Peyton's?"

"Nope." Brodie walked away. He didn't know where he was going, he just knew he needed to go somewhere far away from here.

He walked back to the house, packed a bigger bag, and threw it into the back of the Porsche. On his way out, he stopped to see his ma.

"Come sit with me, Brodie."

"I can't Ma. I just wanted to see how you were feeling."

"What's happened?"

"Nothing. I rescheduled several sales meetings due to Peyton's son's accident, so I'll be out on the road for a few days." He looked into his mother's eyes. "But if you need me, call, or have Da call or Mad or Naught, and I'll come right back. Okay?"

"What about Peyton?"

"She was Kade's girlfriend, Ma. She has her own life now that he's gone."

"Brodie?"

He leaned down and kissed his mother's cheek. "I'll call from the road."

—:—

"You weren't kidding. What did you do to him?" Alex was standing in Peyton's kitchen unpacking groceries.

"What is all that?"

"Stuff."

"Frozen pizza? Burritos? Mac n cheese?"

"I'm hungry."

"Is that an apple pie?"

"I'm really hungry."

"We had an argument, and I asked him to leave."

"The state?"

"What does that mean?"

"By the size of the suitcase he had with him when he left, I think he's planning to be gone a while."

Alex was quiet while Peyton told her about the last conversation she and Brodie'd had.

"Well? You're not saying anything."

"You're the one who texted me and said you think you f'd things up."

"So you agree? You think I was wrong?"

"Wrong? I don't know. Too tough on him? Definitely."

"Really?"

"Go look in the mirror, Peyton. You're still you."

Peyton checked her phone, both to see if it was time for her to pick Jamison up from basketball practice, and also to see if she'd missed a call or text from Brodie. She hadn't.

"You want me to go get Jamison or stay here with Finn?"

"I'll go. Thanks for coming over, Alex."

"I'm here almost every day, Peyton. What would I do with myself if I wasn't here?"

"Yeah but you only have a couple of days of amazing sex left before your next dry spell, so I owe you."

Alex was sticking a spoon into what looked like a gallon of ice cream. "Whatever. I have junk food. I'm good."

Peyton had a few minutes to kill before Jamison would be ready to go, so she walked from her house to Moonstone Beach Road and watched the sun going down. A week ago she met Brodie here and wound up spending the whole day with him. Now he wasn't speaking to her, and she wasn't sure what to do about it.

Part of her could see Alex's point, that maybe she'd been too hard on him. On the other hand, he'd really overstepped. She was just about to jump off the rock and go get Jamison, when a familiar orange sports car pulled up.

She turned around and waited for him to get out. When he didn't, she walked over. "Hi."

"Hi."

"Uh, I have to go get Jamison."

"Please get in."

"Brodie, did you hear me?"

"I heard you. Please, Peyton."

Peyton climbed in, and Brodie drove to the school. Jamison was walking out the gym door when they arrived.

"Where's Finn?"

"He's home, honey, with Aunt Alex, who raided the junk food aisle at Louie's."

"Cool! Am I going to be allowed to have any?"

"If she'll share."

Brodie drove to Peyton's. "Hey, Jamison, can you tell Alex your mom and I had a quick errand to run?"

Jamison looked at his mom. "It's okay, honey. We'll be back soon."

"Okay, I'll tell her."

Brodie backed up the car and drove the block and a half back to the beach.

"What's going on, Brodie?"

He parked the car and turned to face her. "You were right. When I said I was sorry earlier, I only said it because you were mad."

"And?"

"I was wrong. I don't know shit about parenting, except what I learned from my own parents. When I said what I said, I was thinking about how they'd handle something with us. It took me a while to see it from your point of view. I get that I don't know your boys, and just because something worked with me and my siblings, doesn't mean anything."

"I overreacted. It wasn't bad advice. I had more of a problem with the way you said it than what you said."

"I'm pushing too hard. I get that, and I wish I understood it enough to explain it."

"What are you afraid of, Brodie?"

—:—

"Everything. I don't recognize myself lately." No one got under his skin the way Peyton Wolf had. It wasn't a misguided sense of responsibility either. His fear was over not having her in his life. Her boys, too. He could mentally reason away the irrationality of it, but it didn't stick.

"I said something similar to Alex."

"I'm supposed to be on my way to the Bay Area, but when I got to Monterey, I turned around and came back." Brodie looked at Peyton. "I'm not like this."

"I'm not either."

"When I left your house this morning, I convinced myself that time away from you would be the best thing for both of us. I planned to stay gone long enough that my obsession with you would abate. I couldn't do it." Brodie rubbed the back of his neck.

"Right or wrong, I'm in this with you, Peyton. I don't know how to get out, mainly because I don't want to. I want you, and that doesn't just mean sexually, although even if we made love ten times a day for the rest of our lives, it still wouldn't be enough for me."

Peyton was looking out at the sea. He couldn't see enough of her expression to know what she might be thinking, and she wasn't talking.

"Can you please say something?"

"Your instincts are right, Brodie. Time apart will help us both get perspective."

"I told Alex I was more into you than you're into me."

"I'm sorry I leaned on you as much as I did these past couple of days. It wasn't fair to you. I gave you the wrong idea."

"So I'm right."

"I'm afraid so. I let you take Kade's place in my life, because it was easy, and it felt good to have someone to lean on. You aren't him, Brodie, and you never will be."

"I see."

Peyton got out of the car. "Bye, Brodie."

"Where are you going? I can take you home."

"I'll walk, it isn't that far."

"Peyton—"

"Really, Brodie. Let me go."

He watched her walk out of his life. Nine days, start to finish, and yet Brodie didn't think he'd ever get over Peyton Wolf.

15

Rather than go inside, Peyton circled around and walked back to the beach. Brodie was gone. She heard his car speed off—her ear followed the sound of the powerful engine as he turned onto the highway and drove away.

It was time to get her head back on straight and live the life she'd made for herself. She liked her independence, and her relationship with Kade had allowed her to hang onto it. For eight weeks, he'd be with her, and then for eight weeks, he'd be gone. The first few days had always been difficult, but once she'd gotten past waking up at night and reaching for him, her life had returned back to the comfortable rhythm that she and her boys had shared since Lang left them.

Jamison and Finn had no recollection of their father, living with them or otherwise. She had photos stashed away, and was willing to talk about him if they ever asked, but so far they hadn't.

They'd have questions about Brodie. Even though he'd been a part of their lives such a short time, it felt like longer. Her biggest regret, now, was she'd allowed it to get as far as it had, at least where her boys were concerned. It became too familiar, too fast, and they'd be the ones to pay.

Brodie would move on. He said he was struggling with it, but Peyton knew better. It was about the chase. She learned that from Lang.

Kade may have thought he wanted to marry her, but what had he known about real life? He'd never really lived it. Maybe he'd talked to her father about it, and to his family, but Peyton wasn't truly convinced he ever would've proposed.

When it came to men, her instincts sucked. What would've happened with Brodie had she allowed things to continue with him? He told her his plan was to leave, until his "obsession" with her went away. That meant he didn't want whatever this was, to last. If she were alone, she might be able to risk it, but she refused to put her boys through the loss of yet another man they looked up to.

Peyton walked back into the house and picked up the phone she'd left in the kitchen. "I'll be right back," she told Alex. She went into the bedroom and closed the door.

"Peter? I'm glad I reached you."

"Peyton, how's your son?"

"He's good. Home. Thanks for asking. I, uh, wanted to get back to you about dinner next week. I'd love it."

"Great, I'm looking forward to it. Should I make a reservation somewhere in town?"

"We wouldn't need it on a Monday, but I was thinking maybe we'd go down to San Luis Obispo." From now on, she wouldn't date in her own backyard, and whoever she was dating, would never meet her boys, because she'd never allow another relationship to get serious enough to warrant it. Before she went back out to the kitchen, she called Sam and asked if she'd babysit Monday night.

"Of course, I'd love to."

Sam didn't ask any questions, and Peyton didn't offer any information. She could pick the boys up from school, feed them dinner, and get them into bed. If they wanted to know where she was going, she'd tell them she had to work late. Compartmentalizing was going to be her new MO.

When she came back into the kitchen, Alex pushed a piece of pizza in her direction. "You look very pleased with yourself."

Peyton looked around to see where the boys had disappeared to.

"Both in their rooms, doing homework. I'm turning into the perfect surrogate mom lately. Maybe I'll consider having one of my own in ten or twenty years."

"Better make it closer to ten, Alex, or you'll have to hire a surrogate."

"Yeah, yeah. So what's going on?"

"I have a date with Peter Wells Monday night."

Alex raised her eyebrows, shook her head, and put a giant spoonful of macaroni and cheese in her mouth.

"What?"

Alex pointed to her full mouth and shook her head again.

"Chicken shit."

"Pot," she pointed to Peyton, and then pointed to herself, "meet kettle."

—:—

What the hell had he been thinking by turning around and driving back to Cambria? If he hadn't, he'd be all the way to San Francisco by now. Instead, he wouldn't get there until well after midnight, which would put a damper on the plans he'd had before his misguided attempt to salvage his *relationship* with Peyton Wolf.

"Hey, sweetheart, change of plans." Brodie left a message on Dominique's cell.

As owner and chef of one of the hottest Michelin-starred restaurants in the city, she wouldn't be answering her phone. Instead, she'd be waiting for him to walk in the door sometime tonight, and he hated disappointing her.

"Getting a later start than I anticipated. I'll crash at Kabuki and see you tomorrow, baby."

Brodie and Dominique went way back. They met when he paid a sales call to her first five-star restaurant, Dom Nom, and had been bed-buddies since. Dominique was the one who'd said they'd never be more than that. She was married to her restaurants, she'd told him then, and he didn't try to sway her into more. She was smart, beautiful, independent, and loved sex. If anyone could get his mind off Peyton, Dominique could.

He was just past the turnoff for Adelaida Trail when he turned around. There was something he forgot to bring, that he needed. He pulled up to the house he shared with Naughton, went inside, and grabbed the box that was still sitting on the kitchen table.

He wasn't sure what he'd do with it yet. Maybe he'd throw it off the Golden Gate Bridge, and really close that chapter of Kade's life. With the box in the passenger seat, he got back on the road out of Peyton's life.

He checked into the hotel that felt like a second home to him. Nestled in Japantown, Kabuki was a world-away departure from his life in the Paso Robles wine country. Whenever he was in the Bay Area, he booked the same suite. It had a Japanese-style, deep soaking tub, en-suite sauna, and king-size bed he and Dominique made good use of.

He had everything off but his jeans when he heard a knock at the door. He opened it without looking to see who it was, and Dominique fell into his arms.

"You don't know how badly I need this." She had her fingers on the button on his jeans before the door closed behind her.

An hour later, she rested her back against his knees. "What's her name?"

"Dom, don't go there."

"Come on, Brodie. In all the years I've known you, the sex between us has been mind-blowing. We don't *talk*, Brode. We fuck. I didn't come here to talk."

"It was a long drive—"

Dominique threw her head back and laughed. "I don't care, Brodie. If you've found someone, I'm happy for you. There is no reason to lie to me. It wasn't the drive that turned you off."

"You didn't turn me off."

"I didn't say I did. I just didn't turn you on."

Brodie rubbed her shoulders, but even that simple act reminded him of having his hands on Peyton.

"Tell me about her."

"I gotta go, Brodie." Dominique kissed his cheek and rolled out of bed. "Dinner later?"

He nodded his head. "Sure, sweetheart. Thanks."

"Don't thank me. Apologize to me," she laughed.

When he started to, she put her fingers on his lips. "It was a joke, Brodie. I'm fine. A little sexually frustrated, but fine."

"Dom—"

"Seriously, honey, you don't think you're the only one who knows how to scratch my itch?"

"I know."

"There is a sous chef at Dom Nom who I can't stop thinking about. Maybe it's time I gave him a performance review."

"I'll see you tonight, sweetheart."

"Sit at the bar. There are a few new dishes I want to try out on you. You're still good for eating, right?"

Brodie reached over and swatted her behind. "Watch it."

Dominique laughed and closed the suite door behind her.

Brodie had a full day of meetings ahead of him, but after talking to Dominique most of the night, he needed some sleep. He checked his phone. Ten in the morning, no messages, no texts. If he was lucky, he'd sleep two or three hours without dreaming about Peyton.

—:—

It was a normal day, except that Finn still wasn't ready to go back to school. He'd wanted to, but Peyton thought he should stay home one more day. She doubted that was the reason he'd been sulking all day though.

"Why isn't he coming back today, Mom?"

"I told you, Finn. He has work to do. Just because I'm off today and tomorrow, doesn't mean everyone has that luxury."

"Why can't he come for dinner?"

"Finn, stop it. Brodie has his own life. I've explained this. It was great that he stayed to help us as long as he did."

Finn folded his arms and looked out the car window.

There was no reason to tell him it was worse than he thought. Both her boys would find out soon enough that it wasn't just that Brodie wasn't "coming back for dinner." He wasn't coming back at all.

Jamison wasn't much better when she picked him up from school, although he didn't ask about Brodie, he just sulked.

At least they weren't heartbroken. Sulking would stop after a day or two. The heartbreak they'd experienced when Kade died still hadn't stopped.

Peyton jumped when her cell phone rang. She half hoped it was Brodie, but was relieved when she saw it was Alex.

"Hey, girlfriend. Whatcha' doin'?"

"The boys and I are about to make dinner."

"Whatcha' makin'?"

"Chicken parm." It was one of their favorite "comfort" meals, and all three of them needed it.

"I'll grab a Sangiovese on my way."

"See ya, Alex."

She'd tell the boys Alex was on her way over, but they'd already figured it out, and neither looked happy.

"They're pissed," Alex laughed.

"No kidding." Peyton loaded the last of the dishes in the dishwasher. "I'm going to let Finn go to school tomorrow. It'll be easier than having him scowl at me all day."

"Have you heard from him?"

"No, and as much as I want to, it's better this way."

"Yeah, I get that."

"What about you and Maddox?"

"Done."

"Already? What happened?"

"I told you, it never lasts more than a week."

"Why not?"

"Every once in a while, we think we like each other, but really, we don't." Alex sighed. "Okay if we don't talk about it?"

"Of course." Peyton understood. She didn't want to talk about Brodie either.

—:—

"Go home." Dominique stood behind Brodie and rubbed his shoulders. "And by home, I don't mean back to the hotel."

"I can't. I'm in the valley tomorrow, and then up in Mendocino on Saturday."

"How far north are you runnin'?"

"Oregon. Maybe Washington."

Dominique sat next to him at the bar. "Brodie, go home. Talk to her."

"It's over, sweetheart." He hated the sound of his own voice. He sounded like a girl.

"It isn't."

"You talk to her or somethin'?"

"Now there's an idea."

"Dom—"

"I'm kidding. Can you imagine? 'Hi, Peyton, this is Dominique, the woman whose bed Brodie ran to when you dumped him...'"

He wanted to go home. Not to the hotel, and not to the house he shared with his brother. He wanted to go home to Peyton. How he could feel this way after a little over a week with her, and yet not sink into the comfort of a woman he'd known for years, he didn't understand.

"You're a mess."

"Thanks."

"I know I've been teasing you, Brodie. But I'm not anymore. Go home. I'm serious. Go talk to her. I've known you a long time, and I've never seen you like this. You're in love with her."

"Do you not remember *anything* we talked about last night? She was with Kade, Dominique. She actually told me I'd never measure up to him."

"My guess is that's not what she meant."

"I was there. You weren't. I didn't misunderstand." Brodie stood and threw some money on the bar. "See ya, Dominique."

"Don't leave in a huff."

"I'm not. I just don't feel like talking about it anymore. I'll be in touch." Brodie didn't slam the door on his way out, but he thought about it.

He wasn't mad at Dominique. She only wanted the best for him. He was mad at Kade. If Kade hadn't been involved with Peyton, if he hadn't died, Brodie wouldn't be feeling as though he was breaking in two again, like he did when his dad called him to tell him Kade was gone. The heartache he felt was different, but it hurt just as bad.

—:—

Peyton felt warm and safe. She dreamed she was in bed with Kade, snuggled up against his bare chest while he ran his fingers up and down her arm. She loved these dreams and never wanted to wake up from them.

"He loves you," Kade said in the dream.

"Who loves me?" She looked up into his deep blue eyes.

"Brodie does."

Peyton tried to turn away, pull herself out of this dream, but Kade wouldn't let her go.

"He loves you in a way I never could."

Peyton shook herself, trying to wake up.

"Give him a chance, sweetheart. He'll love you and take care of you and the boys. He'll make you happy."

What the hell, as long as this dream refused to end, she'd get some answers.

"He's a player, Kade. Just like Lang. The boys will get attached to him, and then he'll leave them, just like Lang, just like you."

"I'm sorry I left you, Peyton."

God, she loved the sound of his voice. The dream was so real, she could feel the vibration of it throughout her body.

"Why did you talk to my dad? He said you wanted to marry me."

"I did, but now I see how wrong it would've been."

"Thanks, Kade. Great dream this is."

"I was never the right man for you." Dream-Kade tapped her forehead. "You knew that. And even though I didn't want to admit it at the time, I knew it too. That's why I never told you about the agency."

"I loved you so much, Kade. I can't love Brodie the way I loved you."

"No, you can't. You can love him more than you loved me. He's always been the one for you. He said it the other night. If he'd met you first, you wouldn't have been available to date me." Dream-Kade laughed. "He's got it bad for you, Peyton. But then, so did I."

When Peyton reached up to kiss him, Dream-Kade kissed her forehead instead. "Go back to sleep now, Peyton. Sweet dreams."

When Peyton woke, the sun was shining. In her dream, it was still dark. Damn Kade. Damn Brodie too. What did she have to do to stop thinking about them? See a hypnotist?

Peter excused himself and went to the men's room, giving Peyton time to take a deep breath. Dinner was nice, but as Alex had said about her date with him, it just wasn't *there*. She was bored out of her mind. She cringed when he drove up to Mama's Meatballs. Of all the restaurants he could've chosen, why this one?

She heard the vibration of her phone that was stuffed inside her purse. She never ignored it, in case it was one of her boys. Peter walked back to the table just as she ran her finger across the screen and saw a missed call from Brodie.

"Something important?" he asked when he sat back down.

"No." It was a lie. She only hoped her phone would vibrate again, indicating he left a message. "I'm sorry, Peter. I need to return this call—you know, the boys." Another lie.

Peyton excused herself to the ladies' room and waited. Her phone didn't vibrate, which meant he hadn't left a message. She waited for a text, but that didn't come either.

"We should head back," she said when she returned to the table.

"Everything okay?"

"No, not really." That wasn't a lie, it just wasn't what he meant, and she knew it.

The waitress brought the check, and when Peyton offered to pay her share, Peter refused.

"I enjoyed having dinner with you, Peyton. I'd like to say I hope we can do it again, but I sense that won't be happening."

"I'm sorry, Peter."

"Don't be. I mean it, I enjoyed this very much."

"You're a good guy, Peter."

"Yeah, yeah," he laughed. "Alex said the same thing."

Peyton winced.

"No worries, I'm sure I'm not the only guy turned down by both of the hottest women in San Luis Obispo County."

"Thanks, Peter."

"I'll take you home."

She'd left her car at Stave. Even that hadn't felt right. She wanted to follow him down, so he didn't have to drive back to Cambria after dinner, but he insisted.

"Good night, Peter, and thanks again. I'm going to head inside for a minute and make sure everything is cleaned up. We're closed tomorrow."

"Would you like me to come in with you?"

"No, but thanks. You should get on the road. You have a long drive ahead of you."

"Thanks again for joining me tonight, Peyton. I'll see you in a couple of weeks."

Peyton unlocked the front door and slipped inside. Peter was gone before she locked it behind her. Kade never would've let her come in alone after dark, or even during the day. It wasn't as though Peter hadn't offered. She had been relieved when he accepted her refusal. It was just another reminder that Kade had been a gentleman, unlike so many other men she knew.

Everything had been put away before they'd left for dinner, but Peyton wanted a minute alone before she went home. It was only a little after seven, so both her boys would still be awake. She didn't anticipate they'd ask her any questions though. They hadn't been very talkative since Brodie left. Correction—since she made Brodie leave. It was as though they sensed it was her fault he was gone, not his.

She poured a finger of Port, downed it, and rinsed the glass before setting the alarm and going out the back door. The motion light Kade had installed came on when she walked outside, illuminating the man leaning against the orange Porsche parked next to her BMW.

"Peyton."

"Brodie. What are you doing here?"

"I called."

"You didn't leave a message."

Peyton stood where she was, unsure whether she should walk over to him, or her car. Had he gone by the house? Did he know she'd been out with Peter? No one other than Alex knew about their dinner plans, and she doubted Alex would've told him.

"Brodie, what do you want?"

When he moved out of the shadows, Peyton saw his clothes were disheveled, and he hadn't shaved. It didn't look intentional. He looked as though he hadn't slept. Brodie stood in front of her, but didn't speak. He reached out, and she took his hand.

"Do you want to go inside?"

"Would you mind?"

Peyton unlocked the door she'd just come out of, and went inside to turn off the alarm. Brodie waited until she held the door open for him.

"Peyton, I..."

She waited, but he didn't finish his sentence.

"Can I get you something to drink? I was going to have a glass of Port." She already had, but that didn't matter, she could use another one.

"Sure. Thanks."

She poured two glasses, walked over to the sitting area by the fireplace, and set them down on the table. Instead of sitting, she walked over and hit the switch, igniting the gas fireplace. Brodie waited, and when she sat on the couch, he joined her.

He picked up the wine glass and swirled it gently. He took a sip, and then ran his finger around the rim, staring into the fire.

Peyton longed to touch him, but with his mood, held back. More than touch, she sensed he needed comfort, but would he accept it from her? Some of the last words she'd said to him were that he'd never be Kade. She hadn't meant it the way she knew he'd take it, but she'd had no intention, then, of explaining. The words had hurt him, and she knew they would. Her goal had been to push him away, and she'd succeeded.

She leaned back and rested her head against the leather sofa, wishing the fire were wood, so instead of the hiss of the gas, it would crackle. Any noise would be welcome. She moved to stand, intending to turn on some music, but Brodie held her arm.

"Don't go," he murmured.

He left his hand where it was on her arm. His touch was warm, but soft. She covered his hand with hers, shifting her body so she faced him. He didn't turn his gaze from the fire, but his eyes drifted closed. Peyton rested her head against his shoulder.

She lost track of how long they sat that way, in silence. Instead of drifting, her thoughts stayed on Brodie, listening to him slowly breathe in and out. When he moved and gripped her face with his hand, bringing his mouth to hers, she didn't fight him. She didn't pull away. She opened her mouth to his and drank him in.

"Peyton," he groaned when she shifted and rested her body on the couch, giving him room to lie on top of her. His hand slid under her sweater and covered her breast, squeezed her, and slid his fingers inside her bra, molding her to his hand. Peyton pulled his shirt from the waist of his pants, and ran her hands over his back.

"I need you, Peyton." Brodie's hand moved between her legs, rubbing her body through the suede skirt she wore.

Peyton dragged the fabric up so she could feel his hand against her skin. With her hand so close, she lowered his zipper. Brodie freed himself, and moved her panties to the side. Peyton gasped as he entered her. He stilled, and then slowly moved in and out.

"So good," he whispered.

Peyton grasped his behind with both hands, urging him deeper.

"Baby," he breathed into her mouth before his tongue did battle with hers.

She moved against him, wanting him deeper still. Brodie grabbed her leg and brought it around him. When he slammed against her, she felt her body flood, not knowing whether she came first, or he had. She wrapped her arms around him, and held him as tightly to her as she could, not wanting to ever let him go. She kissed the side of his face and reached up to run her fingers through his hair.

Brodie captured her mouth with his, and kissed her hard enough that it hurt. She didn't care. She wanted to feel him everywhere. She didn't want soft or slow; she wanted Brodie to lose himself in her. He started to move inside her again, more forceful this time, until she felt him drench her for the second time.

"Again." He looked into her eyes, and she nodded.

"Again, Brodie."

Peyton lost track of how many times they came together, Brodie's body never separating from hers. Finally he shifted, and rolled so she was on top of him. He held the sides of her face with his hands and looked into her eyes. When she looked in his, she saw regret. "Peyton, I—"

"Please, Brodie. Whatever you say, don't let it be that you're sorry."

"But—"

Peyton climbed off of him, adjusted her clothes, and ran to the ladies' room before he saw her tears. After something so beautiful, something so perfect, he was filled with regret? She held the edge of the sink, as sobs wracked her body. She heard the back door open and close, and the sound of Brodie's car speed away.

She cleaned herself up as best she could. There'd be no hiding how hard she'd been crying, no matter how long she waited to go home. At least now she knew her boys would be asleep. She'd do her best to avoid a conversation with Sam, so she could retreat into her shower, and wash the memory of Brodie from her body.

—:—

Brodie drove straight to the airport in Los Angeles, parked in long-term parking, and brought his suitcase, and his brother's box, to the ticket counter.

"Where to?" The agent smiled at him.

He looked at the board. "Has the flight to Buenos Aires boarded?"

The ticket agent picked up the phone and asked the gate agent how soon they'd be closing the door.

"You're in luck," she said when she set the phone down. "The flight has been delayed. You should make it through customs in enough time, provided your paperwork is in order."

Once on the plane, Brodie settled into his first class seat, allowing his body to feel the pain of knowing he'd never again make love to the woman who owned his heart, and would, for the rest of his life.

—:—

She didn't need a test. Peyton knew she was pregnant. She'd known for days. Soon, Alex would know too, because if this pregnancy was anything like her other two, there'd be no hiding her morning sickness.

She hadn't told Alex what happened with Brodie the night before he disappeared from her life. Soon she'd have to tell the story, as little of it as she could get away with.

Where Brodie was concerned, Peyton was numb. She didn't look for him or expect to hear from him—she knew he was gone from her life. A part of her wondered if she'd ever see him again. She'd felt this way after Kade died too. She'd dream it was a mistake, that he hadn't really been killed, but inside, she felt the separation, the finality.

There was no question, though, that she'd have this baby. It was her baby, just like Jamison and Finn were. Their father wasn't part of their lives, and this baby's father wouldn't be either. For someone who Alex accused of caring too much about what people thought of her, in this case, she didn't give it any thought at all. She was pregnant, and she refused to hide it, or herself, from anyone. If someone dared to ask about the baby's father, she already knew what she'd say. She'd tell them it was none of their damn business.

Peyton washed her face, brushed her teeth, and surveyed her reflection. With both boys, she remembered looking haggard. Maybe she wouldn't have noticed if Lang hadn't pointed it out to her. This time, with no one to shame her, Peyton felt beautiful. Soon her body would change and grow, and she'd feel the miracle of the new life growing inside her. It was a feeling she'd never expected to have again.

She didn't know yet what she'd tell the boys, but her mom would help her through it. No matter what, she knew she had her parents' support. Their love for her was unconditional. Maybe without it, she wouldn't be able to be as brave as she was.

When she walked into Stave, Alex was already there. She looked exhausted, as though something heavy weighed on her.

"What's up?" Peyton asked, feeling anxiety flood her body.

"It's Brodie, Peyton. I don't know how to tell you this."

Peyton's hand flew to her mouth, and she ran to the restroom, getting there right before she lost the contents of her stomach. When she came back out, Alex was waiting, and pulled her into a hug.

"Tell me."

"Maddox called this morning. Brodie was traveling to a remote vineyard in Argentina. The small plane he was in lost contact. Maddox and Naughton are making arrangements to leave now."

Peyton rested her hands on her stomach and took several deep breaths. The tears she expected didn't come.

"Peyton, are you okay?"

"I don't know."

"Do you want to sit?"

"I think I better." She held onto Alex's arm, but when Alex tried to get her to sit on the sofa near the fireplace, Peyton let go, and moved to the other side of the room.

"You better sit too, Alex. I have something I need to tell you."

16

Brodie felt the small plane surge, and knew the moment the wing clipped the mountain peak. Seconds later, the right wing severed, and was thrown back with such force that it left a gaping hole in the rear of the fuselage. The aircraft hit the ground and slid. That was the last thing he remembered.

Of the forty-five people aboard the plane, Brodie was one of twelve remaining survivors. Fifteen were killed instantly, and eighteen others died from their injuries within days of the crash. The co-pilot, one of the survivors, believed the crash site was only miles from the Chilean mountain town of Parrado, but Brodie sensed they were much farther west. However, with frigid spring temperatures, he had little hope any of them would survive, unless they were rescued within the next two or three days.

Three of the twelve decided to set out in search of Parrado. Brodie volunteered to join them, but after a short distance, he realized the injuries he'd sustained to his leg were worse than he'd initially thought. He turned back alone, unsure if he'd make it back to the crash site. He found his way to an area beneath several trees, pulling low branches down to the ground to provide warmth.

He knew better than to sleep, but his exhaustion was too great. Covered in branches, Brodie let himself drift off, doubting he'd still be alive by morning.

—:—

Alex made the decision to close Stave indefinitely. The sign she put on the door said they were closed for remodeling, but only the tourists who visited Cambria were unaware of the real reason.

There were days when Peyton felt certain she was going to lose the baby. She'd gone to the emergency room twice because the cramping had gotten so bad she couldn't stand the pain. They kept her overnight both times, releasing her when the ultrasound showed the baby was fine. After her last trip, the doctor recommended temporary bed rest.

Peyton went to stay with her parents, who took responsibility for getting the boys back and forth to school every day.

Communication from Maddox and Naughton was limited. The search for the plane wreckage was extensive, and that was all they knew at this point. Only Sorcha believed her boy was still alive. Laird had given up hope, but kept his belief from his wife.

"He's alive," she insisted. "A mother knows. I *know* my Brodie is alive and nothing anyone says will change my mind."

Alex visited Sorcha and Laird every few days, although neither knew yet of Peyton's pregnancy.

She'd stopped dreaming. Neither Kade nor Brodie came to her when she slept. Instead, she woke each morning with no recollection of dreaming at all. When she slept, she saw nothing but darkness.

"Do you want me to go to your doctor's appointment tomorrow?" Alex asked.

"Would you mind? I feel as though my parents never get a break."

"I don't mind, and I doubt they do either. I'd just like to be there."

"You're at the ten-week mark," the doctor told her without needing to. Peyton knew exactly how far along she was.

"Can you tell if it's a boy or a girl?" Alex asked.

"Not yet. Closer to twenty weeks for us to know for sure."

Peyton didn't need the doctor to tell her that either. She was certain she was having a girl.

After her appointment, Peyton waited out front, in the wheelchair, while Alex went to get her car. The sun felt warm on her face, and she let her eyes drift closed.

"Peyton?"

When she opened her eyes, Sorcha Butler stood in front of her. She knelt down, and Peyton's eyes filled with tears.

"Peyton, why are you here?"

Alex pulled up, saw Sorcha, and jumped out of the car.

"Ready, sweetie?" She wheeled Peyton toward the car, leaving Brodie's mom without an answer.

Alex closed Peyton's door and turned back. "We'll talk later, okay?"

"Alex?" Laird Butler walked up behind her, and saw Peyton sitting in the car. "Is she okay?"

"She's okay, but I need to get her home. I'll stop by later."

Peyton rolled down the window and motioned for Alex to come closer. "Invite them to the house, if Mrs. Butler feels up to it."

"Are you sure?"

Peyton nodded and rolled the window back up.

Neither spoke on the ride back to the house. Alex came around the car to help Peyton, who swatted at her.

"I'm fine, Alex. I'm having a baby. I'm not paralyzed, for God's sake." Peyton slammed the car door.

Alex had her hand over her mouth, and Peyton expected her to bitch at her, or cry, as she was prone to do lately. Instead, Alex was laughing.

"What?" Peyton laughed too.

"It's so good to see Peyton-the-bitch is back. I hate the milquetoast version of you."

"Milquetoast? What the hell is milquetoast? Although, it sounds kind of good. Like toast and warm milk?"

"Hungry too? I'm so happy right now."

"What possessed me to invite Brodie's parents over?"

"You did what?" Peyton's mom came out the front door of the house.

"I need to tell them, Mom. Seriously, they deserve to know."

"I wondered."

Peyton looked at Alex. "But she didn't say anything. She never says anything."

"Don't complain. Spend a week with my mom, and you'll realize how good you have it."

"Yeah!" Her mom fist-pumped the air, which only made Alex and Peyton laugh harder.

"Did I hear you say you're hungry?"

"Starving. Can you make me some toast? And some warm milk?"

"Good Lord, Peyton. Where did you come up with that craving?"

"Blame her." Peyton pointed at Alex, who shrugged.

—:—

Two of the other survivors found Brodie in the woods and carried him back to the camp they'd built from the wreckage.

For two days, they told him, he'd slipped in and out of consciousness. They were certain he wasn't going to make it, but today he felt better. He remembered dreaming about Kade and Peyton—crazy dreams born of his delirium. Most of his dreams were about being rescued, and then going home to find Peyton waiting for him. Some of his dreams were so far out there, he gave them no credence. The ones about being rescued though, he clung to.

He drifted to sleep again, and dreamed he heard the *thwpthwpthwpthwp* of a helicopter flying low. It was the shouts and screams he heard seconds later that brought him fully awake.

—:—

"Thanks for inviting us to your home, Mrs. Wolf."

"Sorcha, please call me August. You know my husband, Jamison."

"Laird, Sorcha," Peyton's father greeted Brodie's mother and father. "Can I bring something to drink?"

"Whatever's open, Jamison, thank you."

Her dad came back in with an unmarked bottle of red. He poured everyone a glass but Peyton.

"I have something to tell you," she began.

When Laird's phone pinged, he apologized and took it from his pocket.

"I'm sorry," he said. "I have to take this."

As he walked out of the room, Peyton took a deep breath. She leaned forward and held Sorcha's hands.

"Oh, thank the Lord," they heard Laird shout from the kitchen. He came running back into where his wife waited with Peyton, Alex, and her parents. *"They've found him. He's alive! Sorcha! He's alive!"*

Hearing Brodie's father's news, Peyton felt the darkness pull her under.

"Peyton?" Alex was tapping her face with her finger. "Peyton!"

She opened her eyes and looked over at Brodie's parents who were handing the phone back and forth.

"They're talking to someone with the search party. Evidently, Maddox radioed that they've located the crash site, and by some miracle, Brodie is still alive. They're trying to determine his condition now."

A few minutes later, Sorcha wiped her happy tears and sat down next to Peyton. "What did you have to tell us, lass?"

Peyton looked at her mom, who nodded her head through her own tears.

"Sorcha, Laird. I'm pregnant. And Brodie is the father."

At first Peyton thought Sorcha might faint, as she had herself only a few minutes earlier. She didn't, but she didn't say anything either. She reached for Laird's hand and gripped it hard enough that he winced.

"I told you," she whispered, before she stood and left the room.

Laird sat down next to Peyton and hugged her.

"Is she okay?"

"Oh, yes, she's fine. Just overwhelmed. You see, she told me Maddox and Naughton were going to find Brodie. She also told me that when they did, you would tell him he was going to be a father."

Peyton felt light-headed again, which Alex noticed. "What do you need, Peyton?"

"I'm okay."

"You sure?"

"It might be a good idea for me to lie down for a bit."

"I'll help you upstairs."

When Peyton started to protest, Alex put her hands together. "Please," she mouthed.

"Seriously, are you okay?"

"Can you close the door?"

"Sure, of course, sorry. God, this is crazy, isn't it? He's okay! They found him. He's coming home."

"Alex..."

"What? Jesus, this is a frickin' miracle!"

"Alex."

She sat at the end of Peyton's bed. "What? I'm sorry. Go. Talk. Say whatever you're going to say."

"He left me long before he was in a plane crash, Alex."

"But don't you think this changes things?"

"Why would it?"

"Peyton, how could it not?"

"He left me, Alex. How are you not hearing me?"

"I hear you, but I don't understand."

"I think I'd like to be alone for a while. Tell my mom it's okay for them to tell the boys."

"Peyton—"

"Leave me alone, Alex."

—:—

"You aren't well enough to travel, Brodie. As soon as you are, we'll get you on the first flight home. I promise."

No amount of pleading made any difference. Nothing he said swayed his brothers. He couldn't make them understand how important it was for him to get back to Peyton.

He spoke with his parents yesterday, and as much as they wanted to get on the next plane to Argentina, his mother's heart wasn't healthy enough yet for travel.

He tried to contact Peyton, but she didn't answer or return his call. He asked Maddox if he'd talked to Alex, and while he said he had, he knew nothing about Peyton. Finally, when they were alone, he begged Naughton to be straight with him. Had something happened to her? Were they keeping something from him? Naughton shook his head and told Brodie he didn't know, but when his brother wouldn't look him in the eye, Brodie knew there was something they were hiding from him.

"Give it three or four days," the doctor told him when he came in this morning. "I'll release you to travel then."

Maddox sat near the end of the hospital bed, staring out the window.

"If you were in my place, I wouldn't do this to you."

"No one is doing anything to you, Brodie."

"I need to talk to her, Mad. You don't understand how important it is that I talk to her."

"Why now, Brodie? You went weeks without talking to her, from what I understand." Maddox got up and walked out of the room. Brodie didn't see either of his brothers until the next morning.

"We've made arrangements for a medevac flight," Naughton told him. "It's essentially an ICU in the sky. The doctor said those were the only conditions under which he'd release you."

"Thanks, man. I appreciate this."

Naughton sat on the edge of the bed, wrapping his hand around the back of Brodie's neck. "I'm just so fucking glad we found you. For now, that's all I can think about. There will come a day though, Brodie, when I have every intention of kicking your sorry ass."

"I'm sorry, Naught."

"I'm not the one you need to apologize to."

"What aren't you telling me?"

"It isn't my story to tell."

"Tell me this much, is she okay?"

"Okay is relative, brother, and that's all I have to say. If you keep pushing me, I'll cancel the medevac, and you can stay here until the doctor thinks you're well enough to fly commercial."

Naughton got up and walked out before Brodie could respond.

—:—

"Can I come in?"

"Of course, Dad. I was about to come downstairs anyway."

"I'd rather talk privately."

Peyton sat up in bed, scooting over so her father could sit next to her.

"I received a call from Laird Butler. Brodie will be home tomorrow. They flew him to Miami yesterday. He'll stay in the hospital there until tomorrow morning."

"I see."

"He'll be in the hospital here for several more days. From what I understand, he was very close to death when they found him."

Peyton's hands rested on her stomach. It was too early for her to feel the baby move, but there were times she could swear she felt her kick.

"Have you made any decisions, Peyton?"

"No, Dad. I haven't."

"I'd like to suggest you consider going to see him."

That was her dad's way. He never told her she *had* to do anything. Instead, he suggested she consider doing what he asked.

"I'll think about it."

"That's all I ask.

Instead of getting up, Peyton decided to say in bed longer. The boys were off school today. Soon, they'd come tumbling in, excited to talk more about Brodie's rescue.

They knew he had been in Argentina when the plane he was on crashed. Their assumption that Brodie would never return, like Kade hadn't, left them giddy with the excitement of his homecoming. They understood their mom was having a baby, but had few questions about what that meant for them as a family. Again, they incorrectly assumed that once Brodie returned, they *would* be a family.

They fought over who would be her primary caregiver on the weekends. Finally, in order to stop their bickering, her mom assigned Saturdays to Jamison and Sundays to Finn. On their "day" they brought her meals either in bed or on the sofa, and were responsible for checking on her at least once an hour to see if she or "the baby" needed anything. While Peyton thought her family was taking her bed rest a little too seriously, the two times she thought she was losing the baby, had devastated her. If keeping the little girl growing inside her safe meant she had to stay off her feet, avoid stress, and allow her family to care for her, that was what she would do.

Jamison came in, sat on the side of her bed, and snuggled her. "Morning, Mama."

"Hi, sweetheart. You could've slept a little later this morning. I know you were up late last night."

"It's my day."

"I know, honey, but I'm fine, and so is our little miss."

"How do you know the baby is a girl?

"I just do. It's called mother's intuition."

"Can I feel?"

Peyton moved the blanket aside and raised her pajama top. Her tummy was only slightly protruded, but soon, it would begin expanding. With Jamison, she hadn't started showing until she hit the four-month mark. With Finn, it seemed her stomach had started to grow as soon as she realized she was pregnant.

Jamison's hands were cold, and Peyton giggled when he rested them against her. He leaned over and kissed her tummy.

"Good morning, baby sister," he whispered.

Peyton cupped the back of his head with her hand. Her eyes filled with tears, in part because her child was so sweet, and also because the emotional roller coaster she was on brought giggles and tears together so often.

"What's her name?"

"Hmm. I'm not sure yet. Do you have any ideas?"

"You should ask Brodie what he thinks."

Peyton didn't respond. There was no need to drag Jamison into the turmoil she felt whenever she thought about Brodie.

"What do you want for breakfast? Eggs, like every other day?" he smirked.

"No, I think I'll mix it up today. How about some yogurt?"

"You need to eat more than yogurt, Mom."

"From Grandma's mouth to yours."

"It's my day. I'm responsible for you today."

"Yes, Jamie. Tell you what, I'm so hungry this morning, I'll eat whatever you bring me. You decide what you think will be the best breakfast for me and your baby sister."

He shot off the bed and ran downstairs. Lord knew what he would come back with.

"Knock, knock," Alex tapped on the bedroom door.

"Come in. You're here early."

"I'm opening Stave today. I think we should, especially with the festival next weekend."

"Oh, okay. That's good. I, uh—"

"I'm just opening on the weekend for now. Friday through Sunday. Sam and Addy are excited for the hours. I was a little worried they'd both find other jobs, but so far, they're waiting it out."

The news of Brodie's rescue had likely spread throughout San Luis Obispo County. It was right to open Stave and give people a place to celebrate.

"I talked to Maddox last night."

"Are you on again?"

"Maybe. I'm not sure yet."

"Does he know about the baby?"

"Yeah."

"Does Brodie?"

"Not yet. He wanted to know if you were going to tell him."

"He isn't even back yet."

"I don't think he's pressuring you. I think he just wanted to know. He said Brodie asks about you constantly."

"Why?"

"Do you want to have this conversation again?"

"Nope."

"Didn't think so." Alex kissed Peyton's forehead. "I'm off to bring wine to the masses. I'll be by tomorrow."

"Hey, Alex?"

"Yeah?

"Can you bring some clam chowder back with you? And some garlic bread?"

"Sure you can wait until tomorrow?"

"No, but since I'm not supposed to leave the house, I doubt my parents or the boys will let me drive to Cambria."

"I'll see what I can do."

Peyton picked her cell phone up off the nightstand and scrolled through Brodie's messages. Thus far they'd all said close to the same thing. He begged her to get in touch with him, begged her to allow him to explain why he'd left the way he had after they'd made love. Each one ended the same way. He told her that, whether she believed him or not, he loved her, and he'd spend the rest of the life he'd been spared, proving it to her, whether or not she could ever love him in return.

He'd left two since she fell asleep last night. She brought the phone to her ear and tapped the first one.

"Peyton, it's Brodie." His voice sounded stronger than it had in his first few messages. "I have something I need you to know, and since you won't return my calls, this is the only way I know to tell you. It's about the last night we were together. You see, that night—"

Peyton couldn't listen to another word. She deleted that message, the one that followed, and all those he'd left before it. She refused to listen to him tell her he regretted their night together, the one that gave her the precious gift growing inside her.

Peyton wrapped her arms around the place where her baby girl grew. "You will never know you weren't wanted. You will never know that one of your parents didn't love you. Never."

Her arms were still holding her stomach when the cramping pain woke her. She felt sticky wetness between her legs, and stumbled to the bathroom in the hall. She screamed when she saw the amount of blood seeping through her pajama bottoms, and fell to the bathroom floor.

"Peyton!" she heard her dad yell, his footsteps getting closer.

"Hurry, Dad!" she screamed. "I think I'm losing the baby."

An hour later, the nurse ran the fetal monitor over her stomach, and shook her head. "I'm not hearing a heartbeat, Peyton. I'm sorry. I'll give you some privacy."

Her mother held her as she sobbed. Her mother knew this pain—how many times had she felt it herself? It was worse than Peyton had ever imagined. She didn't feel any different than she had when she heard Kade had been killed. Her baby was dead. It wasn't a "miscarriage"; it was a death.

The nurse came back in the room to discuss whether Peyton wanted to go through a natural miscarriage, or through the medical dilation and curettage. Her mom explained the difference, telling Peyton that with her own first miscarriage, she'd let things happen naturally. The pain was intense, and the risk of infection was high. The next two times, she'd opted for the medical procedure. She wondered still, she told Peyton, if the first miscarriage had compromised her uterus, resulting in the subsequent losses. There was no medical evidence to prove her theory, but it didn't change her mother's belief that had she done things differently, she may have been able to have another child.

Peyton still hadn't made up her mind when the doctor came in.

"Peyton, I need to examine you, and then we can discuss your options."

"Will you stay?" Peyton held her mother's hand and wouldn't let go.

"Of course, sweetheart."

The doctor stretched latex gloves over his hands and asked Peyton to rest her feet in the stirrups. Tears streamed down her cheeks. There was physical pain as he performed the examination, but it was a fraction of the emotional pain she felt.

The doctor removed her feet from the stirrups, told her to ease back, and covered her with the blanket. He left the room and, when he returned, ran the fetal monitor over her abdomen.

Whoosh, whoosh, whoosh. Peyton heard the sound of her little girl's heartbeat.

"Order an ultrasound," he told the nurse.

Peyton's mom held her hand tight, and smiled when Peyton looked up at her.

"There are times we can't find the heartbeat," the doctor started to explain. "You remember from your first pregnancy."

The same doctor with her today, had been her obstetrician with both Jamison and Finn.

"With the amount of bleeding—"

Peyton held up her hand. "I understand."

The tech rolled the ultrasound machine in, and the doctor spread the cool gel over her tummy. He ran the wand back and forth, stopping to tap the computer's keyboard, or to click the mouse. Peyton recognized that he was taking measurements, and also recognized movement.

"Do you want to know the baby's sex?" he asked.

"It's a girl," Peyton responded.

"It's early, but I think you're right. I'm sorry to have put you through the scare, Peyton."

She shook her head. She understood. There were times the symptoms indicated more than what actually happened.

"I want to admit you. At least overnight. Maybe longer."

She'd be on the labor and delivery floor, where she'd been the last two times they had admitted her, far away from where they'd bring Brodie, but in the same hospital nonetheless.

17

The aroma of clam chowder and garlic bread filled the hospital room.

"I love you so much right now." Peyton smiled at Alex.

"You only say that when I bring you food. It's starting to bother me."

"Get over it." Peyton laughed. "How many people are you planning on feeding? The entire nursing staff?"

Alex was unpacking brown paper bags emblazoned with the Sea Chest's logo.

"Is that all chowder?"

Alex pulled out four quarts, along with several foil-wrapped pans.

"And other delicacies. Your parents will be here shortly with the boys."

"I do love you, and not just because you bring me food."

"Yeah, yeah. I know. Don't start in with all that pregnancy-induced, emotional shit."

Jamison bumped into the back of Alex and held his hand out. This time when she reached into her pocket, she pulled out a twenty. "Can that cover my bad language at least for tonight?"

Jamison shrugged and stuffed the money into his front pocket. "We'll see."

"Hey!" Finn punched Jamison.

"I'll share it, you little bugger."

Alex held her hand out in Jamison's direction. "Bugger? Now you owe me."

"That isn't a bad word."

"Sure is, especially in my house." Maddox Butler walked into the room, and over to Peyton. "Hey there, pretty little mama." He leaned down and kissed her cheek. "How are you feeling?"

"Hi, Maddox. I'm doing okay, thanks for asking." Peyton tried to be polite, but inside she was fraught with anxiety.

"I'm parking the car, getting some coffee, and calling the winery," he offered.

Peyton looked over in time to see her parents and Alex usher the boys out of the room, and close the door behind them.

"So he's here?"

"Brought him in about an hour ago. They have him in the ICU, but it's only precautionary. They expect to have him in a regular room later tonight or tomorrow."

"Does he know?"

"No, Peyton. We discussed it as a family, and we all agree it's up to you to tell him. Only Naught and I, and our parents, know. We haven't told Skye or Ainsley."

"I appreciate it, Maddox."

"Alex told me what happened earlier. Sounds like you had quite a scare."

"It was…horrible." Peyton's eyes filled with tears she brushed away.

"I'm sorry. I shouldn't have brought it up."

"It's why I'm here, so it's hard to avoid the subject."

"Right." He smiled.

"How is he?"

"Better every day. Stronger. More obstinate."

"Mad?"

"Yeah?"

Peyton laughed. "Sorry, I meant is he mad?"

"Oh, gotcha. I wouldn't say he's mad. He's worried. Beatin' himself up pretty bad. Naught and I aren't letting him off the hook either."

"Did he tell you what happened between us?"

"Promise *you* won't get mad?"

Peyton nodded.

"Alex told me."

"I see."

"You promised you wouldn't get angry."

"I'm not angry with Alex." Her best friend only knew part of the story anyway. She'd refrained from sharing the part where Brodie left her in a *shit pile* of humiliation. All Alex knew was that she and Brodie had sex, she ended things, and he left the country. She'd fudged the order a little, but it was mostly the truth.

"Do you want to know what I think?"

"Sure."

"You sure?"

"Yes, Maddox. Tell me what you think." No wonder Alex couldn't stay away from this guy. He was hotter than hell, gruff as all get-out, with a heart bigger than Butler Ranch.

"He really regrets whatever happened with you two."

Wrong word. She had no room for regret, his or anyone else's. If he regretted having sex with her, why in the hell was he so relentless about wanting to talk to her? Did he want her forgiveness? She'd never forgive him for something she'd never regret.

"Can I ask you a favor, Maddox?"

"Of course."

"Would you please tell Brodie he doesn't owe me a damn thing. He doesn't need to apologize, or feel regret, or even feel any responsibility for my baby. I'm raising two other precious children without their father's involvement, and we're doing just fine. There is no reason for me to believe it'll be any different with my daughter."

"Two things. What did I say? And, you know it's a girl? Shit, Peyton, that's wonderful."

"I don't need anyone's regret, Maddox. If he's ashamed or embarrassed about what happened between us, that's between him and the reflection he sees in the mirror. And as far as knowing my baby is a girl, I've known for weeks. It's a feeling, Maddox. One that is born out of love for my child."

"I didn't come here to cause more trouble, Peyton."

"I know that, and I'm sorry I'm taking my anger out on you. Nothing that's happened is your fault. I don't need any of this...this...*bullshit* from your brother. Please tell him to move on with his life, and stay the hell out of mine."

"Can I visit you again, or are you banishing me from your life, too?"

How could this man smile at her when she was treating him so abhorrently?

"You're a good man, Maddox, and you can visit me whenever you'd like. You might want to consider purchasing protective gear before you see me again."

Maddox leaned over and kissed her cheek for the second time. He grabbed her hand and put it near his chest. "If you need somebody to beat on, sweetheart, I can take it."

—:—

Brodie slept for most of the day. The travel took more out of him than he'd expected it to, and was glad the Argentinian doctor had insisted he go by medevac. If he had tried regular travel, he might not have lived through it.

Maddox came in and pulled a chair closer to Brodie's bed. He leaned forward, rested his forearms on his knees, and then gripped the back of his neck with his hand.

"What's bothering you, Mad?"

"Tell me what happened between you and Peyton."

"It isn't any of your business—"

"Tell me!" Mad bellowed. "*Right now.* Or I won't help you, brother. And whether you've figured it out or not, you need a helluva lot of help."

By the time Brodie finished recounting his last night with Peyton, Maddox understood why the word "regret" had set her off the way it had. She had it wrong, and so did Brodie, but once they understood how wrong they were, they'd find their way back to each other. They didn't need Maddox's interference.

"Are you going to help me?"

"Nope. You're good. Just remember this—no woman wants to think she was a mistake. Be mindful of that when you're groveling."

"Why would she think she was a mistake?"

"You mull that over for a bit. When you're certain you're ready, I'll make sure you get to talk to her."

—:—

Alex peeked her head in Peyton's door. "Safe to come back in?"

"God, yes. I'm starving."

"Good. I was afraid Mad might've ruined your appetite."

"Not a chance." Peyton looked behind Alex. "Where are my boys?"

"Right here." Finn walked under Alex's arm and over to the bed. Jamison followed and sat on the other side of her.

"When will the baby come out of your tummy?" Finn rested his hand on her stomach.

"Sometime in December. Maybe she'll be a Christmas baby."

"Really? That would kind of suck."

"Why, Jamie?"

"Cuz then she'd only get presents once a year."

"But she'd get twice as many presents, right, Mom?"

Peyton pulled Finn closer to her. "That's right. We'll make sure she never forgets how special she is to us."

"We could give her presents every day."

"That's stupid," Jamison said to his brother.

Alex held her hand out to him.

"What?"

"Stupid. That's a bad word. Hand back some of that money, cowboy."

"Stupid isn't a bad word. Right, Mom?"

"If Alex says it is, it is. Pay up, buddy." Peyton looked over at Alex. "See what a good mom you're going to be?"

Peyton didn't like the look that flashed across Alex's face. She'd try to remember to ask her about it once her parents took the boys home.

—:—

"Do you still talk to Alex?" Brodie asked Maddox.

"Yeah, why wouldn't I?"

"Think she'd talk to me?"

"No."

"Why not?"

"She's not who you should be talking to."

"Peyton won't talk to me."

"She will. When you're sure you're ready. I've told you this."

"I'm ready."

"No. You're not."

"How do you know?"

"I'll know when you're ready."

"You're so full of shit."

"That'll cost you another day."

"Asshole."

"That's two more."

"Why don't you make it easier on me, Mad. Just tell me where you think I went wrong."

"Nah, Brode. You gotta figure it out for yourself."

"Okay if I think out loud?"

"Do whatever you want. I can leave."

"I'm not this guy, Maddox. I've never had a woman have the upper hand with me."

"There's your first mistake."

"Letting her get the upper hand?"

"Thinking there is one."

"I hate what I did to her."

Maddox got up and walked out of Brodie's hospital room.

Brodie had no idea what Maddox was trying to get him to see. He hated what he'd done. He was being honest, and he wanted Peyton to know how sorry he was. He'd never before been so profoundly ashamed of himself.

There were probably women he'd been involved with who'd wanted more from him than he was ready to give, but he was honest about his feelings. How would he have felt if a woman had tried to trick him into a relationship he didn't want? He wouldn't have liked it. He would've been angry, as much at himself as the woman.

These were all the reasons why he regretted what he'd done. Peyton had every reason to be angry with him, even to hate him.

—:—

Peyton shifted in the small hospital bed, and knocked over the pitcher of water on the bed tray. The icy cold water hit her legs, and she shrieked.

"Here." Maddox came out of the bathroom holding a bunch of towels. He tossed two at her while he stopped the flow of cold water dripping onto her from the edge of the tray.

"Maddox? What are you doing here?" she asked once they had the watery mess cleaned up.

"I came down to talk, but you were asleep, so I've been sitting here, watching you." He smiled, but was obviously embarrassed.

"Alex calls Naughton the dark and broody Scottish guy."

"Yeah? Does she call me the creeper?"

"She hasn't, but after I tell her this story, she'll probably start."

Maddox laughed. "I like you, Peyton. Not very many people can hold their own against Alex Avila, but I bet you give her just as much shit as she gives you."

"We've been friends a long time."

"She's not one for spending time with people she doesn't like."

"I'd ask you about your relationship with her, but I doubt that's why you were watching me sleep."

"No, that wasn't the reason."

"What can I do for you?"

"They moved Brodie out of the ICU, and into a regular room late yesterday afternoon. It looks like they're going to be able to save his toes."

"Frostbite?"

"Yeah. Listen, I promised myself I wouldn't do this, but here I am anyway."

"You sure you want to make a pregnant woman angry again?"

"The thing I said a couple of days ago, about Brodie regretting what had happened between you two. That's the part that bothers you, isn't it?"

"How would you feel if I told you Alex regretted her time with you, Maddox? Come on, this is pretty obvious stuff here."

"What if she didn't regret our time together? What if she regretted how she handled something? That would be different."

"Of course it would be. However, if Brodie regrets how he handled leaving, that wouldn't be different at all. At least not how I'd feel about it."

"I have other questions. If you don't want to answer them, you don't have to."

"That's a given, Maddox. I am completely capable of telling you something isn't any of your business, or saying no. That shouldn't surprise you."

"Is there any way you can forgive him?"

"Brodie?"

"Not Brodie."

"Kade?"

"No. Lang."

"That's the last question I expected you to ask me. And I'm not sure. I guess it depends on what for." She forgave Lang a long time ago for leaving her. When she said she blamed herself as much as she blamed him for things not working out between them, she meant it. If she had listened to her instincts, she never would've married him to begin with. She doubted she'd ever forgive him for walking out on his sons. Even she wouldn't have predicted he'd be able to do that.

"Why do you ask, Maddox?"

"I wanted to watch your expression while you thought about it."

"What did you learn?"

"Nothing."

"I'm not following you. If I were having this conversation with anyone else, I'd tell them to stop with the games, but you're not playing games, are you?"

"No, Peyton. No games."

When the nurse came in to see if Peyton needed anything, she asked for more ice water. When she came back with the ice water, she asked for a wheelchair.

"Where to?" Maddox asked when the nurse left the wheelchair near the door to her room.

"You don't have to push me. I can get around pretty good on my own."

"Yes, Peyton, I'm aware of that. Where to?"

"You're so much like your brother."

"Thank you."

"Aren't you going to ask which one?"

"Nah. I like all of them."

"You're sweet."

"Shh. Don't let *that* get out."

"I want to go look at the babies, Maddox. What if that gets out?"

"Damn, even worse."

Maddox pushed her over to the nursery window, and grabbed a chair out of one of the nearby rooms.

"Do they let you hold them?"

"No. I think they look for volunteers in the NICU, but you have to go through a bunch of training to hold the preemies."

"I'm lost, but before you offer to explain, I'm good not knowing. No was an adequate enough answer for me."

"What's going on, Maddox?"

"You're not that far apart."

"What does that mean?"

"You and Brodie. I think if you'd just talk, you could work it out."

"Are you trying to get me to go talk to him?"

"No. He's not ready."

"Then why did he call me incessantly?"

"He thinks he's ready, but I told him he isn't."

"I'm getting tired of asking you questions, Maddox. Do you want to explain, or are you going to continue being evasive?"

"Brodie hasn't pulled his head out of his ass yet, but he's close. I promised him that I'd get you to listen to him when I think he's ready."

"Quite a promise to keep given you're not the decision-maker."

"I'll make you a promise too, Peyton. If he figures it out, you'll want to talk to him. If he doesn't, I won't be knocking on your door asking you to."

"That's fair."

"The nurse told me you were down the hall, looking at the babies with a guy that looked like a lumberjack. Had to see it with my own eyes. Is that really Maddox Butler checking out babies?"

"Hi, Alex." Maddox stood and offered her his chair, but she waved him off and leaned down to kiss Peyton's cheek instead.

"How's our girl today?"

"Me, or the baby?"

"Both."

"Better now that you've delivered whatever food is waiting back in the room."

"I didn't bring food today."

"You're a liar. I can smell it."

"No, you can't."

"Pregnancy superpower. You can smell deep dish pizza from miles away."

"Damn. That is a superpower."

Peyton watched as a funny look flashed across Alex's face. The same one as the other night.

"Time to go check on my baby brother. Alex, can you get Peyton back to the room okay?" Before she had a chance to answer, he held up his hands. "I was just being polite. I know you can get her back to the room okay."

He knelt down and kissed Peyton's forehead. "I'll see you later, sister." Maddox walked down the hall and turned near the bank of elevators.

"What's with the two of you?"

"It's weird right now."

"Does it have anything to do with the freaky expressions I see move across your face sometimes?"

"Like when?"

"Like just now, with the aroma superpower."

"Ready?" Alex released the lock on the wheelchair and pushed Peyton toward her room.

"Alex?"

"Yes?"

"Is there anything I can do?"

"Not yet."

—:—

"I'm goin' home," Maddox told Brodie.

"I thought you'd already left."

"No, I went for a walk. Ma said she and Da will be here later tonight. She'll sing you a lullaby or somethin'. I think Skye is coming too."

"Maddox?"

"Yeah, Brodie."

"I can't figure it out."

"You will."

"You're talking to her, aren't you?"

"Yeah, I am."

18

"Bet it's going to feel good to sleep in your own bed."

"It is, although this isn't my own bed, Mom."

Peyton's mom fluffed her pillows and opened the bedroom window. "It used to be."

"Actually, it didn't. This was my bedroom, but this is a new bed."

When her mom straightened the books on the nightstand for the second time, Peyton put her hand on her mother's arm.

"What's wrong?"

"Oh, Peyton." Her mom sat down on the bed and put her face in her hands.

"Are you crying?" Peyton tried to pull her mother's hands away from her face, but her mom wouldn't budge. "You're scaring me."

"I'm sorry, sweetheart." She stood and wiped her tears away. "Let me go get your father."

"Didn't you hear the doctor say I'm supposed to avoid stress?" Peyton shouted at her mother, who was already partway down the stairs.

She didn't feel any better when her father walked in a few minutes later. He held an envelope in his hand, and his face was ashen.

"Dad, what is it? You're scaring me now too."

"I'm sorry, Peyton. There's no easy way to tell you this."

"Just tell me, Dad."

"Lang has filed a petition for joint custody."

"Over my dead body."

"That's what we're afraid of."

"This is ridiculous. He wouldn't know the boys if he saw them."

"He has seen them."

Peyton flew out of the bed, but her father grabbed her arm and made her sit back down.

"When?"

"He's been going to their basketball games."

"Oh my God. What have the boys said? Has he approached them?"

"Not yet, or at least not that anyone saw. I'm so sorry, Peyton."

"They know better than to talk to strangers, and that's what he is to them."

"He's also their father, Peyton."

"No, Dad. He isn't. He's their sperm donor. He doesn't know anything about those boys. He hasn't seen either one of them in seven years. Seven years, Dad. Two or three basketball games don't make up for seven years."

"I know, honey. But they're granting him a hearing."

"When?"

"In two weeks. I'll call Stan."

Stan was their family attorney. He'd handled her divorce from Lang, and the subsequent hearings when Lang got behind with child support payments. Stan would understand that Lang had no business asking for visitation, let alone joint custody. If she wasn't so scared that something would go terribly wrong, and he'd somehow manage to get the judge to side with him, she'd laugh this off as being as ridiculous as it really was. What judge in his or her right mind would give a man who had abandoned his children joint custody?

Alex answered on the third ring. "What's up girlfriend? You bored out of your mind yet?"

"Alex, Lang wants custody of the boys."

"I'll be right there."

"But—" Too late, Alex had already disconnected the call.

Peyton lay back down on the bed and looked at the ceiling. If Kade were alive, he'd know exactly what to do. Her parents were wonderful, but they'd encourage

Peyton to handle this the "right way." They'd tell her to let the courts do their job, and surely everything would go the way it was supposed to. Unfortunately, Peyton knew of too many horror stories where a parent's rights were respected more than the child's. If they were to get a judge sympathetic to Lang, who he managed to convince that he'd made a mistake, and wanted a second chance, he may be given it.

The back door slammed, and Peyton heard Alex take the stairs two at a time.

"No f'in way this is happening. Over my dead body, Peyton."

"I said the same thing to my dad. He's talking to Stan now, I think. How did you get here so fast?"

"I was with Maddox."

"Oh. Is that on again?"

"Not exactly. It's complicated. By the way, Brodie is coming home today."

"That's nice."

"Yeah, that's what I figured you'd say. Maddox won't tell me what the two of you cooked up. He just tells me to stay out of it, and it'll work itself out."

"Stop right there. I don't have anything cooked up with Maddox Butler. He has some twisted idea that Brodie is going to have an epiphany in which he sees the error of his ways, and for some reason, when that happens, I'll forgive him."

"Would you?"

"It isn't about me forgiving him, Alex. He left me. Even if he tells me he's sorry, what difference would that make? He left. It's something he can apologize for, but he can't change what made him leave in the first place."

"Maybe he was scared."

"You wanna know what really happened, Alex? We had sex, and when we were done having sex, Brodie apologized for it. He regretted having sex with me. He regretted it so much, he left the country. He didn't come out and say it, but the part he probably regretted the most was having *unprotected* sex with me. And sure enough, his worst fear is coming true. That sex he regretted so much, resulted in a pregnancy. Do you think there's a chance in the world that I would accept that he didn't regret it the way he told me and Maddox that he did. Because...why? Because I am pregnant? Or maybe he'll look at me and decide he has to do the *right* thing. God, it makes me sick to think about it."

"I didn't know."

"No, you didn't. Do you have any idea how ashamed I am to know a man found me that distasteful? Could you really expect me to admit what happened between us?"

"No, Peyton. I'm so sorry."

"Now that you know the whole story, you can understand, I'm sure, how it would be impossible for me to ever talk to Brodie Butler again, let alone *forgive* him. What the hell is there to forgive him for?"

When Peyton began to cry, Alex reached to hug her.

"Don't. Don't touch me, Alex. Don't pity me. Don't feel sorry for me."

"I don't pity you, Peyton. I'm sorry you've gone through this alone. That's all. I wish I would've known sooner."

Peyton rested her head on Alex's shoulder. "I know, and I'm sorry. I have far worse things to worry about than Brodie Butler. Right now the evil bastard I have to figure out what to do about is Lang Becker."

—:—

"I hate you," Brodie spat at Maddox.

"Right back at ya, brother."

"Broderick Laird Butler! You dinnae speak to your brother that way."

"Fucker," he mumbled under his breath.

"I'd watch it if I were you, Brodie."

"You're not me, Maddox, and I'm sick of this game you're playing."

"No games, brother. What you did to Peyton is all on you."

"Maddox?"

"Stay out of this, Ma. I don't mean any disrespect to you or Da, but Brodie has to figure out his relationship with Peyton all on his own, with *no interference* from anyone. Do you understand me?"

Brodie couldn't believe his eyes. His mother, the one capable of actually breathing hellfire and brimstone, curled her shoulders forward and walked away from Maddox in defeat. She actually nodded her head and walked away.

"Maybe they shouldn't have released me from the hospital."

"Why not?"

"Because I think I'm losing my mind."

"I'm sorry, Brodie, but what you don't seem to understand is that while you were in Argentina, Peyton's life went on."

"I do understand, Mad. And I swear to God, if anyone would let me have the keys to *my* automobiles, I'd be in Cambria, on her doorstep, faster than those wheels would take me. She's blocked my calls. She'll talk to you, but she won't talk to me. What am I supposed to do?"

He'd never felt so powerless in his life, and his brother refused to help him. Not just Mad, Naught would barely talk to him. Skye came to see him, but when he asked her about Peyton, Skye asked who she was. Ainsley called a couple of times, but she didn't know anything about Peyton either.

Now that he was home, there was a chance he'd be able to convince one of his friends to take him to see her, since his family refused.

He sat down and put his head in his hands. This was as close as he came to crying in front of someone since he'd been rescued. He did plenty of it when he was alone.

Brodie stormed out the door of his parents' house, went out into the field, and screamed at the top of his lungs. He screamed, and screamed, and screamed, until he fell to his knees, and sobbed.

When he felt a soft hand on his back, he was certain it was his mother. He kept his face buried in his hands.

"Brodie? What's going on?" He recognized the voice, and it wasn't his mother's.

"Leave me alone, Alex."

Instead, she sat down next to him and crossed her legs.

"Seriously. Please, leave me alone."

"You really screwed things up, Brodie."

"I know I did. *Jesus.* If I knew how to fix it, I would. And all of you telling me that as soon as I figure it out, you'll let me talk to Peyton, is bullshit. I can't figure out whatever the hell it is I'm supposed to figure out, Alex. I can't."

He put his face back in his hands and cried. He couldn't give a shit who saw him now.

"I'm not part of this, Brodie. Look at me."

She didn't speak again until he looked at her.

"I don't know what's going on with your brother. My guess is he's trying to keep you from making things worse. I know that's hard to understand, but I honestly don't think he's trying to stop you from talking to Peyton."

"Why won't she talk to me?"

"It's complicated, Brodie, and I'm not sure I can explain it to you."

"How about this? Why don't you or Maddox or Naughton just say, 'she hates you, Brodie'? Or 'she never wants to see you again, Brodie'? Instead, you say it's complicated, or 'as soon as you figure out what you did wrong, we'll let you talk to her.'"

"That isn't what I'm saying."

"You just did. You said it was complicated. Even my own ma walked away when Maddox told her to stay out of it. I feel like I've entered an alternate universe. Am I in hell, Alex? Is this what hell is? Did I die, and instead of being at home, like I think I am, I'm really in hell?"

Brodie followed Alex's line of sight. Maddox was standing near the barn, watching them. He had his arms folded in front of his chest and a scowl on his face.

"If this is hell, he must be Satan, because he's made it his personal mission to torture me. Do you know he talks to her? Can you believe that? He talks to her, but he won't let me talk to her."

"He can't stop you, Brodie."

"How can I talk to her, Alex? I've been in the hospital. I've called her a thousand times, and she won't take my calls. I've left her messages. I've tried to explain what happened that night, and nothing. No response. I bled over the phone, Alex. I admitted the absolute worst thing I've ever done in my life, and nothing. *Nothing!*"

"Tell me, Brodie."

"I can't. Don't ask me to do that, Alex. First I tell Peyton, and she doesn't say anything. Nothing. Then Maddox forces me to tell him. And the result? *Nothing.* Again, nothing. Wouldn't you think that if you admitted the absolute worst thing you've ever done in your whole life, someone would say *something?*"

"I think you should tell me, Brodie. I'll say something. I might even be able to help you."

"Stay out of this, Alex."

Neither he nor Alex had noticed Maddox walk over.

"You stay out of it, Maddox. Leave me alone, and stay the hell away from Peyton. You can scowl all you want. I'm a Butler too, and I know how to scowl right back at you."

"Maddox, I'm trying to help."

"Alex." Maddox looked down at her.

"This is ridiculous. I know how Peyton feels, because she told me. Brodie is obviously tortured by this. Why does it have to be this difficult?"

"He's going to make it worse."

"See, Brodie? I told you that your brother was trying to protect you, not keep you from Peyton. Right, Mad?"

"It's true, Brodie. I don't want to see things get so bad, they're irreparable."

"Go away, Maddox. Let Brodie talk to me."

Mad huffed and shook his head, but he did as Alex asked. Alex grabbed Brodie's hand. "Come with me."

"Where are we going?"

"For a ride."

"I can't tell you how much I appreciate this, Alex." They were sitting on a bench near the boardwalk on Moonstone Beach. "Just getting away, feeling the ocean air on my face, I feel like a different person."

"Brodie, tell me what happened that night at Stave."

"Alex, please."

"Brodie, I asked you before to look at me. I'm going to ask you to do that again."

He turned his body so they were face-to-face.

"She needs you. There's a lot of shit happening in her life right now, and she needs you to help her through it. In order for you to be able to do that, I have to know what happened that night."

"Okay, I'll tell you, but if you do to me what Mad's been doing, I swear I'm going to lose my mind."

"I won't, Brodie. I'll be completely honest with you."

Alex was leaning forward, with her head in her hands.

"You told me you were going to be honest with me."

"Did you tell Maddox everything you told me?"

"Yes. Jesus, Alex. Don't do this to me."

"I get it. Now I'm going to tell you how Peyton sees it."

19

Brodie walked into his parents' house feeling more like himself than he had since before he left for Argentina.

"We need to talk," he said to his parents. "All of us. I'm going to find Maddox and Naughton and ask them to come up to the house. Okay?"

"You get Maddox, and I'll find Naughton," his father offered.

"I'm already here." Maddox walked out of the kitchen.

"And, Ma, can you, please, start acting like yourself again? It's almost like I don't know who you are anymore."

"Brodie, I—"

"Let her be, son."

Brodie shook his head. He planned to get to the bottom of all this craziness today, with his parents, and with Peyton.

When his father came back to the house with Naughton, Brodie asked everyone to sit at the kitchen table. He stood.

"To begin, things between Peyton and I are not resolved. I haven't spoken with her, but I intend to, very soon. There is something happening that she needs our help with. You may tell me that you don't think this is any of our business, but as Kade's brother, I've made it our business."

"Go on, son." Laird raised his hand when Maddox began to say something. "Let him finish."

"I spent a couple of hours with Alex Avila, and she told me Peyton's ex-husband filed a petition asking for joint custody of her boys."

His mother gasped, and both his brothers stood and paced the kitchen.

"Go on," his father repeated.

"Her father asked their lawyer to fight it, but I want to ask that we support her in any way we can."

"Of course we will." His mother spoke, and for the first time since he came back from Argentina, he saw the fire return to her eyes.

"I'll know more later in terms of what she's facing, but for now, I just want to make you aware of it. Also, I understand that Lang has been going to the boys' basketball games. I'd like to start going myself." He looked at his two brothers, who nodded in agreement.

"Finally, I'm going to see Peyton as soon as we're finished. She and I have a lot to talk about. I've been made aware of an issue with her health, and my guess is that is why Lang was able to blindside her with this custody petition."

"Brodie—"

"Ma, Alex wouldn't elaborate. She said Peyton needed to tell me herself."

Brodie looked from Maddox to Naughton, neither spoke.

"Mad, am I ready?"

"Yes, you are."

"Alex told me you mean well, and for now, I'm going to take her at her word."

"Good."

"Can I have my keys, please?"

His father walked over to the drawer in the kitchen. "They've been in here all along. Well, since your brothers went to the airport in Los Angeles and brought your car home."

In the weeks between the plane crash and today, his body had been ravaged to the point of near death. Whatever health problems Peyton faced, he'd help her. He knew what it was like to fight to stay alive, to keep his body from succumbing to overwhelming odds against him. The advice Kade had given him in his dreams kept him going.

"Get up, get moving," Brodie had dreamed Kade told him. "Keep hydrated. Keep warm." The dreams he'd had of Peyton gave him the will to listen to the ones he had of Kade.

Whatever was wrong with Peyton must be bad, maybe even life-threatening. He couldn't imagine any other circumstance in which she'd stop working entirely, or allow Alex to close Stave even temporarily. He couldn't fathom her missing her boys' sports events, and have no knowledge Lang had been there instead.

Brodie pulled up near the Wolfs' house, turned off the truck, and took several deep breaths. Here he was, in the place he'd wanted to be for so long. This was it—either she'd forgive him and let him be in her life, or she wouldn't.

Alex had told him to remember two very important things when he talked to Peyton. Apologize last, after he told his story, and refrain from saying he regretted anything.

Peyton never struck him as being an insecure person. She couldn't possibly think he regretted having sex with her? It wasn't the sex he regretted. It was the under-handed way he went about seducing her into it.

"I get that, Brodie," Alex had said to him. "But tell it the way it happened."

When Brodie opened the truck door, he saw Peyton's parents sitting on the front porch of their house. They reminded him of his parents. Before he climbed the steps to where they sat, Peyton's father approached him.

"Welcome home, son," he said.

When Brodie held out his hand, Jamison Wolf pulled him into a hug instead. "We prayed for you every day."

"Thank you, sir." Brodie's eyes filled with tears. "Sorry. Emotional these days."

"Don't apologize," Peyton's mom said, hugging him the same way her husband had.

"I guess you know I'm here to see Peyton."

"She's upstairs, Brodie. Has anyone...uh...prepared you?"

"Yes and no, Mrs. Wolf. Alex explained she's had some issues with her health."

"Let me show you where she is." Peyton's father led Brodie inside. "First door on the left when you get to the top of the stairs."

"Do you want to let her know I'm here?"

"It's better this way. Just...try not to upset her too much."

"I don't want to upset her at all."

"Good luck."

Peyton was asleep when Brodie walked into her room. He didn't expect the deep, dark circles under her eyes, or for her to be as pale as she was.

There was a chair by the window, which Brodie pulled closer to her bed. She opened her eyes and blinked.

"You're not dreaming, sweetheart."

"Brodie." She sat up and clutched the pillow in front of her. "What are you doing here?"

"I came to talk to you, Peyton. How are you?"

"I'm okay." She shifted and held the pillow closer.

"Alex told me you've had some health issues."

"Is that what she said?" Peyton smirked and looked away from him.

"I'm not here because you're ill."

"You shouldn't be here at all."

Brodie closed his eyes, focusing on all the things Alex told him not to say.

"Peyton, the last time I saw you—"

"I don't want to hear this, Brodie."

He leaned closer and tried to hold her hand, but she yanked it away.

"I need to tell you, Peyton. It's important that you know what happened that night."

He took another deep breath. "I was traveling on winery business in San Francisco, and drove back to

Cambria. I stopped by your house, and Sam told me you weren't home. I went to Stave and saw your car, but you weren't there."

Brodie heard Alex's voice in his head. *"Do not say you're sorry until you've told her everything."*

"Before I left for up north, you told me that I wasn't Kade, and I never would be."

Peyton nodded, but still wouldn't look at him.

"I waited. I didn't know where you were, but something told me to wait." Brodie looked up. "Or someone."

He cleared his throat and said a silent prayer that he wouldn't cry when he told her what he'd done. He wouldn't ask her forgiveness. He'd tell her, and then she could decide what was next for them.

"I didn't say much when you invited me inside. God, Peyton, this is so hard. When I made love to you that night, I didn't use a condom."

He didn't look at her. He couldn't. He had to keep talking, or he'd never tell her the truth.

"I did it on purpose, Peyton. I made love to you without a condom because I wanted to tie you to me, forever, whether you wanted me or not. It was the only way my deranged brain could think of."

She was crying, but he couldn't stop now. This was his one shot to tell her everything, and no matter how hard it was to continue, he had to be man enough to admit what he'd done.

"I didn't ask if it was okay. I didn't ask if you were on birth control, because I didn't want you to stop me. I've never had sex with anyone without a condom. Never.

"After, when you looked into my eyes and begged me not to say I was sorry, God, Peyton. I've never felt like such an asshole. I took your choice away. I forced myself on you, into you. And the first thing you said to me was for me not to be sorry."

Peyton turned her body away from him, sobbing into the pillow she held so tightly against her.

"When I heard you sobbing that night, like you are now, my heart broke over what I'd done. I was filled with shame, not because I was with you, but because of what I had done to you. I knew what I was doing, and I did it anyway."

There was more. He had to finish, and when he did, he'd walk away. It was clear to him now that she'd never forgive him, and why should she? He was a lying, conniving bastard.

"I drove as fast and as far from you as I could. When I got to the airport in Los Angeles, I got on the next international flight available. That's how I ended up in Argentina."

Brodie cleared his throat and wiped away the tears he couldn't stop from falling. "I fled, knowing I couldn't stay away from you. I couldn't. I was too weak. And Peyton, I couldn't apologize either, because if I had the chance to go back and undo it, I wouldn't. What kind of man does that make me? I tricked you and manipulated you. I was ready to beg you to let me be a substitute for the man you truly loved. I knowingly tried to force you to have my child."

It was a long time before Peyton turned her body toward him. She wasn't crying as hard, but tears still rolled down her cheeks. He looked into her eyes. "I'm sorry, Peyton, but not for making love to you. The only part I'm sorry for is trying to manipulate you into spending your life with me."

"Brodie..."

He loved hearing his name on her lips, but there was more he had to tell her.

"I came very close to dying after the plane crash. I dreamed about you, and about Kade. I dreamed he was telling me how to stay alive, but you were the only reason I wanted to. I slipped in and out of consciousness, and if the search party hadn't arrived when it had, I'm not sure I would be here."

Brodie moved closer and rested his hand beside her, hoping she'd reach out to him, but she didn't.

"There's more, but it isn't important, Peyton. The only thing that is important is that you know this—I love you. It may seem crazy, that we haven't known each other that long, but I love you, and nothing can change that. I love you so much that I fought to stay alive so I could come back and tell you how much. More than anything I want to spend my life with you. I want to be a father to your boys, and I want to make more babies with you. I want you to choose to be with me, not because I forced you, but because you want to. I want you to be with me because you love me, Peyton."

Brodie rested his head on the bed, next to where she lay. Telling her everything that had weighed so heavy on his soul had taken every ounce of energy in his body. His fatigue was the same as it had been when he was rescued and the helicopter flew him away from the plane's wreckage. He was about to push his chair back and stand, when he felt Peyton's fingers run through his hair. He couldn't move, even to breathe, for fear she'd stop. His body craved her touch, and the loss of it so soon after he'd felt it, would devastate him. The place where he rested his head was damp with his tears, but he wasn't ashamed of them. Crying meant he was alive.

He thought back to the day he met Peyton. The cold wind from the ocean had stung his face with sand, and he remembered being grateful to be alive that day too.

"Brodie," she whispered. "Please look at me."

He raised his head, knowing what she was going to say. He'd prepared himself. It wasn't unexpected. He just hadn't expected the depth of hurt that pulsed through his body, anticipating, *knowing*, she was going to ask him to leave. His gratitude for being alive dissipated. Without Peyton in his life, he'd rather he'd died in the crash.

Peyton rested one hand on his while she shifted the pillow away from her body with the other. She tossed it to the floor and moved the blankets that covered her body away. She reached down and raised the oversized T-shirt she was wearing, took his hand, and brought it to her bare abdomen.

"She's fought to stay alive too, Brodie."

20

Peyton studied Brodie's face, waiting for the moment he realized what she was telling him. His eyes, already red from tears, filled again as they looked from her face to her belly, and back again.

"Peyton…I…"

She shifted on the bed and pulled him toward her. "Hold me, Brodie. Hold us." She leaned forward so he could put his arm around her, and nestled close to him. He splayed his fingers on the place their daughter grew inside her, and Peyton felt his warmth spread throughout her body.

"I'll never be cold when I sleep with you, Brodie. You keep me warm."

He cried again then, his head resting against hers. "I don't know what to say."

"There isn't anything more to say."

—:—

Brodie heard the bedroom door creak, and opened his eyes. Alex peeked inside, smiled, and closed the door behind her. He wasn't sure how long he and Peyton had been asleep, maybe a few minutes, maybe an hour.

The fatigue he'd felt earlier was gone. The hurt that had pulsed through his body was replaced by an energy so powerful, he worried he'd scald the woman sleeping in his arms. *His woman.* The woman carrying his baby. From his most shameful act, came the most precious love he'd ever known.

"I love you, Peyton," he whispered before he let his heavy eyelids close again.

"Mom?"

Brodie woke at the same time Peyton did, and saw her two boys standing in the doorway. He motioned for them to come closer. When they came over, taking turns hugging him, he prayed he wasn't dreaming. The scene that surrounded him was almost too good to be true. He looked at Peyton, feeling the love he saw in her eyes.

"Did you tell him about our baby sister, Mom?" Finn asked.

"I did," she laughed.

"Did he think of a name yet?"

Brodie laughed too. "Not yet, buddy."

Finn was wearing shorts and pointed to his leg. "Look, you can hardly see my scar anymore."

"Wow, that's amazing. I hope my scars heal as well as yours did."

Brodie's eyes met Jamison's, who hadn't said anything since he came into the room. "Come back over here, buddy." Brodie pulled him close so the boy's head rested against his chest. The same dampness he'd felt earlier from his own tears spread on his shirt.

Peyton rested her hand on her son's head. "It's okay, Jamie. Everything is going to be okay."

"Don't leave again," Jamison said against Brodie's chest.

"I'm not going anywhere. I promise."

The bedroom door flew open, and Alex spilled into the room. "Told ya," she jabbed Maddox, who followed her.

"Yes, you did." He smiled.

"Someday you'll learn."

"What will I learn, Alex?"

"That I'm always right."

Maddox looked at Brodie and Peyton. "What I'll really learn is to tell her she's always right, whether she is or isn't."

"This room is getting crowded," Peyton's dad said, shifting so her mother was standing in front of him. "How about we take this party downstairs?"

Peyton tightened her grip on Brodie's arm. "We'll follow in a minute, okay?"

"Of course. Come on, everybody." Her father herded everyone out of the room and closed the door behind him.

"I almost lost the baby a couple of times, Brodie, so the doctor recommended bed rest. That's why I'm staying here with my parents. They've been a huge help with the boys, so has Alex."

"Whatever we need to do, Peyton, I'm with you every step of the way."

"I'd like to go home."

"We can make that happen."

"But—"

"When I say every step of the way, I mean *everything*. Whatever you need or want, I'll take care of."

"Let's go downstairs. We can talk about all of this later. You may want to take some time to think about it before you jump into this with both feet."

"How long did you think about jumping in when you realized you were pregnant?"

"If you mean how long did I think about keeping the baby, I didn't think about it at all. There was never any question that I would."

"Same for me, sweetheart. No questions, no doubts, no nothing. I love you, Peyton. There are things we need to talk about. We went from no communication at all, to me taking you home. There's a lot in between we didn't say."

"You mean there's a lot I didn't say."

"By your actions alone, I'm assuming you want me in your life. For now, I'll take whatever you're willing to give."

"I'm not ready to say the words you want me to say."

"I'm not pushing, sweetheart, but there is something I need to know."

"What's that?"

"Have you forgiven me?"

Peyton breathed deeply and looked into Brodie's eyes. "Forgiven you? No. I knew what we were doing that night, too. You didn't trick me or manipulate me. I wasn't intentionally trying to get pregnant, but I didn't stop you from making love to me without protection. So what's to forgive? I misunderstood your reaction that night. I hated thinking you regretted what we'd done. I hated you for leaving me too, but that wasn't what you were doing."

"It wasn't. It's so cliché, but it wasn't you, it was me."

"I understand that now. It might be more difficult to leave it behind us and move on with our lives, but there are two things...more really, that I've learned in the last few months. Life is short, and those you love can be taken from you in an instant. I lost Kade, and then I thought I lost you. When I believed I'd lost our baby, I was devastated. I don't want to waste any more precious time, Brodie."

Brodie lowered his head and covered her mouth with his. He dreamed so often of kissing her. Just having her in his arms felt like some kind of miracle, but the intimacy of sharing a kiss, one filled with passion, and even love, was more than he'd ever expected. If they didn't stop now, he wouldn't be able to walk down the stairs without embarrassing himself and everyone else. He pulled away, but held her close.

"We should go downstairs," Peyton sighed.

"Should I carry you?"

She laughed. "As I told Alex, I'm pregnant, not paralyzed. I can walk. I just need to stay off my feet as much as possible."

—:—

"There they are." Peyton's father stood and motioned for them to sit on the sofa. "As you can see, the party has grown somewhat."

Between the time her boys woke them and now, Brodie's mother, father, and Naughton had arrived.

"Our daughter Skye is on the way with her family too, but if it gets to be too much, Peyton, just let us know, and we'll go back to the ranch," Laird told her.

"She's pregnant too," Brodie whispered to Peyton. "They're having a boy." He rubbed his chest, near his heart. "And we're having a girl."

Peyton rested her head against his shoulder and put her arm around Brodie's waist.

"I've prayed for this, lass," Sorcha said through her tears. "I knew my Kade would bring you two back together."

"Ma—"

"It's okay, Brodie," Peyton stopped him. "I believe there's some truth to what she's saying."

"I do too, actually. I'm just not sure how much you like to talk about him."

There was a knock at the door. "I'll get it," Maddox offered.

"It's probably my mom. I'll get it." Both Alex and Maddox walked toward the door. Peyton saw the look that passed between them, and noticed they stood close enough to each other that their arms touched. Soon she'd corner Alex and force her to tell her what was going on between her and Brodie's brother.

"We didn't expect to see you, little sister." Maddox wrapped someone Peyton didn't recognize in a hug.

Brodie jumped off the sofa, hurrying to the entryway. He held the woman who was crying, tight in his arms.

"That's Ainsley, lass," Sorcha told Peyton. "Have you met my youngest?"

"I haven't. She's beautiful."

The woman walking toward her, with her arm wrapped around Brodie's waist, was stunning. She was tall and thin, like Peyton was, with the same fiery red hair as Sorcha's. It was wavy and long, reaching all the way down to the curve of her back. She had the same deep blue eyes as her siblings, and her face was covered in freckles. She wore a knee-length, deep emerald green dress with long-sleeves, over black tights, and funky patterned socks were peeking over her caramel-colored boots.

"I'm Ainsley." She leaned down and hugged Peyton. "About time we met," she laughed. "Ma's told me so much about you."

"It's nice to meet you, too."

Ainsley sat down on one side of Peyton, and Brodie sat on the other.

"Where's Skye?"

"On her way. I didn't know you were coming too. I've missed you kiddo."

Ainsley leaned into Peyton. "I'm twenty-seven years old, and he still calls me kiddo."

"You'll always be my baby sister, Ains. Doesn't matter if I'm seventy-five and you're seventy."

When they heard another knock, Peyton's father got up. "I'll get it, and we can leave it open. Who knows who else might show up today?"

Peyton's mother stood when she saw it was Lucia Avila.

"Welcome, dear friend." She leaned forward, and the two women hugged.

"Quite a gathering you have here today, August."

When Peyton shifted to stand, Brodie did instead. "Mrs. Avila, it's good to see you."

"And you, Brodie." Lucia smiled and leaned down to hug Peyton. "If I were thirty years younger, I'd hook one of these Butler boys myself."

"Mama!" Alex shook her finger.

"Now, now. I'm not, so Maddox is all yours." She winked.

Peyton couldn't have predicted she'd ever see Maddox Butler blush, but Alex's conversation with her mother had him turning almost red.

"Is this getting to be too much?" Brodie whispered to Peyton when he sunk back down on the couch.

"I'm okay, just a little tired."

He leaned in closer. "Let me know when you want to go back upstairs. Don't feel as though you need to stay down here if you don't want to."

"I want to go home, Brodie."

"Today?"

"If you don't mind. If you do, I can stay here a few more days."

"What's going on over there? August, didn't you tell your daughter it isn't polite to whisper?"

"She's a grown woman, as you are, Alex."

"We're talking about Brodie taking me home." Peyton looked over at her mother, to gauge her reaction.

She simply smiled.

"I think that's a wonderful idea, don't you boys?" When August addressed Jamison and Finn, they both stood.

"Should we pack up our stuff?"

"We're not leaving yet, but if Brodie doesn't mind, maybe we can get him to take us home after dinner." Peyton squeezed Brodie's hand.

"Whenever you're ready, sweetheart."

Brodie's sister Skye arrived less than half an hour later with the most beautiful little girl Peyton thought she'd ever seen.

"This is Spencer," Skye said. "Spencer, can you say hello to Miss Peyton?"

Spencer hid behind her mother's legs, but her blue eyes met Peyton's. Skye looked like a slightly older version of Ainsley, but her hair was a little lighter, not fiery red like Sorcha's and her little girl's. Peyton imagined Spencer looked a lot like her grandmother might've looked as a child.

"What are you thinking about?" Brodie caught her staring.

"What this one will look like. Will she look more like me or someone from your family?" Peyton rested her hands on her tummy.

"She'll be beautiful, with blonde hair and green eyes, just like her mama. That's my prediction."

"Seriously? I think you two should just leave now. You're so annoyingly happy," Alex scowled.

"Jealous much?" When Naughton nudged her, Maddox shot him a look both Peyton and Brodie caught.

"What is up with those two?" he whispered.

"I don't know, but I'm going to find out tomorrow," Peyton whispered back.

"When are you due?" Peyton asked Skye.

"Another month. You?"

"December."

"You're almost out of the first trimester, then. Have you been sick much?"

"Not as much as with my boys."

"You're glowing. I felt wonderful when I was pregnant with Spence, but this little guy is kicking my butt. I feel as though he's aged me twenty years."

"Nonsense. You're just as beautiful today as when I met you ten years ago. More beautiful, in fact," said a man with the same accent as Sorcha.

"Peyton," Skye smiled, "this is my husband, MacLayne Campbell. Mac, meet Peyton."

Mac shook her hand, but his eyes barely left his wife's.

Lang had been wretched when she was eight months along with both Jamison and Finn. He'd never failed to mention she looked "haggard." When he asked her how long she thought it would take her to lose weight after Finn was born, she wanted to slug him. To think a man who cared so little about his then wife, wanted custody of the two boys he'd abandoned when one was a toddler and the other a baby. Her blood boiled thinking about it.

Brodie's hand rested on the back of her neck, his fingers softly stroked her skin. "Everything okay?"

"Sorry, I was just comparing your brother-in-law's behavior with Lang's when I was pregnant."

"Something else we need to talk about, Peyton."

"So you know?"

"My parents and my brothers know too."

"I can't believe he would do this." She shook her head. "Can we change the subject?"

Skye leaned over and put her hand on Peyton's arm. "Is there a place you and I could speak privately?"

"She isn't supposed to be on her feet," Brodie answered.

Peyton smiled at him, but stood. "Of course, follow me. I need some fresh air anyway."

The two walked out the front door to the porch. Peyton closed the door behind her.

"Spencer was two weeks early," Skye began after they sat in two big wicker chairs. "I've wanted to discuss this with you, but I wasn't sure how to handle it."

"What did you want to discuss?"

"Mac and I want to name the baby Kade. We want to talk to my family about it, and since everyone is here, the timing would be good. However, I told Mac I needed to talk to you about it first."

"Skye, you and your husband do not need to discuss your child's name with me. You should name your son whatever you want to. But since you asked, I think it would be a wonderful tribute, not only to your brother, but to your whole family."

"Mac said you wouldn't mind, but I feel a lot better asking."

"I appreciate it."

"Should we go back in?" Skye asked after a few minutes of silence.

"I'd like to stay out here a little while longer, if you don't mind."

"Would you like to be alone?"

"No, there's something I'd like to talk to you about, too."

21

Alex sat on the couch, next to Brodie, and elbowed him. "How are you doing with all this?"

He ran his hand through his hair and blew the air out of his lungs. "I feel like I just ran a marathon, or survived a plane crash."

"Right?" She laughed. "So it never dawned on you she was pregnant?"

"Nope. It should've, but it sure as hell didn't." Brodie leaned in closer to her. "I don't know how to thank you."

"You may need to return the favor one day."

"What do you mean?"

"There may come a day you need to pull your brother's head out of his ass for me."

"Sure he's worth it?"

Alex's mood turned serious quickly. Instead of being playful, she seemed sad. "Yeah, Brode, I am."

Alex stood and went to sit next to her mother. Brodie tried to catch Mad's eye, but his brother looked lost in thought, and no happier than Alex.

"Join me, son?" Jamison Wolf motioned for Brodie to follow him into another room.

There would likely be many private conversations like these today, and in the days that followed.

"You're aware of Lang Becker's petition to the court," he began after closing the door behind Brodie.

"I am, sir."

"From what our lawyer has been able to find out, it appears that Lang is getting married again, and there is a child on the way."

Brodie kept his sarcastic thoughts to himself, but, jeez, who would marry and start a family with a man who had abandoned his first wife and kids? Probably someone after the Becker family's money, he'd guess. Lang Becker had no idea what he lost when he left Peyton, and Brodie intended to help her forget her ex-husband's existence. The first thing they had to do was get this petition thrown out, so she didn't have the stress of it hanging over her.

"My understanding is the new wife's family disapproves of his lack of a relationship with Jamison and Finn. I doubt Lang would've initiated this without their prodding."

"How well do you know his family?"

"The Beckers? Not well at all. We had the usual interaction with them when Peyton married Lang, and then again when each of the boys was born. Their own lack of interest was baffling. August and I have a difficult time understanding people who have no involvement in their grandchildren's lives."

"I was going to ask you about that."

"It's as though Jamison and Finn don't exist."

"Why does Lang think he has a prayer?"

"The judge who signed the petition is his future wife's uncle."

"Does Peyton know this?"

"No, and until we have a better idea of how to fight this, I would appreciate you not mentioning it."

Brodie didn't want to disrespect Peyton's father, but it didn't feel right to keep this from her, or to start their relationship with secrets. As hard as it was, he had to speak his mind. "I can't promise that, sir. I understand your reasons for asking me not to tell her, but Peyton needs to be able to trust me."

"I see." Peyton's father turned away to open the door, but Brodie thought he caught a quick smile on his face. Had he just passed a test?

"Sir?"

"Yes, Brodie?"

"Are we good?"

"Better than."

Yep, he'd just passed his first test. The next would be to figure out a way to tell Peyton what he knew, without wreaking havoc on her already taut nerves.

"Wait." Brodie paused while Jamison closed the door. "Can't we get this moved to another judge, claim bias or something?"

"That is exactly what Stan is working on now."

"Stan?"

"Our lawyer."

"I love her," Brodie blurted.

"That's obvious. I think you'll be very good for her, too. Peyton hadn't found anyone truly worthy of her until she met you, at least that's what her mother and I believe."

"Not even Kade?"

"You can form your own opinion on whether you believe he would've been good for her in the long run."

"Yes, sir, I can."

"Shall we go back and join the others?"

Brodie started to follow the man who he hoped would be his father-in-law one day soon, but then stopped. "Wait, Mr. Wolf, there's something else I'd like to discuss with you."

"Call me Jamison, and if it's our blessing you're looking for, you have it whole-heartedly."

"Thank you. I'll do everything I can to make her happy."

"I know you will." He smiled.

—:—

"To answer your question, Kade and I were never close. That may surprise you, given Mac and I want to name our son after him. Maybe that's even the reason I suggested it in the first place."

"I didn't really know anyone in your family until I met Brodie. Kade never gave me the impression he was close to any of you, at least not like I am to my parents."

When Skye's eyes teared up, Peyton thought maybe she'd gone too far. "I'm sorry if I've upset you."

"No, it isn't what you said. It's just that his behavior always bothered me. He was never around, and then when he would come home, he'd turn right around and leave again."

"He spent a lot of his time with me. It makes me sad to think I kept him from his family."

"But you didn't. If he wasn't with you, he would've been somewhere else. Before he met you, he wasn't around either. It isn't something you should feel sad about. Maddox is the only one who really got to know him. Kade spent more time with our brothers than he did with Ainsley and me, but I don't think Naught or Brodie would say they felt close to him either."

"Your family has been so accepting of me..."

"Why wouldn't we be?" Skye laughed. "I met you a couple of hours ago, and already feel as though I know you. You're very easy to accept, Peyton."

"Thanks, but—"

"Stop. I know you're worried about what we all think, but you shouldn't be."

"What's up, girls?" Ainsley came out the front door and sat down in one of the other wicker chairs.

"I'm assuring Peyton that no one in our family has any issue with her relationship with Brodie."

"Oh, God, no. Personally, I'm thrilled. The first of our brothers is getting married. I never thought I'd see the day! Wait, you are getting married, aren't you?"

Peyton laughed. "What time is it?"

"I don't know, around four maybe. Why?"

"Give us a couple of days. It hasn't been more than a couple of hours since he found out he's going to be a father."

"Oh, gotcha." Ainsley laughed.

"Where are all my girls?" Sorcha opened the front door and started to come out when Skye stopped her.

"We're coming inside now, Ma. Ready, Peyton?"

When Peyton stood, Sorcha walked over and rested her hand on Peyton's cheek. "You're one of my girls now too, lass."

"Thank you, Mrs. Butler."

"*Sorcha*, please. You have a choice. You can call me Sorcha or Ma, whichever you prefer."

"You'll call her Ma. Everyone does." Skye smiled.

Peyton felt the emotion of the day weighing on her, something Brodie picked up on when he met her near the front door.

"What would you like to do, sweetheart? Go upstairs and rest?"

"I'd rather go home, Brodie. Can we, please?"

"I'd prefer it too, Peyton, but I think we should talk about how this is going to work. I'll need to stay with you."

"I don't care what anyone thinks, Brodie. I've spent too much time worrying about it. I want to go home."

"You got it."

—:—

Brodie went upstairs with Peyton and found Alex already packing her stuff.

"I just need to grab what's in the bathroom, and you'll be set to go."

"Thanks, Alex. I'm so tired."

"I know you are. You'll feel much better, sleeping in your own bed. Plus, no stairs at your place. That'll be better too."

"Brodie, can you ask the boys—"

Alex held up her hand. "The boys have plans tonight."

"They do?"

"Yep. Slumber party with Uncle Maddox and Aunt Alex."

Peyton and Brodie both raised their eyebrows.

"We'll talk about that tomorrow. You need to get our girl home," Alex said to Brodie. "We'll bring the boys home tomorrow afternoon, and I'll call you in the morning."

Peyton nodded her head and sat down on the bed.

"I'll bring all this down. You get her in the car."

Rather than waiting for further direction, Brodie picked Peyton up and carried her down the stairs. When they got to the bottom, she wriggled.

"Put me down, Brodie. I'm heavy."

He ignored her and held her still.

"I need to get my girl home. We'll see all of you soon."

He didn't wait for anyone to answer. Instead, he walked out the front door. Moments later, Maddox followed with Peyton's things while Alex ran ahead to open the door of Brodie's truck.

"You're making too much of this," Peyton said, but when she rested her head on his shoulder, he knew he was right about how exhausted she was.

Alex closed the door after Brodie helped Peyton inside, and rested her arm on the bottom of the open window. "You're in good hands, or I wouldn't let you leave," she teased before her eyes filled with tears. "I'm so happy for you both."

"Thanks, Alex." Peyton leaned back and closed her eyes.

"Get her home, Brode." Alex backed away from the truck and into Maddox, who wrapped his arms around her waist. They both waved as Brodie drove away.

—:—

"What else can I get you?"

"Seriously, Brodie, nothing. I've already told you that ten times." Peyton patted the mattress. "Would you please just get in bed?"

When he rubbed the back of his neck with his hand, Peyton threw a pillow at him. "I'm done sleeping without you next to me, Brodie. *Get. In. Bed!*"

"Are you sure it's okay?"

"Yes I asked my parents before we left, and they're fine with it." She smirked.

"That isn't what I meant, smartass. What about the baby?"

"It's okay with her too."

"Peyton..."

"If you don't get in bed by the time I count to three, I'll get out and make you."

"Okay, but if you're at all uncomfortable, just say so, and I'll sleep on the couch." He toed off his boots and lay next to her.

"What are you doing?"

"Getting in bed. Isn't that what you told me to do?"

"No clothes allowed in bed, Brodie."

"Oh, yeah?" Brodie lifted the blanket Peyton had covering her up to her shoulders. "You're naked. Have I told you that's my favorite?"

She smiled. "It's my favorite too, Brodie. Now lose the clothes and get in bed."

He climbed back out of bed and pulled his shirt over his head.

She gasped. "Brodie!"

"It looks worse than it feels, sweetheart." He rested his body next to hers and wiped her tears away. "All I need to heal is feeling your body next to mine."

"I don't want to hurt you."

"You aren't going to. I'm more worried about hurting you and the baby."

Peyton moved into his arms and rested her head near his heart. "I'm sorry I'm so tired," she sighed.

"Sleep, sweetheart." He closed his eyes and felt her breathing even out. He couldn't control his body's natural reaction to having her naked and pressed against him, but within minutes, he felt himself drifting off to sleep too.

—:—

Peyton opened her eyes and looked at the clock. It was just before ten in the morning, and Brodie was still sound asleep next to her. She'd slept fourteen hours straight, and wondered if he had too. The blanket had fallen away from his body and rested just above his pelvis.

Even with the scars and marks from the injuries he'd suffered in the crash, his body was still beautiful. Careful not to wake him, Peyton got on her knees and then climbed over so she straddled his waist. She leaned forward, resting her body against him. She was kissing the soft area between his neck and shoulder when his hands gripped her hair and brought her mouth to his.

His hands held her close as his mouth ravaged hers. "I don't want to hurt you," he groaned, "but, God, Peyton, I can't hold back."

"You won't hurt me." She pressed her mouth to his, kissing him harder.

Brodie gently moved her off of him and pushed her down on the mattress. "Let me look at you," he breathed, moving the sheet and blanket away. "Are you cold?"

Peyton shook her head.

Brodie started at her shoulder and kissed his way across her body. He lifted one of her breasts and closed his mouth over its pebbled nipple, nipping at it. When Peyton gasped, Brodie lifted his head.

"They're very sensitive. Part of pregnancy," she explained.

"I'll be gentle, then." Brodie laved her with his tongue, rather than nipping.

Peyton's back arched, and her hands held him close.

"Don't stop," she murmured.

"Never, sweetheart." His lips trailed down her body to where her tummy protruded, his peppered kisses driving her mad. He shifted farther down her body, stopping at the apex between her legs.

"Can I kiss you here, Peyton?" He ran his fingers over her swollen sex.

"Yes," she pleaded, trying to bring his mouth closer to her.

—:—

Brodie tried to be gentle, running his tongue softly through her delicate folds, but couldn't ignore Peyton's pleas for him to go deeper, harder. He settled between her legs, and brought his mouth down to her again, while his hands slid up her body, each grasping her full breasts. Her hands, which had been holding him so tightly to her, moved up to cover his. When he gently kneaded her fullness, her fingers urged him to be rougher. Brodie heard her cry and felt the wetness of her climax at the same time.

"Brodie." She reached for him, pulling him up her body until his hardness rested where his mouth had just been.

"Peyton?"

Instead of answering, she pushed him to his back and covered him with the warmth of her mouth. He couldn't last when her tongue swirled around him.

"Peyton—" he groaned, trying to stop her, but she refused to cease her torment.

Moments later his body jerked against her, but she still wouldn't relent. She stilled when he came, running his hands over her skin.

"Jesus, that was good, sweetheart."

Brodie let his eyes drift closed, but woke when he felt her shudder against him. "Everything okay?" he asked before he realized she was crying. He gently eased both of them, so he was sitting against the headboard and could see her face. "What is it, Peyton?"

She shook her head, and tried again to hide her face from his view. He leaned forward and kissed her forehead. His fingers came under her chin, forcing her to look at him.

"Did I hurt you?"

She shook her head again and tried to move away from his grasp.

"You're killin' me, Peyton. Please tell me what's wrong."

She wiggled away, but didn't get up. Instead, she turned her body around, so she was facing him. Brodie held his breath and waited.

"It's just that...I never thought...I mean I never realized that I could feel this way."

"What way, Peyton?"

"I thought I loved Lang, and I thought I loved Kade, but...I don't think I ever really did. Ya know?"

He nodded, although he had no idea where she was going with this.

She took a deep, deep breath, drawing so much air into her lungs that her naked breasts rose with it. It was all he could do not to pull her close to him and ravage her body. Instead, he closed his fists and kept them tucked next to his body.

"Brodie..."

"Yes, sweetheart? Please, whatever it is, just say it."

"I love you. I love you more than I've ever loved anybody, except my kids, of course. I didn't even know that I could love someone as much as I love you. Ya know?"

This time he did know, because he felt the same way. He had no idea feelings like these were possible. "I do know, because I love you, Peyton."

The worry he saw etched in her forehead fell away, replaced by the smile he loved so much.

Peyton rolled off the bed and took a robe from the hook on the back of her bedroom door. She grabbed his hand and pulled him out of bed.

"Whoa, slow down, there, cowgirl. Where're we going?"

"I'm starving. Here, put this on. And don't worry, he never wore it."

"Who, Kade?"

"Yeah. Sorry, I probably shouldn't have told you that."

"Don't care, honestly." Brodie tightened the sash on the terry-cloth robe. "Wouldn't have cared if he had." He was here, and Kade wasn't. And if it had bothered him even in the slightest, knowing that Peyton loved him was all that mattered to him now.

Peyton was halfway down the hallway when Brodie caught up to her. "You're supposed to be waiting for me to bring you breakfast, sweetheart."

"I can walk around, Brodie, I just can't overdo it."

Brodie reached his arm around her and lifted her into his arms. "Not on my watch. You need to go somewhere, I'll be the one taking you there."

"Oh!" she gasped. "I almost forgot. I have an appointment today with the obstetrician."

"What time?"

"Uh, eleven." Peyton started to laugh when she looked at the clock. They had twenty minutes to get dressed and get to the office, which was only a few minutes away.

Brodie carried her back to the bedroom, where they both threw on the clothes they wore the day before, not that he had any choice. Last night, he hadn't given any thought to stopping at his house to get any of his stuff.

"Mind a drive to my place after your appointment?"

"Only if you promise to feed me first," she grinned.

Brodie thought his heart would explode. What had his sister said yesterday? That Peyton was glowing? She was. She was beaming, and happy, and it was in part because of him.

"I love you." She smiled, standing on her toes to reach up and kiss him. "We better go. You aren't going to *believe* this, Brodie."

He sat in stunned silence, watching the screen, and seeing their baby, his baby, move inside of Peyton.

"She's thriving," the doctor told them both. "Growing right on schedule."

"Can he hear her heartbeat?" Peyton asked once the doctor finished the ultrasound.

"Of course," he smiled. "I'll be right back."

Brodie came over to where Peyton rested on the gurney, still too stunned to speak. He took both her hands in his and stared into her eyes.

"What?"

Brodie shook his head, smiling, but unable to find the words to describe how he felt, seeing their baby.

"I know." Peyton smiled back at him. "I told you, didn't I? Unbelievable, right?"

Brodie nodded and tried to blink his tears away before Peyton realized he was crying.

"Wait until you hear her heartbeat."

The doctor came back in and showed Brodie how the fetal Doppler worked.

"It'll sound like whooshing," Peyton added. "It's the best sound ever. Right, doc?"

"Especially the first time you hear it."

Peyton pulled her shirt up, and Brodie closed his eyes, wanting to focus only on sound. His eyes flooded again, as Peyton had predicted, when he heard the sound she'd described.

Peyton held Brodie's hand tightly in hers. "I think I know how you felt when you were rescued."

"You do?" He was having a hard time speaking.

"I dreamed this. You and me, seeing our baby, hearing her heartbeat. Never, for one minute, did I think it would happen. Now that it is, I keep hoping that I'm not dreaming. I don't want this to be a dream, Brodie, I want it to be real."

"Me too, sweetheart. And you're right, it's exactly how I felt. Even now, I pray I'm not dreaming."

The doctor asked Brodie to step out while he examined Peyton, but she asked if he could stay. "I want you to hold my hand," she explained.

—:—

"That was amazing," Brodie repeated several times over breakfast. They were at the Ollalieberry Diner on Moonstone Beach Road, which reminded Peyton there was something she wanted to ask him.

"How did you know about the rock?"

Brodie had just put a heaping forkful of berry-laden pancakes in his mouth. "What rock?" he asked between bites.

"That morning. You were sitting on the same rock where Kade and I would watch the sun set."

He shook his head. "No idea. Just a coincidence, I guess."

Peyton doubted it was. There had been too many things that happened since the morning she and Brodie walked into Louie's Market at essentially the same time. More and more she believed that Kade truly had a hand in bringing his brother to her, and then making sure he came back to her.

Brodie leaned back and rubbed his belly. "I haven't had a meal that good since we were at Big Sky."

"Seriously?"

Brodie leaned forward and gripped her hand. "Food tastes better when you're happy."

She laughed, but agreed.

"You ready to head out?"

"Sure, but can we swing by Stave on our way?"

Brodie leveled his eyes at her in a mock scowl.

"He said I could go back to work."

"He said you could *think* about going back to work, and he told you to take it easy. I believe his recommendation was one or two days a week."

"I'll take it easy, I promise, but I miss it."

Brodie brought her fingers to his lips and kissed each one. "I liked the idea of keeping you in bed, days on end, waiting for me to do your bidding."

"We can still do that on the days that I'm not at Stave. I like the idea of you doing my bidding." Peyton wiggled her eyebrows. "Especially now that we've been given the green light for..." she looked around to see if anyone could hear her, and then whispered, "*Sex.*"

Brodie laughed out loud, and then reached over to cup her neck with his hand. He drew her close and kissed her the same way he would've if they'd been alone.

"Jeez, Peyton," Helen, the waitress who had worked at the Ollalieberry Diner since Peyton was a teenager, admonished them. "Get a room, girl."

—:—

Brodie stopped on the way over the pass to Butler Ranch and took the dirt road up to where they could see the view of Morro Bay. Instead of getting out of the truck, they sat inside and looked out at one of the best views in all of California.

"I loved you then," he murmured. "Even then, I knew."

"I think I did too. I just fought it harder than you did."

"And later, when I told you I wanted to make you mine, I knew I wanted to spend my life with you, Peyton. Does that sound crazy?"

"It doesn't to me. I felt the same way you did. Except I had too much history believing I made bad choices when it came to men. When I finally found the right one, I didn't trust myself."

"Should we get going? I know you still want to go to Stave, and I'd like to have a little more time alone with you before Alex brings the boys home."

"I don't even know where they are. Alex didn't say, did she? All she said was they were having a slumber party. Maybe they're at the ranch. And if they are, who's at Stave?"

"We'll soon find out."

They were quiet the rest of the way to the ranch. When Brodie pulled in, they saw Alex's car parked near Maddox's house. "Guess that answers one question. Do you want to go see them while I pack up some stuff?"

"No, that's okay. I'd rather come with you. I've never seen where you live."

"I don't live there anymore, sweetheart." Brodie pulled her close and brought his lips to hers.

"Damn, Brodie, you can kiss." She put the back of her hand against her forehead. "Those women who call you 'Brodie the Booty' must not know how good you are with those lips."

"And they never will, darlin'." Brodie opened the door and turned on the light in the kitchen. "I apologize if it's a mess—wait, *what the hell?*" Brodie stopped before Peyton could get in the door.

"What's wrong?"

"Sorry." He moved forward so she could come inside. "I can't believe this." Brodie ran his hand over the box that sat on the kitchen table.

"What is that?"

"It's Kade's box."

Peyton gasped and sat in a chair near the table. "Where did it come from?"

"The woman who owned the house I rented in Argentina must've sent it."

"You took it to Argentina with you?"

"Yeah." Brodie's hands still rested on the top of the box. He had no idea what he should do with it. He'd told her that if she ever wanted it, she should let him know. Should he take it upstairs and store it? Should he get rid of it? He had no idea what she'd want.

"Let's open it together." Peyton stood and rested her hands on his.

"Are you sure?"

"Would it bother you?"

"No, but..."

"It isn't a secret, Brodie. You knew your brother and I were together. You know I loved him, but you also know I love you, more than I loved him."

"I don't want to intrude on your privacy."

"But I want you to. I don't want there to be any secrets between us, Brodie. I don't want you to hide things from me, not even to protect me, the way Kade did."

"Peyton—"

"What, Brodie? You have that same look on your face. That look of regret." Peyton started to back away from him, but he grabbed her arm and pulled her up against him.

"There is something I didn't tell you, but only because I forgot, not because I meant to keep it from you."

She tried again to pull away from him.

"It's about Lang and the petition. Your dad's lawyer is trying to get the petition denied, or at least to get the judge who signed it to recuse himself."

"Why?"

"Because he has a connection to Lang."

"*I knew it.* I knew he'd find a way to work the system against me and for him. He's a lying, cheating bastard."

"He isn't going to win, Peyton. I promise you. If we can't get the petition denied now, we'll keep at it until we do."

"What else?"

"What do you mean?"

"What else didn't you tell me?"

"That was it."

"I don't understand."

"Yesterday, your dad asked to talk to me privately while you were outside, talking with Skye. He told me, and then he asked me not to tell you until we knew more. I told him I couldn't, that I wouldn't keep things from you."

Peyton threw her arms around his neck and kissed him. "And when I said that, it reminded you."

"Yes, and I'm sorry. I had every intention of telling you."

"I know, Brodie. Now let's open it and get it over with."

—:—

There wasn't much in it that Peyton didn't expect there to be. Kade had saved the letters she wrote to him, and there were photos of him with her and her boys. Near the bottom of the box, there was a case that held the Legion of Merit Bronze Star that he'd been given for exceptionally meritorious conduct.

"Your mom should have this," she said, running her fingers over the clear box.

"If that's what you want, Peyton."

Below it, were other awards Kade had been given, along with his diplomas, and newspaper articles written about him through the years. She was about to put the rest of the contents back in the box, when Brodie stopped her.

"There's something under the papers, Peyton."

He took the papers out, and there sat an envelope with her name on it, and a ring box.

"Brodie, I...I can't." Peyton stood and backed away from the box. "I don't want this." Her eyes filled with tears.

"You should read the letter, Peyton. He left this box for you, knowing you'd only see it if something happened to him."

Peyton knew he was right. "Can you give me a few minutes?"

"I'll check on the boys." He picked up her phone and added his name to her "favorites" list. "You need me, press this, and I'll come right back."

Peyton threw her arms around him again and kissed him. "I love you, Brodie."

"I love you, Peyton."

Brodie closed the kitchen door behind him.

Peyton pulled the envelope from the box and held it. She knew Brodie was right. She had to read it, no matter how hard it was. She had loved Kade, and Kade had loved her. Now he was gone, and he wrote this to say goodbye.

My dear Peyton,

As I've asked that this letter be given you in the event of my death. I understand it will be difficult for you to read, and I'm sorry.

There are things you need to know, about me, and about yourself, that are important for me to tell you. Things I couldn't say when I was alive.

I knew my time on earth would be short. I always knew, from when I was a boy, and I accepted it. I also knew I'd die doing something I dedicated my life to, something I believed in, something bigger than me. To serve my country, to protect the rights and freedoms of those I love, was what drove me to keep going, keep living, and in the past couple of years, to keep leaving you and the boys.

I want you to know I love Jamison and Finn as though they are my own flesh and blood, and when I'm gone, I'll continue to look down on them, and you, and protect and love you.

I do love you, Peyton, but I realized that I'd never love you the way you needed me to. I knew I could never give up the life I chose, even for you.

A few days ago, I found the ring my grandmother asked my father to give me, before she died. He told me she wanted me to have it, and I'd know when I met the woman who deserved to wear it. You are that woman, Peyton, even though I am not the man who was meant to give it to you.

The love you deserve is so close. The man who truly deserves you, hasn't met you yet, but you and he will meet soon. He will be the one who gives you this letter, and he will be the one who gives you our grandmother's ring. Give him a chance, Peyton. I know he'll love you in a way I never could.

I'm okay, my dear Peyton, and you will be too.

All my love,

Kade

Peyton felt for her phone, through her tears, and pressed the screen where Brodie had showed her to. She set the phone back on the table, knowing he wouldn't answer. Instead, any second, he'd come through the door, because she needed him.

Kade knew. Brodie was the man she was always meant to be with. He was the man she was meant to love and who was meant to love her.

She heard the door open, and felt Brodie's arms around her. She leaned back against him and felt his warmth flow through her body.

—:—

"He knew, Brodie," Peyton said when she handed him his brother's letter.

Without reading it, he knew what she meant. So many of the dreams he'd had while struggling to stay alive after the plane crash, came flooding back to him. He knew what the letter said without reading it.

"She needs you, Brodie. You have to stay alive. Maddox and Naughton will find you, and they'll take you back to Peyton." How many times had he dreamed Kade saying those words? Countless.

He set the letter aside and reached inside the box. He pulled out the light green velvet box, the color of which reminded him of Peyton's eyes. He had no idea what it held, but he couldn't overpower the need he felt to kneel before her.

"Peyton, you and I are destined to spend the rest of our lives together. I know it deep in my soul. I've never been so certain of anything. I love you now, and I'll love you forever, until the end of time. Please marry me, Peyton."

"Yes, I'll marry you, Brodie. Yes, and love you forever—until the end of time."

Brodie opened the box and pulled out his grandmother's ring. He slipped it on Peyton's finger, and it fit as though it were made just for her. The center diamond was flanked by two rubies, and there was an inscription on the gold band.

"What does it say, Brodie?"

He turned her hand and read around the band he hadn't set eyes on until moments ago.

"*Love forever—until the end of time.*"

Keep reading for a sneak peek

at the next heart-poundingly sexy novel in

Heather Slade's

Butler Ranch Series,

available now.

Maddox

1

If he weren't in someone else's house, Maddox would put his fist through a wall. He'd put up with Alex's shit for almost twenty years, and he was just about done.

He'd been done before, yet somehow, he always circled around and ended up right back where he was now.

Her latest? Offering to babysit her best friend Peyton's kids at his house. His house. Not hers. His. As far as kids went, they seemed okay, but Maddox never babysat anyone's kids, not even his niece, Spencer. His sister Skye never asked. She was too smart to consider leaving a child in his very incapable hands.

Alex had been avoiding him since this morning, when he'd tried to stop her from interfering with his brother's relationship with her best friend.

She ignored him, as usual. And she'd been right, as usual. He'd been trying to get Brodie to pull his head out of his ass and fix things with Peyton for days, and in two hours, Alex had managed what he couldn't.

Now Peyton and Brodie were reunited and about to leave for her house while Peyton's two sons were packing their stuff for a slumber party with Uncle Maddox.

That's what Alex had called him, and while it was likely Peyton and Brodie would be married sooner rather than later, especially given she was pregnant with Brodie's child, wasn't calling him the boys' uncle taking things too far?

Maddox followed Brodie and Peyton down the stairs and carried her bags to Brodie's truck.

Alex closed the door after Brodie helped Peyton inside, and rested her arm on the bottom of the open window. Maddox couldn't hear what she said to Peyton, but he could see her eyes fill with tears.

When Alex backed away from the truck, he was right behind her and wrapped his arms around her waist. They waved as Brodie drove away.

"We need to talk," he whispered.

When she tried to escape his hold, he tightened his arms.

"You're not goin' anywhere, Alex. We're gonna talk."

"No, we aren't, Maddox."

"What's this Uncle Maddox crap?"

"Seriously? It isn't going to kill you to do something nice for your brother, especially with all you put him through."

He let go and spun her around. "What did you say?"

"You heard me. You could've helped him, Maddox. Instead, you played the almighty omniscient, telling him he had to figure things out for himself. Meanwhile, my best friend was as heartbroken as Brodie was."

"If I had to do it over again, I wouldn't change the way I handled it."

"Of course not."

"You can't admit that if Brodie had gone in guns blazing, the way he planned to, he would've driven Peyton further away?"

"You could've told him how she felt."

"No, I couldn't have, because I don't know Peyton the way you do. You may say it was that simple, but you know damn well it wasn't."

"It doesn't matter. They're back together now, and her boys, who happen to be my godsons, are standing on the porch of their grandparents' house watching the guy whose house they're sleeping at tonight argue with their aunt.

"I'm honored to be their aunt, Maddox. They're amazing boys who are about to watch a shitstorm custody fight go down between their mother and a father they've never known. Do I want them to have a night away from all the crap that's been going on in their lives? You bet I do. I'm going to make this the best damn sleepover they've ever had. If you can't help me make that happen, at least stay out of the way and don't spoil it for them."

As much as he wanted to wring her neck, it was this fire in her he couldn't resist. She'd stand up for the defenseless, soothe the pain of those who hurt, and fiercely protect those she loved. There were times he wished she loved him, but more often, the idea that she might scared the living shit out of him.

When Alex walked over to where the boys waited, Maddox stayed where he was and watched her joke and laugh with them. She had a smile that never failed to knock him on his ass. It had since the first time he'd met her.

Her long brown, almost black, hair hung straight today, the ends just kissing the curve of her ass—another thing about her that never failed to knock him on his.

She was wearing jeans, rolled up far enough above her ankles to show off her hotter-than-shit, red suede boots with the three-inch heels. The cream-colored, sleeveless, silk and lace blouse she wore was long in the back, but short enough in the front that when she stretched, Maddox caught a glimpse of her tan belly. Her eyes, the same color as her hair, danced as she talked with the boys.

Maddox finally joined them on the porch. "Ready, guys?"

Jamison, Peyton's oldest son, was ten. His brother, Finn, was eight. When he and his brother Kade were their age, they had their own "best damn sleepovers"—ones Alex couldn't even imagine. They'd have fun; he'd make sure of it. The same kind of fun he and Kade used to have.

Before he was killed in Afghanistan on what was to be his final mission with Delta Force, Kade had dated the boys' mother. Maddox knew that, even though they welcomed Brodie's role in their mother's life, they still missed Kade. How could they not? He was the coolest guy who'd ever lived.

If Alex wanted them to have fun tonight, they sure as hell would. She might not, but they would.

Maddox loaded the boys' bags into his truck and told them to climb in the back seat of the big SUV.

"Ready?" He winked at Alex.

"What are you up to, Mad-man?"

"You'll see, Al. You wanted fun, right?"

—:—

Oh, Lord. What had she started?

It had always been this way with them. She'd challenge him, and then he'd step up and blow her away. Maddox Butler was the least boring man she'd ever met and, by far, the hottest. He'd rocked her world since the first time she laid eyes on him.

She was fourteen; he was seventeen, and it was more than his age that kept him off-limits. He was a Butler—an unmentionable name in the Avila home.

Even then, Maddox was all man. Six feet three, with steel blue eyes that danced when he smiled, Mad always looked as though he knew something scandalous that no one else did. He'd always kept his dark hair short, even when he was younger.

His rock-hard torso would rival any gym rat's, but his body was that of a man who hoisted barrels full of wine like they were ten-pound bags of potatoes.

His face was chiseled, rugged, and weathered from days spent in the vineyard heat—with a mischievous smile framed by a dark beard that hid the dimples she sometimes forgot were there. While the women in the Butler family were fair with vibrant red hair, the men wore their olive skin like a suit of armor. His trail of dark hair was perfectly placed, trailing down from his brawny neck, over his rough-hewn abs, to his pelvis.

The full-sleeve tattoos on both of his arms married traditional tribal with Celtic designs, and stopped just short of his hands. Splayed, those hands could cover her ample breasts, their power seeping into her, driving her to the edge with little but their heat, and then be equally gentle when his calloused fingers rolled her nipples.

Alex sighed, knowing those hands would not cover her body tonight. Missing them, missing the fullness she experienced only when Mad's body penetrated hers, was what kept her coming back to him, even when she knew they were destined to combust.

About the Author

USA Today and Amazon Top 15 Bestselling Author Heather Slade writes shamelessly sexy, edge-of-your seat romantic suspense.

She gave herself the gift of writing a book for her own birthday one year. Forty-plus books later (and counting), she's having the time of her life.

The women Slade writes are self-confident, strong, with wills of their own, and hearts as big as the Colorado sky. The men are sublimely sexy, seductive alphas who rise to the challenge of capturing the sweet soul of a woman whose heart they'll hold in the palm of their hand forever. Add in a couple of neck-snapping twists and turns, a page-turning mystery, and a swoon-worthy HEA, and you'll be holding one of her books in your hands.

She loves to hear from my readers. You can contact her at heather@heatherslade.com

To keep up with her latest news and releases, please visit her website at www.heatherslade.com to sign up for her newsletter.

MORE FROM AUTHOR HEATHER SLADE

Butler Ranch

Kade's Worth

Brodie

Maddox

Naughton

Mercer

Kade

Christmas at Butler Ranch

Wicked Winemakers' Ball

Coming soon:

Brix

Ridge

Press

K19 Security Solutions

Razor

Gunner

Mistletoe

Mantis

Dutch

Striker

Monk

Halo

Tackle

Onyx

K19 Shadow Operations

Code Name: Ranger

Coming soon:

Code Name: Diesel

Code Name: Wasp

Code Name: Cowboy

The Royal Agents of MI6

The Duke and the Assassin

The Lord and the Spy

The Commoner and the Correspondent

The Rancher and the Lady

The Invincibles

Decked

Undercover Agent

Edged

Grinded

Riled

Handled

Smoked

Bucked

Irished

Sainted

Coming soon:

Hammered

Ripped

Cowboys of Crested Butte

A Cowboy Falls

A Cowboy's Dance

A Cowboy's Kiss

A Cowboy Stays

A Cowboy Wins

Made in the USA
Columbia, SC
22 April 2022

59331741R00215